T0303035

# Provenance

Paul M. Levitt

TAYLOR TRADE PUBLISHING
*Lanham • Boulder • New York • London*

TAYLOR TRADE PUBLISHING
An imprint of Rowman & Littlefield

Distributed by NATIONAL BOOK NETWORK



British Library Cataloguing in Publication Information available

**Library of Congress Cataloging-in-Publication Data**

Names: Levitt, Paul M., author.
Title: Provenance / Paul M. Levitt.
Description: Lanham : Taylor Trade Publishing, [2016]
Identifiers: LCCN 2016012446 (print) | LCCN 2016015651 (ebook) | ISBN 9781630761493 (hardcopy) | ISBN 9781630761509
Subjects: LCSH: Art—Fiction. | Louisiana—Fiction. | LCGFT: Historical fiction.
Classification: LCC PS3612.E935 P76 2016 (print) | LCC PS3612.E935 (ebook) | DDC 813/.6—dc23
LC record available at https://lccn.loc.gov/2016012446

∞™ The paper used in this publication meets the minimum requirements of American National Standard for Information Sciences—Permanence of Paper for Printed Library Materials, ANSI/NISO Z39.48-1992.

*For Victoria Tuttle, whose literary sensibility made this book possible.*

# Contents

# Acknowledgments

"All art," said J. M. Synge, "is a collaboration." Sadly, the collaborators are often unrecognized. Standing behind this book are several people to whom I am indebted.

Scot M. Levitt, my elder son and Director of Fine Arts at Bonhams & Buttterfields, schooled me in art history and rendered me countless favors. His expertise as an art appraiser and auctioneer is beyond measure.

Daniel G. Levitt, my younger son, shared his knowledge about geology and plant life.

Andrea J. Stein, my daughter, always appeared when most needed and never failed to volunteer her help, legal and otherwise.

Sandra Levitt, my sister, provided wit and good cheer to rebalance my sanity scales.

Nancy Levitt, my wife, enabled me time to write by uncomplainingly assuming all the household responsibilities.

Carl Manthei, attorney, patiently tried to lead me through the labyrinth of the law. Any missteps issue from me.

Gary Gautier, a native of New Orleans, who read the manuscript and made several valuable observations about life in the South, is an accomplished writer and a loyal friend.

Katie Sharp, copyeditor extraordinaire, not only corrected my infelicities but also improved the text.

Ellen Urban, assistant managing editor, gently held my hand throughout the publishing process and never once made me feel anything but welcome.

Rick Rinehart, my longtime publisher, encouraged me to undertake this project and patiently waited until I could steer a safe passage through the shoals.

Maria Krenz, who corrected my imperfect Hungarian, has been unfailingly helpful and generous with her time. Any errors are my own.

Susan Zucker, who designed the cover, has imaginatively united the visual and the verbal.

Any resemblance to persons living or dead is purely accidental, except where name recognition is intentional.

# Sorrow Drowned

For three days in June 1988, police cars wailed, bloodhounds bayed, and mounted troopers cantered through the town and woods of Hungamon, Louisiana searching for Immanuel "Manny" Crenshaw. Eighteen months before he had been found guilty of manslaughter and sentenced to serve fifteen years in a correctional center near Monroe, Louisiana. Having escaped from the exercise area by cutting through the bottom of a fence, he presumably took refuge with friends or family in his hometown of Hungamon. The police bulletins described Manny as black, twenty years old, six feet tall, 182 pounds, and presumed dangerous.

In the beginning Adam Shaw tried to persuade himself that the sound he heard at two in the morning came from a dream and not from the dock. His house, one of several in a wooded area west of Coburn Creek, on the eastern edge of Hungamon, looked out on a lake maintained for the recreational use of the homeowners. When the cry rang out again, he thought of a bird. Turning off the air conditioner, he could hear clearly now. "Help! Someone's drowning. Please help!" Adam's wife, Rachel, awakened by the commotion, leaped out of bed and, in her scant pajamas, made for the stairs. Silently chastising himself for admiring her slender half-naked body instead of acting, he reached for a robe and followed Rachel to the lake, where a young black boy, hysterically crying about someone drowning, kept pointing to a particular spot. The hot, muggy air, which felt like a wet surgical mask, captured the smells of mildew and bougainvillea, and the myriad cicadas sounded like an angelic choir. As Adam cradled the lad in his arms, comforting him and attempting to elicit more information, the symphony of frogs made it nearly impossible to hear the boy's murmurings. Rachel leaped into the water, swam to the designated area, and dove to the bottom. When her breath gave out, she surfaced and dove again, dozens of times, but with no success. Exhausted, she swam to shore and emerged completely naked, having lost her pajamas in the lake. Adam threw his robe over her, and she bolted for the house to call 911. He continued to soothe the sobbing boy, who tearfully identified himself as Wayne Hildreth, a last name that gave Adam pause. Wayne had been hunting for night crawlers in Timberlake Estates when he saw an older boy, dressed in an orange jumpsuit, push a beached rowboat into the water, paddle toward the middle, and jump overboard, never to surface again. Terrified of being punished, Wayne said he wished now that he had observed the "No Trespassing" sign.

Within minutes a fire truck arrived bearing an emergency crew, closely followed by an ambulance and three policemen. On the Shaw's lawn they set up klieg lights and illuminated the area around the lake. Adam's neighbors appeared in various states of undress with flashlights, candles, and flares. Word spread through the crowd that a black kid had apparently drowned. "A lotta good our sign did," said one man. "Maybe we shoulda said 'Whites Only.'" The others ignored the crude attempt at humor and silently watched the rescue crew. The long, narrow lake fell off sharply a few feet from shore, deep enough to make the crew's probing poles useless. Going back to the fire truck, the men removed a raft and trawling net. Minutes later they brought up the body of Manny Crenshaw and laid it on the grass. A stunned Adam felt nauseous; he knew Manny all too well. Turning their kliegs on the young man, the firemen applied a respirator and then tried to manually pump oxygen into his lungs. But though he looked asleep, he was immutably dead.

The police, finding the pockets of Manny's jumpsuit stuffed with rocks, began to mumble darkly. Adam thought about the jury that had found Manny guilty, a jury on which he had served. Returning from the house, Rachel kneeled and removed some reeds from the boy's hair. Days later witnesses told the newspaper that Rachel had sunk to her knees to pray. But in fact the innumerable insects roused from their nocturnal slumbers, basking and cavorting in the bright beams, held her mesmerized, and she marveled that this summer night, so alive with midges and moths, hosted a death. As a good Christian she reasoned that death, terrible as it is, led to a rewarding afterlife. But she found it hard to reconcile her religious beliefs with the reality of a dead young man.

Wayne seemed desolate, putting his hands on his head and keening the ancient anguish: Why? Confronted by a cacophony of questions, the boy could only sob. Adam asked his age—eleven. When morning came and his mother found him missing, what would he tell her? And his father? Adam learned that the boy's parents had separated. Although the police would be contacting both of Wayne's parents, Rachel felt obliged to call as well. She took Wayne's hand, led him into the kitchen, and fed him lemonade and cookies. A handsome boy with high cheekbones and perfect skin, he seemed fearful of returning home and uncertain how to behave in this white person's house. She sat down and reached across the table, touching him consolingly. He looked at her hand on his as if viewing a new reality, black and white joined, or was it white and black united against the void?

She glanced at the clock, 4:12 a.m., and the calendar, Sunday, June 12, 1988, the same month, many years before, that she and her mother, Ellen, returning from New Orleans, had been hit by a drunk driver, an accident that had instantly killed Miss Ellen, her beloved mama, and sent her to the hospital for radical surgery.

The accident had changed her life drastically. Her father, unable to cope with her post-traumatic moodiness, had sent her to a private girls' school in Virginia, separating her from the closeness of the Hungamon community, a rupture that made her all the more sensitive to the terrified child now staring at her wide-eyed.

Rachel smiled and asked, "How can I reach your folks?"

"My dad lives in New Orleans. He ain't got no phone. Mom's leavin' 'bout this time for the Grandview Nursin' Home."

"Where's that?"

His mother, Wayne said, worked as a nurse in the retirement home, located sixty-five miles southwest via the Lake Pontchartrain Causeway. She'd arrive there at 6:00 a.m. and return home before 8:00 p.m. His father, Samuel, had moved to New Orleans in 1984, when Wayne turned seven. Only on special occasions did Wayne see him, and recently hardly at all. Samuel had been a Marine in Vietnam, assigned to electronic reconnaissance. Wayne had a photograph of him. He removed a small child's wallet from his overalls. The shirtless man, sculpted with muscles, exhibited a finely chiseled face, except for a splayed nose, which Wayne said resulted from a fight. He resembled a fighter. Rachel, like Adam, knew the man and the name, Hildreth.

The police wanted to take Wayne to the station to wait for his parents, but Rachel volunteered to care for him temporarily.

"Would you like to stay with Mr. Shaw and me," she asked, "until we can reach your mother?"

The boy looked relieved. "If it's okay?"

Rachel urged him to finish the cookies and lemonade. She and Adam watched and whispered as the crew put Manny's body on a stretcher and carried it to the ambulance. Rachel had a preternatural feeling that Manny's drowning would not end the matter. Mrs. Hildreth said she would leave immediately. Rachel gave her directions to the house. Wayne would be waiting and, in the meantime, well cared for.

At 7:30 a.m. the phone started ringing. Rachel and Adam took turns explaining the events of the night. The last of the calls came from Irma Wallace, who reminded Rachel that she had agreed to introduce Mrs. Olsen, who had just returned from East Africa with a summary of the church's good works in helping to alleviate the famine. No, said Irma, she could not, at this last moment, find someone else. Couldn't Adam stay with the boy? Rachel thought it sinful to abandon Wayne when he needed her most, and when the police would want to question her.

Irma said, "It's not like he's your own . . . one of us."

Rachel hung up and told Adam what had just transpired. He assured her that he could look after Wayne and that she should avoid a fight with that sanctimonious Irma Wallace.

Feeling unmanned by Rachel taking the lead in trying to recover the body, he wanted a chance to exhibit a steady masculine hand. He knew that Rachel had married him for his good looks and because she could have her way with him. Indeed, her instincts proved true. She ran his life. On weekdays, when Adam came downstairs for breakfast, she would run her eyes over him like a full-body CAT scan, looking to find an imperfection in his dress, in the way he had combed his hair, in the closeness of his shave. Perhaps he had missed a spot. He always felt skewered by those looks and slightly humiliated when she added, "All right." She dressed stylishly and regarded clothes as one of her strengths, making it a point to buy Adam's clothes and oversee every other aspect of his wardrobe. Given her impeccable manners, notwithstanding her rudeness to Irma, she frequently counseled Adam on how he, a Northerner, should behave in the South. Her friends regarded him as more "European" than American.

The phone rang. Irma. Had they been cut off? Surely Rachel would introduce Mrs. Olsen. Adam gathered from Rachel's remarks that she felt pressured to accompany Irma. He whispered: "Go, I'll stay here." She reluctantly agreed and told Irma to collect her in ten minutes but that she couldn't stay long. As she slipped into a different pair of shoes, Adam assured her that he could "hold down the fort." When Irma drove up and honked, Rachel gave Wayne a hug and told him that his mother would arrive any minute and that she'd return shortly. Adam lifted the box of paper plates and plastic utensils Rachel had volunteered for the reception and offered to carry them to the car. Rachel murmured, "He'll be alone in the house. We don't know what kind of family he comes from."

Her remark moved Adam to a rare rebuke. "He's not going to steal the silver."

Rachel's cheeks were still flushed when she reached Irma's car.

"Got any hobbies?" Adam asked, hoping to take the boy's mind off the drowning.

"Stamp collectin'," Wayne answered dully, still suffering from shock.

"A philatelist."

"I ain't got that one."

"Which is the most valuable?"

"Don't know."

"There are books. You could find out." Adam, aware that stamp-collecting books cost more than the lad could afford, immediately amended his statement. "In the library."

"Never been."

"Let me show you a book, not for stamps, but for paintings."

Adam removed from the shelf a catalogue titled *Hungarian Art*. As he flipped through the pages, the boy slowly emerged from his traumatic trance and stared at the glossy colored photographs. Adam pointed to a picture of a woman resting on a rock, with a bundle of sticks strapped to her back. Dressed in a blue skirt, white blouse, and red cap, she held her folded hands in her lap. Adam said, "The man who painted this, I'm pretty sure, also did the canvas over the fireplace." He pointed across the room.

Wayne stared at Adam's painting and then at the photograph titled *Woman Carrying Faggots.* He shook his head skeptically and asked, "What kind of name is that? It don't make no sense. She ain't carryin' no queer. And she ain't one herself, neither. Boys are called faggots, not girls."

"Faggots are sticks," said Adam.

"Not where I come from."

What would he say to a son of his own? "I'm sure you don't like it when people call you names. So let's not insult others."

Wayne looked away, apparently chastised, an encouraging sign, until the boy blurted, "Our minister says queers ain't right. He says they sin against God."

Adam, tempted to ask him the name of his pastor and church, decided against it. In this part of the country, prejudice was enjoyed equally. "I want to ask you a question," Adam said, changing the subject and leading the boy to the fireplace. "Do you see any similarities between the painting of the woman and this one?"

Reflecting, the boy said, "The light. The way it comes from the side."

"Good eye."

As they stood in front of the handsomely framed painting of a man hunched over a book and writing with a quill, Adam explained that the man probably represented a rabbinical scribe. The candle that illuminated the writing stand, ink bottle, and open tome gave the painting its special quality.

"What's a rabbi? What's a rab-bit-cal scribe?"

"A Jewish minister or priest."

"And a scribe?"

Adam, glad for the chance to instruct the lad, told him that rabbinical scribes hand-copied the Torah, the first five books of the Old Testament. They didn't write on paper, but on sheepskin, called a scroll. How could he tell the man's religion just from a painting? Wayne wanted to know. He guessed that although the man's black frock alone did not mark him as Jewish, other clues included his black skullcap, side locks, beard, and bony nose.

"I'm pretty sure the same man composed the two paintings." Adam pointed to the name printed in the catalogue, the Hungarian master, Mihály Munkácsy. "His last name is pronounced Moon-kah-chee. He lived from 1844 to 1900. I call it 'The Scribe,' and if I can prove it's genuine, well, I'll be rolling in dough."

Wayne tipped his head and scrutinized the painting. "Could be a fake. They sell fake stamps. I got cheated once. Where d'ya buy it?"

"My parents put me up for adoption and, believe it or not, sent along the painting as well." Wayne looked doubtful.

"Well, that sounds pretty stupid to me, 'specially if the picture's really worth somethin'. Why don't you find out? That's what I'd do."

"I'm trying."

Wayne continued to pepper him with questions. Adam explained that one had to depend on books and letters and exhibition histories and word of mouth and, if lucky, bills of sale to determine a painting's provenance. No, not providence, provenance, meaning origin, derivation, source. If an old painting is found, for example, in someone's attic and an expert thinks it might be a Rembrandt, then the only way to learn the provenance of the painting is to trace all of its previous owners, right back to the original buyer, who might have left a record of the purchase.

"Maybe that's what I oughta do with some of my stamps. Who knows, I might own somethin' valuable." He stared again at the wall painting. "You wanna know what I think? I think the frame's worth more than the painting. It's really cool."

"The frame is one of the clues that I have a rare painting. It's done in a nineteenth-century fashion, carved and gilded with twenty-four-carat gold. The wooden stretcher, the pieces in the back attached to the frame, also tells a story."

Before Adam could explain, Wayne suddenly seemed to lose interest. He looked around the room as if trying to locate some familiar point or person. "The only real valuable thing, I guess, is people. Stamps don't mean nothin'. Pictures don't mean nothin' unless a body's there to see them." He sniffled and wiped his runny nose with his arm. "When my daddy comes to visit, we look at my stamp collection together . . . under a magnifyin' glass."

Adam, never feeling safe on emotional grounds, fled the field. Uncomfortable asking others about their personal lives, he ducked the chance to ask Wayne about his "daddy."

"Ever play golf?"

"No, but I seen it on TV"

"Come on. I have a putting area on the side of the house with a cup sunk in the grass."

Taking two putters and a bag of golf balls from the garage, Adam led the way to the site. He pointed out the cup and explained how to grip the club. Wayne, ignoring the mosquitoes, listened keenly and couldn't wait to take his first stroke, which showed a great deal of promise. After several tries, Adam called him "a natural."

"Could you ever take me to a real golf course sometime?"

Adam paused to think about that request. As far as he knew, no blacks golfed at the club to which he and Rachel belonged. "Why not?" he said.

---

On the drive to church, although Rachel pretended to listen to her friend, she could not stop thinking about the drowned man and Irma's rude response. This thought led her to wonder why she had settled in the South. Adam had balked at her decision, preferring the East. But Hungamon was home. Her father, Montgomery F. French, lived here. He offered to buy her a lovely home on a lake and promised to find a good position for Adam. Moreover, she felt drawn to the history and fabric of Washington Parish, one of the so-called Florida parishes (north of Lake Pontchartrain and east of the Mississippi River). At the First Baptist Church she would be reunited with old friends and guaranteed the community of hundreds of others. Social life in the South revolved around the church. She found the North cold, literally and figuratively, a place where Baptists fought over doctrinal matters, divorced from their roots. Planting in alien soil, she told herself, brought forth a bitter fruit. She often repeated to herself, "How can we know where we're headed unless we know where we came from?"

And yet, ironically, she felt adrift, an educated woman without a purpose, and a beautiful one as well. Graceful, athletic, slender, and tall—some of her admirers called her balletic—she turned more than one head with her Mediterranean features, in particular, her marble-white teeth, olive skin, and long black hair swept up in back with expensive turquoise combs. She tried to expel her aimlessness by working for her church and modeling clothes for the Hungamon fashion show. She devoted time to charities, and to golf and tennis. But surely, she told herself, a life comprised more than game, set, and match. Piano lessons proved only that she had no talent. Gardening gave her great satisfaction, but not enough to steady her restless mind. Good works and sports and diversions she treated as toys of the rich. She wanted to put her critical thinking in the service of some worthy project, one that took acumen and imagination, and perhaps even courage, which she had in ample amounts, but most projects seemed to lack substance. On dreary winter days she would stand next to the picture window and watch the rain sheets ripple the lake. In those moments she knew she lived as a dilettante, and disliked the feeling.

It had taken her several months to persuade Adam that once they graduated from Vanderbilt in 1975, they should settle in Louisiana. He had no objections to their marrying in her hometown, but he wanted to join some large New York accounting firm, where the work would be exciting and the city tonic. She objected, painting New York as impersonal, noisy, dirty, expensive, and brash, whereas her hometown presented the opposite in every regard. Finally he reluctantly agreed when her father not only bought them a house on a lake, but also found a place for Adam in the accounting department of a New Orleans hospital with the opportunity to advance.

Rachel often thought back on Vanderbilt, its manicured grounds and hilly landscape, marred only by some tasteless statues someone had donated. She belonged to a sorority, Kappa Gamma, and Adam to some forgettable rugby club, a source of humor among her sorority sisters, all of whom seemed to have checked out the best fraternities for prospective doctors or lawyers or stockbrokers. Though nervy, Rachel didn't have the courage to remain independent of the Greek fraternal system, with all its social connections, even though the best students remained independent. She wondered if her life would ever again be as good as those college days, when she and her sorority sisters wore black cocktail dresses on dates with frat boys to football games and celebrated into the night when one of the sisters received a diamond engagement ring. Of course then the tittering began, since the sorority sisters knew that the young woman would now be serving up her hymen in appreciation.

Rachel had decided that before she would give up her virginity, Adam would have to agree to her demands. She behaved like a street merchant, haggling with him over the social clubs they would join, the church they'd attend, the cars they would drive. Recalling the ecstatic drunken moment when Adam, in light of her father's generous offer, agreed to live in a part of the country he regarded as foreign, she gave him what she had so jealously guarded, her Southern maidenhead, although she had to admit that she had long wanted consummation.

Adam's acquiescence provided the occasion. Their first time proved a comic episode of fumbling and futility. Her membrane had proved hard to penetrate, causing him to spill his seed prematurely. Several days later, on their second try, they prevailed, and to her delight she discovered that she actually liked sex, though not to the degree that Adam subsequently wished to take it: watching "adult" films and trying new positions. She gathered that he had already viewed such films; otherwise how could he talk so knowingly of those "other" ways? Her good manners and discreetness, however, kept her from asking where he had seen them.

Ironically, the subject resurfaced when some of her sorority sisters suggested that they might raise a lot of money for charity—the principal excuse Greeks used to justify their presence on campus—by hosting a showing of *Deep Throat*. The chapter at the University of Colorado, she heard, had raised a bundle that way. But Rachel and others pointed out that among the boys at Vanderbilt they would be raising more than money. After the titters died down, she asked why the "trike" races they traditionally held to raise money for charity weren't good enough. Told that trike races stamped women as children, she felt caught between new feminine attitudes and old values. Rachel couldn't say exactly why she objected to the showing of a blue film, but she intuitively felt it lower class, and she wished to strike a blow for feminism. Although she knew that Southerners, for all their piety, watched porno films in larger percentages than their Northern counterparts, she shamelessly invoked religion, telling her sisters that as a good Baptist she intended to stand at the marriage altar pure of heart. She carefully made it a point not to say pure of heart and body.

In their married life she and Adam always observed the missionary position, which had a certain sanctity to it. Although in college she read magazine, which exposed her to the subject of "oral sex," she regarded it as off-limits and the purview of perverts, even though some of her sorority sisters giggled about it. In other words, she never had been personally involved in what her former minister, Pastor Manders, referred to as that "fiendish filth." So when Adam recently said, "Now that we're an old married couple, a soft porn flick might liven things up a bit," she took the comment as a slap in the face. First of all, they were in their mid-thirties, hardly old; second, she had told him back in college, when he first mentioned the idea, that she regarded such films as smut. So why reintroduce the subject now? Did he wish to indicate his dissatisfaction with their conjugal bed or the frequency of their lovemaking? She took pride in the fact that unlike shy women or those ashamed of their bodies, she readily undressed in front of her husband and enjoyed being fondled. Had she been unable to reach orgasm, she might understand Adam's desire to delve into "that" side of human behavior. Admittedly, she did not experience "explosive finales," the stuff of how-to articles in women's magazines. Her climaxes, akin to a small pleasurable wave that passed over her body, may have lacked thunder, but she rarely failed to have them, and once a week certainly numbered enough for a married woman. Although she would never tell Adam, she associated frequent sex with white trash and blacks. When Adam pressed her to "play" more often, focusing on a word he had discovered in a Hemingway novel, she would teasingly say that too much would sate him and make him lose interest. Scarcity increased desire.

Besides, she told herself, she had a full calendar that kept her busy from morning till midnight. When she returned home in the evening, she longed for sleep, not sex; and in the morning, thank God, Adam left early. Sex took time and energy, with its foreplay and exertions. Her numerous commitments at the country club and health club, her frequent dinner parties for friends and Adam's colleagues, her shopping, her keeping up with the reading for her book club, and, not least, her proving herself a good member of the church, led her to wonder how her women friends had the courage to make babies. Even though the care of them passed to black nannies, mothers did, now and then, have to spend time with their children.

She chastised herself for thinking about sex. Leave that subject to men. So she let her mind wander to something more ladylike: redecorating the house. Her father had bought them a splendid home. It stood on 5.5 acres of woodland and cost $271,500. Many years before, he had sold a pine sawmill on the Louisiana-Mississippi border to the Great Southern Lumber Company, a division of Crown-Zellerbach, making Hungamon's mill the world's largest. A million dollars richer, he invested wisely. His wealth made Rachel feel important and secure, certain that he would see to her future, as well as Adam's. Never one to idle, he now wrote articles for the Hungamon *Daily News* on the history of Washington and Bienville Parishes. Rachel did, on occasion, wonder about his two particular interests: the racial integration of Hungamon, and the gangsters Bonnie Parker and Clyde Barrow, who died in Bienville Parish when their car was surrounded and riddled with bullets, an account her father spent many hours trying to correct, and one he dilated on frequently, especially to his friend Judge Emory Waters.

A dabbler in real estate, the judge, famous for his eccentricities and garrulity, first pointed out the property to Montgomery French. Through one of his innumerable contacts—no reclusive circuit judge, he—Emory heard on the grapevine that the owners of the house needed cash and would be willing to sell below market price. Montgomery readily doled out the bucks. The four-thousand-square-foot house had ceilings ten feet high, granite countertops in the kitchen, fireplaces in the living room and master bedroom, oak flooring, a wrapped porch, a workshop, a boathouse, a dock, and the private lake. In Rachel's estimation the house lacked furniture less fussy and frilly. Her father, having vacated their large family home for a bungalow, moved the period pieces into the house that he purchased for Rachel. Surrounded by all those reminders of her mother's taste had been initially pleasant, but after all these years, she wanted to fashion the house anew, less nineteenth century and more modern.

Rachel took particular pride in the garden. The previous owners had kept the grounds simple: lawns, a few shrubs, and bamboo that had run amok in the swampy soil, requiring her to ruthlessly prune the roots and stolons. To add color and mitigate the nauseating odor from the processing and chemical division of the sawmill, Rachel worked closely with a landscaping company that planted dogwood, azaleas, camellias, daffodils, honeysuckle, and tulip trees. In the low swampy areas around the lake, they introduced pitcher plants with their large yellow flowers. She had professional tree trimmers remove the dead limbs from the pine and cypress trees and give the catkin-covered oaks a stately shape. The landscaping seemed to attract squadrons of cardinals, shrikes, and myrtle warblers; in addition, white egrets flapped around the lake, roosting clumsily in favorite trees along her shore. She refused to let the landscapers remove the rotting logs with their colorful toadstools; they attracted colonies of insects that she enjoyed watching. Having always regarded birders as odd, she imperceptibly became one herself. In the early evening, when the clouds boiled up in brilliant shades of red, she strolled around her property looking for nocturnal birds and the winking lights of the fireflies; she identified the sounds emanating from the deep woods, like tree frogs, coypus, and wild chickens. Yes, she told herself, living in the South had its natural and financial advantages.

Wayne's mother clutched her son to her chest and asked how the drowning had happened. She had driven to the house in a battered red Toyota, which Adam hoped ran better than it looked, and brushed past him, trailing behind her an abbreviated thanks and the scent of lavender.

"I heard on the car radio the name Immanuel Crenshaw. The same one—" She broke off.

Adam gathered that English was not her first language. Her lateness had resulted from her having to deal with an emergency. And then one had to avoid the roadkill: the dead opossums and raccoons. Dressed in a white nurse's uniform, she struck Adam as exceedingly attractive, statuesque even. *High yaller*, he thought, adopting the local language. Introducing herself as Zoe Hildreth—again he started at the mention of the name—she said: "Yes, Mr. Shaw, you and my husband served on the jury together. We're currently separated."

That fateful jury. He could still see the faces of his peers. The panel had been composed of eight whites—five men and three women—and four black males. Adam sensed during the trial that the black jury members wanted to show the white community that they, like all good upstanding Christians, would have no mercy for murderers. Before he could speak—he had contriteness in mind—she began to pace the living room, aimlessly touching pieces of furniture, gesturing, grimacing, glancing around as if in response to some voice, pausing, balancing on one foot and then another, filling the room with a kinetic energy that made Adam feel vicariously buoyant. He also found her presence comforting. She spoke softly, her voice an adagio movement, slow and emotive. The music held his attention, but the words escaped him.

"I'm sorry, would you kindly repeat that?"

"Are you sure he took his own life?"

Before Adam could answer, Wayne whispered to his mother, but not so quietly as to prevent Adam from hearing the word "rocks." Zoe bit her lower lip and followed Wayne to a window with a view of the lake.

All too clearly Adam saw the Sunday morning in 1986 after the Crenshaw trial. He had showered and shaved while Rachel dressed. As he left the house for church, he had told himself that the lawn needed cutting. On the drive, he had ruminated about the chasm between rich and poor, black churches and white, New Jersey and Louisiana. While walking from the parking lot to the entrance, they had stopped to greet friends, hers mostly, and had seated themselves on the wooden benches for a sermon from Pastor Dieter Rominy, the son of a German who had fled the Nazis. Unmarried, the pastor constantly had to discourage church ladies who felt it their duty to introduce him to a prospective wife; but he always rebuffed their advances with a smile and the strange comment, "I wish to die a bachelor." The pastor, who two years before had replaced Pastor Manders, frequently disquieted his more conservative parishioners with his opposition to capital punishment. That day, he had chosen for his sermon the taking of life and what constituted just punishment, using phrases such as "evil begetting evil" and "turning the other cheek." He had mentioned Sister Helen Prejean's family interviews, which had shown that executing criminals rarely brings relief to the victims' relatives. Reminding the congregation that the Lord reserved vengeance for Himself, and that the death penalty constituted a form of revenge, he had concluded with the observation that in the past executioners hooded themselves because no man wanted the reputation of having blood on his hands, and he urged the congregation to resist those who wanted their pound of flesh.

Adam, rightly or wrongly, assumed the sermon applied to the recent sentencing phase of the Crenshaw trial. Manny Crenshaw, a young black man, eighteen, had been convicted of shooting and killing Mr. David V. Dozier, sixty-eight, a lawyer who had been watching a movie at home. Someone hearing a shot had summoned the police, who found Manny on the premises and in possession of drugs that he said belonged to Mr. Dozier. Manny denied the shooting, and the police found no gun. Inexplicably, the day after Manny's arrest, someone vandalized Mr. Dozier's house. The jury had found Manny guilty of murder but could not agree that the crime qualified as premeditated and intentional. By means of secret ballots, it quickly became clear that first-degree murder wouldn't fly. The jurors kept voting the same way, 10-1-1, with the abstention counting as a negative vote. Finally, on a 12-0 vote, the jury agreed on voluntary manslaughter, a lesser offense requested by the defense, and entered that decision on the verdict form. The judge, through friends in the Louisiana Department of Corrections, arranged for Manny to do his time at a correctional center, less forbidding than a prison. Adam had served on the jury. Numerous people angrily denounced the sentence of manslaughter as a miscarriage of justice. On the courthouse steps Vincent Dozier, the son, stopped Adam to ask whether he thought the sentence fair. In front of a phalanx of newspaper reporters and photographers, he publicly apologized for the failure of the jury to find in favor of the greater offense, and opined that the decision "strained comprehension."

In a matter of days, the outraged community held Mr. Samuel Hildreth, Wayne's father, responsible for the lesser sentence. They reasoned that his war experiences had pacified him. Treated like a pariah, he remained secluded at home, leery of venturing beyond his front porch, lest the finger pointing metastasize into something more lethal.

Still looking out the window, Zoe said, "Samuel begged me to move. He said we could start over in New Orleans."

Adam said tentatively, "You mean because of the trial?"

"We separated a year and a half before, after he started screaming. I thought he would stop. But he went on this way every night. I told him he needed to see a doctor. I knew one in Baton Rouge. He refused. So we agreed that maybe it would help if he lived elsewhere. He moved to New Orleans. But he came back for the trial. He knew Manny. I could never figure out why Samuel drew jury duty, except for his still being registered to vote in Hungamon. During the trial he lived at home, with Wayne and me. We all got along fine. And then it started again. The screaming. Vietnam had sickened his head really bad. So he returned to New Orleans."

Adam feared that his standing on the courthouse steps and decrying the verdict had contributed to the mob mentality. "I suppose you blame me," he said.

He felt as if her silence would deafen him. Fortunately Wayne, who understood the situation only partially, came to his rescue.

"Mr. and Mrs. Shaw, they been real nice to me, Mom. She gave me cookies and lemonade." Mrs. Hildreth put her hand on Wayne's head and gently stroked it. "And me and Mr. Shaw been talkin' about oil paintings and playin' golf."

She told Wayne to wait outside and turned to face Adam. The boy stopped at the front door and asked if he could collect the balls and a club from the garage to resume putting. "Of course." Adam liked the boy, a handsome lad, well-mannered, though not well-spoken. His high cheekbones had apparently come from his mother, but unlike Wayne's face, hers, he thought, narrowed to a Modigliani V, with a small red Picasso mouth. A hundred years before she undoubtedly would have been the mistress of some French merchant in New Orleans, living in silken splendor in her own quarters, the envy of the man's wife.

"Wayne said that Manny . . ."

"Yes, I saw them empty his pockets."

She ran the fingers of both hands under her eyes, as if adjusting her makeup, but actually wiping away tears.

"But now go the bells, and we are ready." She halted. "It comes from a poem. I like poetry . . . I even try to write it."

"My wife does too."

"Where is she?"

"Church."

"I'm imposing. You probably want to join her."

She slung her handbag over her shoulder.

"No, stay, please. Sit. I want to talk. Would you like something? Coffee, tea, a fruit drink? We have orange, cranberry, apple, tomato, and probably other kinds in the pantry."

"Cranberry, please."

"Done."

Alone in the kitchen, he steadied himself against the counter. The air seemed filled with electrons, and he, pulsating from the charge, felt light-headed and vertiginous. He tried to diagnose his condition, attributing it first to Manny's death, then to lack of sleep, and at last to the presence of Zoe Hildreth. He likened himself to a snake shedding its old skin, a man showering after weeks in the wild, the recipient of a new brain and central nervous system.

As they sipped their drinks, he wished to say how much he regretted his words on the courthouse steps, but that would have been cowardly. He would earn her respect the hard way, by deserving it. He asked her about herself.

"The long or short version?"

"That's up to you."

Born in Panama in 1957, she could speak Spanish, English, and two Indian languages, Naso and Emberá-Katió. She also understood Guari-Guari, a mix of Creole, English, Spanish, African, and Native American.

"While in Panama, I met Samuel Hildreth, a soldier, five years older than me. My parents died of malaria in 1967. So old-school white Baptist missionaries, a childless couple from Arkansas named the Tarpers, raised me. They allowed nothing, especially to a young girl, not even dresses. I wore overalls and accompanied the Tarpers into the jungle to convert the natives and assist at childbirths. The first and only man I ever dated—we met secretly—was Samuel. One night, after climbing out my bedroom window to meet him, I carelessly left the shutters open. It rained hard, and the wooden shutters clattered. The Tarpers discovered my absence. When they questioned me, I confessed: Had he ever done anything to me? No, but we had kissed. The Tarpers virtually put me under house arrest. I had always looked forward to excursions in the jungle, which took me away from the house and introduced me to exotic ways of life. I took my confinement poorly, and I managed, through a servant, to send a message to Samuel, who appeared at the Tarpers' house in his uniform, declared his intentions, and told the Tarpers he would not be 'talked down.' I cracked the door of my upstairs bedroom to listen.

"The meeting proceeded uneventfully until the Tarpers asked Samuel his religion. Methodist. Not even his Southern background could overcome their objections to this heresy. They told Samuel to leave. Before making his exit, he asked, 'What would it take for you to say yes?' A conversion, they said. A heartfelt longing for the Baptist covenant. Instead, Samuel and I eloped shortly after my seventeenth birthday. He wangled a transfer to Louisiana, and here I am." She paused. "And you?"

Zoe's admission, made simply, free of any pride, led Adam to talk frankly about his own life.

"I'm adopted also, twice in fact, but I never knew my real parents. Born in Hungary, I came to the United States with one set of parents, and shortly thereafter lived with another in Newark, New Jersey." He chuckled self-consciously. "The only interesting thing about my background is that I came to this country owning a painting that my real parents presumably sent with me. To this day I have been trying to discover, through that painting, who I am, my roots."

She smiled and opined that the painting might be valuable. "Why else send it along?"

"I agree." They sipped their drinks in silence, occasionally smiling at one another, but mostly ruminating. Breaking the disconcerting lull, he rashly said, "You work in a retirement home." She nodded. "I know what that's like. I manage Moss Hospital. It's private. We have a number of elderly patients. The nurses who work that duty have a hard time of it."

"Even the young lose their wits. You want to cry for them all, especially when their families stop visiting."

"Are you an RN?"

"I have a degree from LSU," She laughed. "It took me seven years to get it, what with raising Wayne."

Impulsively Adam said, "How would you like a job at Moss? I'm sure it will pay more than the retirement home."

She cocked her head like a bird trying to see a frontal object. "I make twenty-four thousand a year."

"I'll give you thirty."

Zoe's first thought was to tell Adam that he knew nothing about her, that he had no idea whether she had the skills the hospital needed, the temperament for the job, the patience to endure the taunting of private white patients. And would he give her a schedule that allowed her to see more of her son? But she couldn't ignore a 25 percent raise, particularly now that she and Samuel lived apart. She wanted to ask him if she could have time to decide and get back to him. Instead, she asked: "Why are you offering me a job?"

Having acted on impulse, he felt unprepared for the question. With her eyes fixed on him, he had nowhere to go, no time to construct a plausible answer. He had learned from his foster home to answer a question with a question.

"Is there some reason I shouldn't?"

"Don't do it out of guilt."

That damned interview again. Why had he ever given it? Judge Emory Waters had warned the jurists that anyone who spoke about the deliberations would be cited for contempt of court. Those two words, "strained comprehension," had violated the judge's orders and invited the wrath of the other panelists. Had Rachel's father not intervened—he and the judge had both attended Ole Miss, though several years apart, and to this day still fished the Gulf waters—Adam might have been jailed and fined. When the public blamed Samuel Hildreth for the verdict, Adam, astonished, felt guilt ridden. In no time Samuel lost his standing in the white community, which normally had a high regard for people who had served in the armed forces. Naturally the black side of the tracks cheered him for his moral courage, but they constituted a minority of the fourteen thousand people of Hungamon, and as such were completely ignored.

Two days after the trial ended, Rachel entertained the judge and her father at dinner. She had not seen the judge in quite a while. He looked older. The jolly, red-faced man, with wisps of hair that rose from the side of his head like wings, looked his almost seventy years, but his consort, Samantha, though older, looked younger. The judge had earned a reputation in the state for chatting with jurors and witnesses and for ignoring the rules when it served his purposes. His daddy had behaved similarly. But debarment never crossed anyone's mind, even when the judge's fierce temper flared. The members of the state bar association merely chuckled that the fruit never falls far from the tree. Much in his cups before dinner, the judge remarked that Immanuel Crenshaw would be transported to Monroe the next day, and he mused about the trial.

Samuel Hildreth had come to see him. Adam asked for particulars, but Emory refused to divulge them. In a moment of contrition, Adam said that perhaps the judge should have put him, Adam, in the "slammer" and "made him pay through the nose" for his injudicious comment. Rachel, shocked by the idea and Adam's intemperate language, objected.

"You sound like a mobster!"

Although her indignation had put an end to the subject, Adam had been harboring the idea of dropping by Judge Waters's house for a talk.

With Adam still lost in thought, Zoe said: "Mr. Shaw—"

He seemed to regard the name as foreign. Zoe repeated it.

"You can call me Adam."

"A young man drowned himself, Mr. Shaw. As I think about it now, I see a string of events that led to his death: desperation, drugs, and a house with a lone man, a gun, blood, and murder. People scream obscenities at a good man and treat him like a traitor."

Though speaking English, she seemed to think in another tongue, perhaps owing to her exposure to the forest Indians of Panama.

"My wife tried to save him from the lake bottom. She's a much better swimmer than me. I did everything I could to comfort Wayne."

"Samuel's fate was foretold, when he voted as he did."

"He showed great bravery."

She looked at him as if she could see right through his skin to his vital organs. "I don't believe you can ever know why people do the things they do. Motives? What's that? Genes, environment, impulse, chemistry, experience, needs, emotions . . . who can say? Maybe all of it, some of it, none of it. How can you ever know?"

He wanted to say he agreed, but he merely stared.

Given the drowning and the attendant circumstances, Rachel asked a friend who had to leave early to take her directly home. Adam introduced her to Zoe. Each condoled with the other, agreeing that the death had been a tragedy and that Manny's parents would need their kind ministrations. Before Zoe drove off, Adam shook her hand and said, "Think it over."

Sipping chardonnay from a fluted glass, one of an antique set that Montgomery had bought them, Rachel thought of the two men in her life: One wanted her to give more of herself, and the other couldn't give enough of himself. Although Adam had never really broached the subject, Rachel knew he thought her prim. How else to explain his teasing her about sex? Having grown up with a father who principally valued her intelligence, and having attended a private school that frowned on demonstrative behavior, she regarded feelings as private, and hers as a powerful potion, a volatile mixture that she carefully dispensed.

She and Adam retired to the screened porch facing the lake. Given the day's events, they had a lot to say. From the first time she'd met him, Adam had excited her fancy. Unlike the other college boys, he rarely talked about himself. Like her, he had Mediterranean coloring and a yen for ballroom dancing. His black wavy hair, his prominent cheekbones, and his dark eyes brought to mind Bedouins and Arabs. With his thin face and thickly sensuous lips, he could have modeled for a clothing company. His childlike good looks, long eyelashes, and muscular torso—he lifted weights—made him attractive to women. When dressed in one of the fashionable suits she selected, he looked like a poster boy for an MBA program at a prestigious university. Although he had majored in accounting, he preferred art history, a subject that initially brought him and Rachel together. Seated two seats apart in a European Medieval art class, Rachel liked his smile, though she found his laugh insincere. He seemed to use it to ingratiate himself with others. While dating in college, she gathered that he regarded her as a prospective trophy wife. But once she turned her irony onto some of his flippant friends, he discovered she had an independent streak and a first-rate critical mind. For all his physical attractions, she marked him as morally confused, a tortured soul who, like so many people, wanted to be his own person and still remain everyone's friend. His passion, in addition to art, was football, which he had played in high school until he injured a knee. Living in Louisiana he closely followed the fortunes of the New Orleans Saints and frequently drove to the city to watch them play. Rachel wished that he cared less for sports and more for her; but if someone were to ask which attentions he failed to bestow on her, which needs she felt unmet, she wouldn't have been able to answer.

She sipped her drink, studied his dark eyes for a moment, and then turned to the docked motorboat she had christened *The Montgomery* in recognition of the donor. The glass table and handsome deck chairs had also been a gift from her father, as well as the chaise lounge. Her father had showered them with gifts, anticipating her every wish. The mere mention of a raft in her dad's presence had precipitated its purchase. She sometimes thought that her father literally owned her.

"How did church go?" Adam asked.

Rachel told him about the coffee hour, with the usual people and the same predictable comments. "Have you ever noticed people's language?" she asked. "Most don't give a care about diction."

Out of his depth Adam simply nodded, unsure whether diction meant words or intonation or both.

"Mrs. Ambers gushed about the pastor, saying what a good heart he has. I wanted to ask her how she—or anyone else—could prove a good heart, unless she meant his treadmill tests."

Adam, nonplussed, said, "This is the first time I have ever heard you find fault with your fellow parishioners."

"Manny's death . . . I told them about it and suggested we take up a collection for the family. They thought a silent prayer would do just as well."

"You can be sure it's the money."

"I used the word morality, but that only angered Mr. Stoner, who said that people often used morality for their own self-interest. 'Are you speaking of me or yourself?' I replied. He sniffed and walked off."

"It looks as if you'll be dropping your membership in the First Baptist Church and joining Memorial Baptist."

Rachel's silence led Adam to assume that she had just such a move in mind, but to his surprise she asked: "What did you mean when you said, 'Think it over?'"

The non sequitur stumped Adam momentarily. "What's that?"

She held the wineglass to her lower lip, contemplating Adam. "She's quite beautiful. I liked her son."

The afternoon heat had raised the mosquitoes to flight and fury. They banged against the screened porch and hummed their ill humor. Adam thought of them as an omen, a portent of an unhappy truth trying to assault his defenses. But what truth, he couldn't say.

"She works for beans at a private retirement home in New Orleans. I've offered her a job at Moss."

Rachel sipped the wine. "Is she qualified?"

"An RN."

"Don't you normally ask for letters of recommendation?"

"Yes, but in this case—"

"As I said, she's quite beautiful."

"Rachel, the drowning—"

"Suicide. Let's call it by its right name."

"—has upset you more than you realize. First you insult your friends at church, and now you insinuate that I—"

"Zoe. That's what you called her."

The drowning, splashed across all the local papers, did not escape Montgomery French's notice. The next day he telephoned Rachel, and she volunteered to come to his house and share what she knew. When she pulled up to the curb, she chuckled. Everyone in town knew that her father had little use for church and spent Sunday mornings, and many others as well, poring over his collection of Bonnie and Clyde memorabilia. If asked whether he regarded himself as a good Christian, he would treat his interlocutor as mad. Did he not contribute to the poor, did he not support black colleges, did he not help the library increase its holdings with his generous gifts? He appeared particularly proud of having enabled LSU to buy a collection of government documents bearing on crime in Louisiana during the Great Depression, the era of Bonnie Parker and Clyde Barrow, John Dillinger, "Ma" Barker, "Pretty Boy" Floyd, "Baby Face" Nelson, and a slew of other desperados.

A chip off the acerbic H. L. Mencken block, Montgomery often observed that Christians railed against female sin but had an insatiable appetite for it. Since the death of his wife, he had, to the shock of Hungamon, been seeing a black woman, Libby Larkin, who had worked for him and his family years before. His reputation would have suffered immeasurably were it not for his wealth, which he sprinkled like chicken seed.

Irascible by nature, Montgomery had softened with the birth of Rachel; and having two women hovering over him—his wife, Miss Ellen, and the nanny, Libby Larkin—had made him civil. But the death of his wife released all his suppressed hostility. His business successes had given him a poor opinion of his competitors, as well as men in general, whom he often bullied, especially those larger than he. With women he behaved like a gentleman caller: polite, deferential, charming. The men in Washington Parish kept their distance, except for Judge Emory Waters.

Rachel used her key to enter the bungalow, which her father preferred to a large house. Always delighted to see his daughter, he took parental pride in her handsome bearing and tasteful reserve; he even found pleasure in the way she moved, lightly and gracefully, reminding him of his wife, who had aspired in her youth to become a ballerina. He tipped back his 1930s fedora, his "gangster hat," revealing his thick white brows, piercing blue eyes, unruly mustache, and narrow nose. They sat at the dinner table he used as a desk, the one spread with newspaper clippings and articles and photographs of the Depression-Era duo. Rachel smiled and opened a privately printed collection of Bonnie Parker's poems. Reading aloud the last five lines from "The Trail's End," a poem Bonnie had written in prison, Rachel delighted her father.

Some day they'll go down together;
And they'll bury them side by side.
To few it'll be grief—
To the law a relief—
But it's death for Bonnie and Clyde.

Her reading provided him an excuse to visit his favorite subject.

"Those god-damned deputies poured more than 150 bullets into Clyde's car. Hell, they weren't goin' anywhere, in fact, just the opposite. Clyde had stopped his Ford to help a friend, Ivy Methvin, who had jacked up his Model A Ford truck for repairs."

On numerous occasions Rachel had heard her father review the different accounts of the shooting. He treated the story like an onion, carefully peeling off the skins and hoping to find at its core some historical fact heretofore overlooked.

Mr. French's obsession with the story and the car had led him to a Texas collector who sold him the same model car that Clyde drove at the time of the shooting: a Cordoba gray 1934 Ford V8, four-door deluxe sedan, model 730, with three speeds, safety glass windows, a steel cover for the spare tire, a Potter trunk, front and rear bumper guards, and a chrome Greyhound radiator cap ornament. It even included an Arvin hot water heater and Firestone tires. He not only drove it in parades, he also used it in his daily activities.

Before he went any further, she reminded him of why she had come and then proceeded to tell him all she knew about Manny's death by drowning.

"You probably ought to visit the family," suggested her father. "They've no doubt seen your name in the papers."

"I plan to."

Rachel barely listened as her father resumed talking about his favorite subject. She took the occasion to dust sills and tabletops. Since returning to Louisiana, she had made it a point to visit her father's bungalow on a regular basis to "tidy up." Montgomery refused to hire a maid, though he could well afford one. Maids, he had learned from past experience, moved papers, even when told not to. His table might look a mess, but he knew the place of every scrap and scribble. Not even Rachel could navigate the swamp of paper. By habit she peered at the painting of her grandfather, Montgomery Xavier French, who had died just before her ninth birthday. The painting showed a bearded man with piercing dark eyes astride a handsome horse. He wore a wide-brimmed hat, jodhpurs with a silver belt buckle engraved 1933, and riding boots. In his right hand rested the reins, resembling a snake, and in his left, a short whip or crop. In the Edenic background stood several men wearing cowls or hoods. The unsigned canvas, rumored to have been painted by a Negro artist who had moved north, always caught her attention. The bottom of the frame held a small brass plate engraved "Kinsman." Montgomery worshiped his father and often commented that he wished the old man had lived long enough for Rachel to appreciate his patriotism and strength of purpose. He would brook no criticism of him.

"See you next week, Daddy," Rachel said, hugging her father good-bye. "I put some Clorox in the toilet. Let it sit a while." As she sailed out the door, she said over her shoulder, "Give my regards to Libby and also a kiss."

Montgomery smiled.

Libby Larkin was the daughter of an octoroon, Samantha Larkin, who worked for Judge Emory Waters as a cook and housemaid. Rumors circulated that when the judge's wife, Miss Julie, died in her mid-forties from ovarian cancer, his great loneliness and despair drove him to quietly take Samantha Larkin as his mistress. Some people whispered that they had known each other before. She came from Vermilion Parish, in the heart of Cajun country, where her parents, penurious and pious, dug clams and died in a boardinghouse fire. Impregnated by a young man working the legal circuit, Samantha, with his help, supported herself and her daughter. Thankfully Libby's prettiness and good nature caused folks not to dwell on her roots, a subject that could lead to mischief. But her curiosity about her daddy led Libby to ask for details. Samantha told her that he had died in a boating accident, and that his body was never recovered. His name? Emerson Wilson. But for the sake of convenience, Samantha kept her maiden name. Montgomery French met the mother and daughter through the judge. At the time, Libby was seventeen and Montgomery twenty-four.

Now a youthful seventy-three, Samantha still flashed a naughtiness in her eyes, and with her ample bosom and pleasant figure, she teased the young boys and drove the older men to distraction. In her parish they called her a Jezebel; but they might just as well have called her a felon. She learned early on how to make bootleg liquor, which she sold to local bars. From the age of ten, she shoplifted, ran errands for the "leggers," and perfected the fine art of eavesdropping. Hired to sweep and mop the local church, she quickly discovered the heating conduit, large enough for her to crawl through. Among other rooms, it vented the pastor's study. When he and an aggrieved wife or husband disappeared into the room, Samantha squirmed into the conduit and listened. The revelations she heard served her well. On one occasion a teacher threatening to fail her confessed to the pastor about an affair. Soon after, the teacher received a signed note from her student:

*Dear Mr. Sorcell,*

*If you don't quit bothering me about bein left-handed (I came born that way and cant help it), Im gonna tell your pretty wife about you and Miss Hicks. I seen you both making whoopee.*

*Sam*

The next day in class, Mr. Sorcell, as if bewitched, greeted her warmly and invited her to submit an extra paper to improve her grade from an F to a B. For the rest of the term, she became his pet student.

Her larceny—and appearance—suited the judge. As a cousin of his once said: "She had the roundest butt and goosiest tits in southern Louisiana." Whatever else they may have had in common, the judge and Samantha both loved her Bayou booze, which she distilled at the back of the house. Although Hungamon's patience for revenuers was always short, for moonshiners it was long, given the poisonous paper company fumes. So no one took any notice of the foul smells in the woods behind Emory's house. As she mixed her witch's brew in a copper kettle, she sang a favorite ditty:

You lookin' like you need a lift,
The kind that comes from Bayou booze,
And makes the Cajuns drool and wish
For some of it and jazzy blues.

Unlike Libby—her well-mannered, umber-skinned daughter—Samantha relished outrageous behavior. The judge, perhaps to keep alive his wife's memory, gave Samantha permission to wear and alter any of his wife's clothing, which still hung in closets and rested among mothballs in chests. While riffling through Mrs. Waters's clothes, Samantha came upon the judge's old silk top hat, which she immediately donned and jauntily wore at an angle with a pair of Miss Julie's white gloves. To enrich the ensemble, she smoked a corncob pipe. She peppered her talk with salacious comments, but never around Libby, whom she brought up like a white debutante. The judge even paid for Libby to attend a private girls' school, All Saints, in Vicksburg, Mississippi. The school authorities decided she could pass for white because of the green in the judge's wallet.

In fact that's where Montgomery first seriously noticed the handsome young woman, at her school graduation. He had accompanied his Ole Miss friend to the ceremony, expecting to tour some of the antebellum mansions and visit a few Civil War monuments. But instead he spent his time in the company of the enchanting Libby. After her return to Hungamon, Montgomery saw a great deal of her, even after she belatedly attended Sophie Newcomb and accepted a teaching position in the Ninth Ward. But then she disappeared. The judge said she now lectured on a tourist ship, and Samantha refused to say anything.

Montgomery made some inquiries among his friends in the Crescent City, but no one knew anything about a Libby Larkin. A few months later, Montgomery met Ellen Churchill, whose family roots, in one way or another, sprouted from Winston's forebears. She too had attended Sophie Newcomb, but unlike Libby, right out of high school. Her degree in fine arts prepared her for a career as a potter and glazer, but marriage changed her plans. Ellen and Montgomery honeymooned in France, where they remained for over a year. When they returned she cradled, to everyone's surprise, a baby girl, whom they named Rachel Caroline French, the middle name in remembrance of Montgomery's mother. The couple quickly fell in with the Hungamon social whirl, albeit modest, attending dinner parties and country club events and riding on floats for Mardi Gras celebrations. As a result Rachel grew up amid privileged splendor. When Libby Larkin mysteriously appeared for Rachel's first birthday, explaining that she had been working on a cruise ship that ran from New Orleans to Key West, Samantha cried "Hallelujah," and the judge behaved most generously, offering Libby a place in his house. But Montgomery insisted that Ellen wanted her for a nanny to look after Rachel. The judge told Libby that the decision rested with her. She chose the Montgomery household and the care of the lovely child, whom she fiercely protected. In later years Rachel remarked that she had grown up in the best of all worlds: with a father and two mothers. She knew that such a world existed for thousands of children owing to the surfeit of black nannies in the South and a culture that saw no contradiction in allowing the nanny to raise—and, in some cases nurse—the child, and always disappear when guests came to call. The birth mothers made it a point to hug and kiss their children goodnight or to show off the children to friends, at which time the nannies stayed out of sight, knowing their place. But Mr. and Mrs. French treated Libby as a regular member of the family, which made the Montgomery home different and caused their friends no little unease.

# Family, Church, and Private School

A few days after speaking to her father, Rachel telephoned the Crenshaws to request permission for Adam and her to pay their condolences. Marie Crenshaw invited them to the house and indicated that she and her husband had a favor to ask. The Crenshaws lived on the edge of town in a black neighborhood, a fact that made the Shaws' social visit unusual, to say the least. Rachel drove. She turned her Buick onto a leafy street of one-story bungalows with neatly kept yards and stopped at number 1601. A pink flamingo lawn ornament greeted them as they exited the car and made their way up the stoop to the screened porch. The board siding of the house needed paint, and the roof lacked a few shingles. Adam had seen Manny's parents in court, sitting silently and seeming stunned by the proceedings; after all, their son had been raised in the truths of the church and had been a track star.

Al Crenshaw opened the door, which led into a tidy living room. A three-piece maroon set—sofa and two parlor chairs—occupied most of the space, except for a small coffee table and two floor lamps with orange shades. Jam cookies had already been placed on the table. Al directed them to the parlor chairs, a cue for Marie Crenshaw to wheel in a trolley with a coffeepot surrounded by cups and saucers. Adam normally drank tea, but because no one asked, he politely sipped the coffee.

"Manny never misbehaved," said Marie. "An ideal son." She pointed to three pictures on the wall: Manny, in the center, flanked on one side by a velvet-framed Jesus and on the other by a church enveloped in mist. Although religious, the Crenshaws eschewed fundamentalism. As she put down her cup, Rachel could see under the table several novels, all of them apparently written by Saul Bellow and Philip Roth.

"I'm the book reader," said Marie. "Al, he likes magazines. We keep those in the kitchen."

"In college," said Rachel, "I read both of those writers. I majored in English. But I must admit that I can't remember much about them. It's been too long."

Marie smiled and put down her cup. "Well, I'm no college person, but I can tell you this. Both those writers like to put themselves at the center of their books, and then they pull out their insides for everyone to see. If it's color you want . . . if you're lookin' for landscapes and soldiers and armies and generations growing up, you'd better find someone else to read."

Marie poured more coffee. No one spoke. Adam could guess the Crenshaws' thoughts: He had implied that Manny deserved a harsher punishment, the one utterance he feared he'd always be remembered for.

"I didn't know your boy—" said Rachel.

"If you had," Marie interrupted, "you woulda known him incapable of killing anyone. The jury got it all wrong. I admit he fell into trouble after high school . . . lookin' for a path to follow and goin' with drugs. You're probably thinkin', well, an addiction can kill. Surely that's true, but rightly or wrongly I suppose he thought of himself as helpin' people, those hurtin' and needing somethin' to ease the pain. But to shoot down a man in cold blood . . . not Manny."

Adam thought back to the trial and asked, "As far as you know, did he ever own a gun?"

"Never."

"He did business with Mr. Dozier," said Adam, probing.

Al took the bait. "Manny never trusted him. Called him a cheat. I guess he regularly held out on him."

"Did Manny say for sure?" Adam asked.

"Manny kept secrets good. He treated a secret like the grave. You don't ever want to disturb it."

A lull in the conversation ensued, until Rachel broke the silence. "You mentioned a request."

Marie eyed the floor, as if she regarded her request as too controversial for polite company.

"We'd like—" Then she started to cry.

Al hugged her and finished the sentence. "We're hoping that Manny can be buried in the Hungamon Cemetery, with some other black folks. But none of them . . ."

The Shaws said nothing, though both of them understood the allusion. None of the blacks interred in the city cemetery included suicides or convicted murderers.

Marie choked back her tears and continued. "Our own black church has rules about such things, so I thought maybe you could talk to your pastor and see if he could help."

"We have less . . ." Adam started to say defensively and then let the demurral die. He would have said "influence than you might think."

Rachel came to his aid, explaining the quirky land deed that allowed the city to administer the cemetery even though the First Baptist Church owned the property.

"We understand. But you and Mr. Shaw here are outstanding members of the community and church," said Marie. "Al and me thought that if you made the request, well, you understand." To Adam's surprise, Rachel said, "Of course we'll make the request. I'll even ask my daddy to speak to friends of his on the City Council." She would have acknowledged the closeness between her father and Judge Waters, but decided against it in light of his having presided over the trial.

As if to further buttress her belief in the innocence of her son, Marie said, "The police went through all of Manny's belongings, but they couldn't find any incriminating evidence. Trust me, Manny ain't what they made him out to be. And he certainly never acted as mean-hearted as the police in this town. Why, they even confiscated his car—or should I say ours—because of his conviction."

On a sudden impulse, Rachel, who had been angling for a new car, said, "Parked in front of the house, you'll see a blue Buick, in good shape. The car is yours." She handed Mr. Crenshaw the keys.

Adam had hoped to apologize for his ill-considered remarks after the trial, but not finding the opportunity, owing to his wife's astonishing generosity, he added, "I'll transfer ownership and send you the papers."

Marie looked at the Shaws ambivalently. Adam hoped she didn't regard the car as "blood money." So before she could speak, he related an early memory.

"A boy once bloodied my nose. The next day he gave me his favorite agate—to make amends. For a moment, I thought I'd refuse the marble so that his guilt would keep preying on him. But as a poor boy, I knew that I wanted the agate. So I took it. To this day, I'm glad that I did." He reached into his pocket and removed a key ring in which a marble had been set in silver. "Have a look."

Both Crenshaws fingered the marble and returned it. Marie had tears in her eyes. "You're not a bad man. You made a mistake. We're all entitled to a second chance."

Al, like a faithful amen chorus, said, "At least two."

Rachel suddenly realized that they had no means of returning home. "Mr. Crenshaw, would you kindly take us back to our house. I just gave away my car."

Al laughed. "I ain't never driven one in my life. Marie here's the chauffeur. She chariots me around."

On the way home Rachel explained the car's features, and the Shaws patiently listened as Marie recounted Manny's "miracles," like winning the dashes and the hurdles.

At the inquest for Immanuel Crenshaw, Zoe and Samuel Hildreth accompanied their son Wayne. The coroner asked the boy to describe the event, and the Shaws to explain their role in the attempted recovery. Although the coroner ruled the death a suicide, he normally worked as a mortician and had no prior experience with suicide; he therefore passed his findings on to the district attorney, who, in turn, consulted Judge Emory Waters about whether to proceed further. The judge concurred in the finding of suicide and asked to speak to both the Crenshaws and the Hildreths, separately. When Zoe and Samuel talked to the judge, the two men greeted each other familiarly. The judge quickly sized up the situation and saw that Samuel had no inclination to talk, so he filled the void.

"It's useless to pin the blame for the suicide on anyone. When someone dies senselessly, we inveigh against God and ask, 'Where is justice?'" He paused. "But in fact, if we exacted justice for every wrong, the world would perish. We must therefore rule our persons with not only law but also mercy, and let not dreadful truths make us enemies of ourselves. For then . . ." He never finished.

After condoling with the Hildreths, the judge seemed more intent on learning from the Crenshaws whether Manny had ever mentioned his drug contacts than on listening to their request that Manny be interred in the city cemetery. The parents came away from the brief talk persuaded that Rachel represented their best bet.

The service for Manny Crenshaw, held at the African Methodist Church, saw Mr. and Mrs. Crenshaw, clearly overcome by grief, sitting silently in the front row and at the conclusion disappearing into the vestry. Adam and Rachel also attended, as well as Zoe and Samuel.

Whenever Adam looked at Samuel, he thought of a long, thin rope of muscle supporting a cropped head, with a haunted face. For some reason Samuel's facial lineaments reminded Adam of a cracked porcelain vase he had seen in the New Orleans Museum of Art. The Greek vase exhibited several fighting men or warriors. Samuel Hildreth's ramrod, sinewy body bespoke the military, and the sadness in his eyes told of indelible memories.

"Always good to see you, Samuel. When are you heading back?"

"Soon as I can."

"Sad circumstances."

"Could've been worse if we had voted for—"

What could Adam say, having publicly compromised himself?

Samuel turned and walked off, making it clear he had no interest in sustained conversation, at least not with Adam.

The black pastor, substituting for the regular one, asked the congregation not to judge Manny, but to consider the fear and guilt that would drive one to take his own life. Those who saw Manny's death as fitting revenge for his deed had forgotten the words of their Savior.

"The Lord expects all His children, old and young, to have love in their hearts. Those without, let us forgive.

Gentle Jesus, meek and mild,
Look upon this young man-child;
Pity his simplicity,
Suffer him to come to thee."

The choir sang several spirituals and concluded with "Oh, Rock-a My Soul," the congregation joining in on the chorus. At the end, a single soprano voice, not a woman, not a man, no, a boy, sounding like a castrato, added two solo lines, a celestial refrain, the music of the spheres. They had come from a chorister who rose above the choir, descanting melodic lines heralding a new day, ushering in a new world.

"Now if you get there afore I do,
Rock-a my soul,

Tell all my friends I'm a comin' too,
Rock-a my soul."

The voice belonged to Wayne Hildreth.

In the parking lot, Adam took the Hildreths aside and offered to pay for voice lessons. Wayne turned to his mother, who thanked Adam and said it all depended on how Wayne's schoolwork proceeded—and her own schedule.

Although Moss Hospital, on the outskirts of New Orleans, specialized in tropical diseases, it also treated general ills. Designed in the Victorian style, the redbrick building had come into existence through the charity of Margaret Moss, a victim of malaria. While traveling in Central America, she had contracted the parasite, returned to New Orleans, and, finding no cure for her fevers and chills, donated the majority shares of her wealth to the construction of a research center for the prevention, diagnosis, and treatment of tropical diseases. Her husband, Leland Moss, who had preceded her in death, had made a fortune in oil. The childless couple had always been philanthropic, particularly in regard to the arts; but after Leland's passing and Margaret's illness, she rewrote her will, leaving the lion's share to the hospital and a pediatric wing that bore their names.

Adam Shaw was fortunate to have joined the hospital's accounting department right out of college, at a time when the two older men who kept the books had already cut back to half time. Two years later both men retired, and Adam, looking to upgrade his staff, recruited a couple of graduates, a man and a woman, from the Wharton School of Business. They proved so competent that Adam had time to study the workings of the hospital and make several suggestions for cost cutting, capital improvements, fund-raising, and staffing. When the hospital director, in poor health, retired, the board offered Adam the position. Moss had heretofore drawn most of its medical staff from Southern schools, but Adam widened the net, recruiting graduates of the Albert Einstein College of Medicine and other East Coast institutions. Maurice Cohen, the gastroenterologist, came to Moss from Beth Israel Hospital in Newark, because of a personal visit from Adam, who had told him that he had carte blanche to hire the best in his field.

The hospital, with Adam's help, had been particularly fortunate in securing multiyear, multimillion-dollar government grants for research into mosquito-borne ailments: Chagas' disease, dengue fever, Ross River virus infection, and sleeping sickness. In the basement laboratories special receptacles held these deadly insects, which required special handling lest they escape and turn the state of Louisiana into a seething cauldron of illness and death. The basement also held cages of mice and holding pens for stray cats and dogs, all used in medical experiments. Adam had often thought that in some states the animal rights movement would have made Moss's research virtually impossible, but Louisiana showed more interest in the sybaritic life than in animal life.

Zoe Hildreth started work two weeks after Adam offered her the job. He wanted to position her close to his office, but as a nurse she belonged in the wards—the safe ones, which required no special protective clothing. Making a point to regularly visit the nursing stations—a routine he had never followed before—he quickly determined, from the work-schedule sheet hung on the wall, Zoe's assignments. At first their exchanges, formal and brief, lacked any real familiarity. It took a few weeks before he joined her in the cafeteria and several more before he asked her to leave the grounds of the hospital to have lunch with him at a fashionable restaurant. They drove in his car, a two-year-old black Saab convertible. He made it a point not to take the top down.

At the Escargot, his favorite restaurant, he would be recognized; so he chose another, an Italian one, the Pericolo. Sitting at a booth in the back, they both ordered a large side of shrimp.

Dipping a shrimp into a tasty sauce, Adam said, "It probably came from a Vietnamese fisherman. They're rapidly moving into the industry."

"The old-timers resent them."

"That's America, always changing."

"For some."

Adam understood and changed the subject. "I haven't asked you. How do you like the job?"

Zoe put down her fork and, without looking at Adam, replied, "Why don't you take Mrs. Shaw to lunch?"

The implication: Adam chased skirts. He laughed, but instead of his explanation sounding carefree, as he intended, it came out defensive. "We often have lunches together on weekends . . . in Hungamon."

"Hungamon ain't New Orleans."

He had never heard her use slang, which made him feel she had used it to make a point. Ethan and Beverly Dexter, his foster family, had made a great to-do about proper English, observing that swearing and poor grammar indicated that a person suffered from "a paucity of vocabulary." Forcing himself to say, "No, it ain't," he hoped that his repetition of the word would mark it as inappropriate. But she didn't seem to notice.

The silence that followed his comment and her expression indicated she still expected a response to her question.

"Mrs. Shaw has the busiest schedule of any woman in Louisiana." Though the statement contained an element of truth, it sounded to him artificial. So he tried again. "Really, she's very busy, and the few times we go out to eat, her father joins us." There, he told himself, I've said it. Truth is the best policy.

"Mr. Shaw—"

"Must you be so formal?"

"All right, I'll let my hair down. Adam, I think you have a yen for me. Mind you, I'm not angry. Fact is, I'm flattered. But where is this headed?" He seemed puzzled. "Our meeting for lunch, here and at the hospital," she said. "I'm married, you're married."

"Breaking up my marriage never crossed my mind."

She pushed away her salad. "An affair?"

"A mutually satisfying accommodation," he said before realizing how forward and stiff his statement sounded.

She took a couple of deep breaths as if preparing for a run to the board of the long jump. "Your thinking defeats me." She excused herself for the ladies' room. Adam frantically tried to conceive different scripts, sensitive dialogue, bon mots. Perhaps he should mention her electric presence. But on her return, he said nothing, waiting for her to speak first.

"Adam, since you want me to call you by your first name, I will. Surely you realize that between us stands a great divide, and I'm not talking about race. That day on the courthouse steps, when you said what you did, you forever affected my husband's life for the worse." She stopped, knowing the dramatic effect of silence.

He nearly replied, "So why did you take the job?" But realized how crass that would sound.

Back at the hospital he tried to remember what they had said after Zoe had made it clear that, to a large degree, she held him responsible for exacerbating her husband's condition. To his dismay, he could remember only inquiring banally if she had liked the lunch.

That evening, Adam gently kissed Rachel on the neck and wrapped his arms around her. She smiled, stroked his hair, rose from her chair, and started to accompany him upstairs to the bedroom. Suddenly the phone rang, a raucous intrusion into domestic bliss. He vaulted downstairs to grab it in the hallway.

"Yes?" A lull. "Really?" said Adam keenly, his tone changing from annoyance to interest. "Where is the preview? In LA or San Francisco?" Pause. "I'll be there."

Rachel had come to the foot of the stairs. Adam explained, "That was Scot Marco. Butterfields just acquired a Munkácsy for sale. He said the provenance would interest me and might help with my painting. The auction takes place two weeks from Saturday, the preview the Wednesday before. I'm sure I can get away for a few days. I'll call the airline now."

Rachel looked downcast, either because of the missed intimacy or because of what she said next. "I hope you're not planning to buy another painting. We have no more wall space."

"Scot said that he wanted to show me some important similarities between my canvas and the Munkácsy coming up for auction. The styles and colors correspond. Same period. Apparently a few valuable letters came with the painting." He pirouetted around the room. "Do you realize, Rachel, this may be the clue that I've been looking for all these years?"

Scot Marco, the head of painting at Butterfields, learned his craft at Sotheby's in London and had become a prominent art appraiser and auctioneer on the West Coast, stationed in Los Angeles. Adam had dealt with him before, having purchased two canvases of the California Impressionism movement, sometimes called California *plein-air* painting. Scot had told him that someday the paintings would be quite valuable. He hadn't misspoken. More than one museum had contacted Adam about selling the Guy Rose and the Edgar Payne that hung in the living room.

He dashed to his art catalogs, set up his stand and magnifying glass, caressed the pages, and completely forgot about making love, at least to Rachel.

Seated at the Shaw's kitchen table, Rachel and Libby held hands as Rachel asked for advice. Of all the people she fondly regarded, she loved Libby best. How many times had the hands she now held held hers? Libby had been her nanny and, after the death of Miss Ellen, she had become her mother and confidante. Never affectionate in public, they hugged and giggled in private, sharing private thoughts about friends, family, and foes. Rachel had been granted permission to speak to the City Council about the burial of Manny Crenshaw in the city cemetery. But she felt at a loss for what to say. When it came to black and white relations, Rachel often sought Libby's clearheaded guidance. Libby, in a house dress, her hair done up in a bun, looked ready to undertake a day's work. Rachel, on the other hand, wore a smart suit and high heels. A stranger looking in from the outside on that September day in 1988 might have regarded the view as a maid taking instruction from her mistress.

"They'll tell you black people have their own cemetery."

"Two miles from town."

"They'll say that the boy committed a murder and killed himself."

"The case might have gone up for appeal had Manny not . . ."

"Escaped, owing to desperation and fear."

"What reasons can I give?"

Rachel studied Libby's face, with its finely etched features. A stately woman and a good one, she would never let you down in time of battle.

Adam had left early for work that morning. Rachel had sought his advice, but he pleaded, as he often did, that the South remained a mystery to him.

"No argument's gonna move them," said Libby. "The only chance you got is money. Offer to buy 'em a new fire engine or a community center, then they'll suddenly discover a reason to let the boy into the Hungamon Cemetery."

Rachel gazed out to the lake. It had rained during the night. The day, beginning to reclaim the light from the overcast sky, promised illumination.

"With my trust fund and my daddy's help . . ."

"My guess is he'd refuse."

Rachel digressed. "Even though you live in separate houses, you care for him. Look after him. Love him. Does he make it all worth it?"

"I wouldn't put it in financial terms." Then she said simply, "Not a day passes when he doesn't show me, one way or another, that he loves me. How many women can say that about their menfolk?"

Libby's observation silenced them both.

"I try," said Rachel, "and so does Adam, but we haven't yet got the knack of it, if that's the right word."

"People marry and they learn to love each other. A pearl has to grow. It's not in the shell from the beginning. From a piece of sand something rare and priceless eventually emerges. That's the way many good marriages work."

"Well," said Rachel sprightly, "at least I don't have to marry a member of the City Council. They're all corpses. So wish me luck."

The women hugged and went their separate ways.

Rachel drove to the edge of town. The City Council met in a former one-room schoolhouse. Small, cramped, and stuffy, the room had no windows, a disused potbellied coal stove stamped "Estate," and walls and a ceiling darkened by the greasy residue of kerosene lamps, which had once lit the classroom. Rachel guessed that the children who studied in this building must have suffered from all manner of bronchial ailments. The air, still today, needed purifying, even though the two ceiling fans, recently installed, labored to dispel the heaviness. A long table at the front of the room served the seven city council members and a secretary, who recorded the proceedings on a computer. Six rows of chairs, which students once occupied, remained mostly empty, filled to capacity only when the subject before the council concerned taxes.

On this day nine people, including Rachel, attended the meeting, three of whom she knew: Samantha Larkin, who no doubt had been asked by Judge Waters to report on the meeting, and Mr. and Mrs. Crenshaw. The other five, she guessed, represented the town newspaper, the Confederate Cemetery Society, a local church or two, and maybe even a member of the KKK. She and the Crenshaws, the only ones who had requested permission to address the council, sat together.

Marie Crenshaw spoke first, pointing out that the family had lived in the community for seventy years and had worked for white folks who treated them as equals, white folks who lay buried in the Hungamon Cemetery. She wanted her son to lie among friends.

Mr. Smalley, a council member, asked, "Why not among black friends?"

"The black cemetery, in all honesty, isn't up to the standard of Hungamon's."

Al interjected. "She's bein' polite. Our cemetery isn't kept up. It's weedy and run-down, littered with trash, and used by some unsavory types for nighttime . . . frolics."

"Where is the boy now?" asked Mr. Piccolo. "I mean the, um, body."

Marie answered in a voice so low, one had to strain to hear. "In the refrigerator at the morgue."

The Crenshaws then drew on their Christian values and begged for understanding, charity, love, forgiveness. But the Council seemed unmoved. Then Al disclosed, to the shock of everyone present, that his great-great uncle could be found in the Hungamon Cemetery. This revelation set the council members buzzing.

"Who precisely is that?" asked an incredulous Mr. Short.

"William 'Willie' Washburn. He fought for the Confederate army and lost an arm at the Battle of Irish Bend. His commandin' officer had all the black soldiers in his regiment change their last names to his, Washburn. Lucky he didn't also insist on them changin' their first names to his, Habaziniah. After the war, Willie resumed his real name."

Mr. Stout nodded toward the secretary, who searched in the computer. Sure enough, a Mr. Washburn fought for the South, died in Hungamon, and was buried in the city cemetery.

Al and Marie Crenshaw looked as if they had just hit the jackpot. With the council now in a state of consternation, Rachel tried to apply the coup de grâce. Following the advice of Libby, she left reason behind and appealed to the council's principal concern: uniting money and morality.

"The First Baptist Church could use a children's center, where parents could drop off preschoolers before work and deposit them during services. I have heard estimates that such a center would cost six figures. If I can prevail upon First Baptist to lend their support to burying Immanuel Crenshaw in the Hungamon Cemetery, with the understanding that the Shaw and French families will pay to construct such a center, will you go along?" She paused, knowing full well that at least four of the council members belonged to First Baptist.

The voice vote stood at five to two in favor, with all four of her fellow parishioners in support. Now she just had to persuade the pastor and five of the nine church elders.

At Louis Armstrong New Orleans International Airport, before boarding his morning flight, Adam called the office to check with his assistant, Mrs. May.

No nothing terribly important, but "the family from Panama that flew here for their baby's treatment—"

"The people Zoe's been translating for—"

"Yes. The parents are now having second thoughts."

"Why?"

"Surgery is recommended."

"Ask Maurice to handle it. I'm sure he and Zoe can bring them around."

He took his seat in first class, sipped an orange juice, and thought of the numerous patients terrified at the thought of surgery. The worst, a Mr. Barish, bolted from the hospital trailing an IV and catheter, grabbed a cab, and went home. The next day his wife had him back in the hospital for a rather routine operation.

Adam drove his rented car from LAX to the San Diego Freeway and headed north. At Sunset Boulevard he exited the freeway going east and wound through an exclusive area of Beverly Hills and million-dollar homes. He had been to Los Angeles three times before, twice to buy paintings and once, in the company of Dr. Maurice Cohen, to interview a radiologist at the UCLA medical school whom he hoped to recruit.

His memory of meetings with Scot Marco induced a smile. A well-spoken, curly headed, round-faced fellow, Scot, always a model of courtesy, told Adam that in his youth he had been unruly; but Adam couldn't imagine the art dealer ever behaving in an unseemly manner. He parked behind Butterfields Auction Gallery, situated just east of Laurel Canyon on the north side of the street. The preview, by invitation only, would undoubtedly attract art dealers, professional collectors, movie stars, and friends of Butterfields, all milling in and out of the rooms and taking notes on those paintings that arrested their interest. Casually making his way through the crowd, Adam saw Scot across the room talking to a famous actress. As he approached, he could hear her say that she wished to buy the painting for her boyfriend, who disliked portraits but loved early American landscapes. The painting in front of them exhibited a white farmhouse and a fence with farm animals and two small figures standing near the front door. Adam guessed eighteenth-century American and looked at the description printed below the frame. "Painter: anon. American primitive. Circa: 1760. Estimated price: $25,000–$30,000." Scot pitched the painting to the starlet by explaining that country scenes rarely included figures in them, and that he thought the painting would probably fetch a little more than the estimate. Adam admired the painting and, to catch Scot's attention, volunteered a gratuitous comment: "It's marvelously evocative."

The screen star smiled at Adam and said to Scot, "I don't like to buy things without knowing where they came from. I won't even buy a blouse unless I'm sure it didn't come from some sweatshop in Asia."

"The family, for personal reasons, wishes to remain anonymous."

Adam suddenly remembered. She had appeared in the Wednesday evening soap opera *The Last of the Lanes*, in which a young woman traces her family roots to the South and slavery. Of course the discoveries she makes are sensational: miscegenation, lost children, passing (light-skinned blacks passing for white), the Underground Railroad and, in each episode, a resolution that hinges on an unlikely *deus ex machina*. He still couldn't remember her name, but he recalled some scenes on a beach that showed her buxom figure to good advantage. Rachel, who normally exhibited impeccable taste, liked the series because, she said, it illuminated a part of American history rarely told.

Eventually the woman consented to go as high as $35,000, but she wanted her bid to remain silent. Scot agreed to arrange it. As she wandered off on her high heels, her blond hair floating behind her, Adam took Scot's expression to mean, *The things a guy has to do to make a living!*

Upstairs, in Scot's office, they sat side by side and looked at two documents, one in Hungarian, a bill of sale, the other in German, an appropriation order. Shortly after receiving the documents, Scot commissioned a UCLA history professor, fluent in Hungarian and German, to translate them. She also included a letter bearing on Jewish names in Hungary and the meaning of the appropriation order.

*Dear Mr. Marco,*

*The problem of Hungarian names has long baffled genealogists. Although Emperor Joseph the second ordered the Jews to take family names—preferably German, the official language—the Jews waited until 1851 to comply. Even then difficulties arose. The Jews of Hungary spoke three languages: Yiddish, Hungarian, and German, so last names often appear with different spellings and diacritical markings. With first names, we encounter even more confusion, because people often used nicknames.*

*The documents clearly state the name of the man who sold the painting, Vilmos Kovács, and the man who bought it, Simon Weisz. But in Hungary, Kovács is a common surname and difficult to trace. As to the buyer, I may have a lead for you. According to the Ellis Island records, a Simon and Piroska Weisz, and their two children, Aliz and Laurenz, immigrated to America in 1944, having come by way of Budapest and Palestine. They listed their city of destination as Denver, Colorado. In my experience, few Hungarian immigrants during this period kept their original last names, owing to American prejudices. Weisz, in all likelihood, would have been changed to White. I'd guess that Aliz became Alice, and Laurenz, Lawrence. The father, Simon, probably kept his name. Piroska? In Hungarian it means "the blushing one."*

*A colleague in modern German history, whom I consulted about the appropriation order, told me that when the Jews of Hungary boarded trains to either death camps or Palestine—a few hundred Zionists escaped for reasons too complicated to go into here—Eichmann ordered all objets d'art confiscated and catalogued. German efficiency! The painting in question by Mihály Munkácsy once belonged to the Simon Weisz family from whom the German authorities in Budapest confiscated it. How the paint-*

*ing came into your possession, I have no doubt, is a story worth telling. Thank you for the check, and I hope one day to hear the details.*

*Yours sincerely,*
*Rosalie Csillag*

Adam's mind raced. In the small prewar Hungarian art collecting world, the Weisz or White family might have known who had eventually purchased *The Scribe*. Private collectors of Mihály Munkácsy's paintings composed a small fraternity. Adam asked Scot about the provenance.

"You said on the phone the story only could have come out of the war."

"The family confided in me because I'm responsible for validating the authenticity of the painting."

"Mum's the word, I promise."

"After the Germans appropriated the painting, they stored it, with thousands of other ill-gotten gains, in a warehouse in Pest."

Adam and Rachel had taken a Danube boat trip, and he remembered that the river divided Budapest. On the right bank stood Buda, built on hills; on the left, Pest, flat. Buda was fashionably residential, Pest, commercial.

Scot continued, "Near the close of the war, in April 1945, the Nazis put the stolen goods on a train for Germany. But the Americans intercepted the train and moved the contents to a warehouse near Salzburg. Many of the items the US Army appropriated, they sold to soldiers."

"Our own people. Who would believe it?"

"A man by the name of Benci Molnar worked in the Pest warehouse, sorting the goods. In the confusion of the war and its aftermath, he managed to keep several paintings. A collector in the American Embassy—in return for a painting or two—helped him and his wife, Erika, immigrate to the United States. Benci, though, kept the Munkácsy for himself. His son, Gabor, who lives in Long Beach, contacted Butterfields and asked us to sell the painting without mentioning the Molnar name.

"Naturally, when we heard the story, we tried to contact the Weisz or White family, but we couldn't find any trace of them in Denver or anywhere else in Colorado. All over the world, paintings taken from the Jews are just now beginning to surface and be restored to them. I wanted to see the same repeated here. No luck. Perhaps if we had looked outside Colorado . . . who knows?"

"To the victor goes the spoils," Adam mumbled.

"No, to the warehouse sorter goes the painting. So the Molnar family receives the check."

"What will it fetch?"

"I would guess almost half a million."

"And mine?"

"As I told you when you first showed it to me. It looks, tastes, and smells like a Munkácsy, but without any evidence of provenance, we can't be absolutely sure. I think yours comes from the salon period in Munkácsy's life. He needed money to maintain his standard of living, so he started to paint portraits of wealthy patrons. But even during this period, he yearned to express higher feelings and thoughts. The result? Realistic moments captured in shaded characters and bright colors encased in a dark base."

"Which describes my painting to a T."

Scot sighed. "There's a forgery industry in Hungary that turns out Munkácsy paintings every several years. With the information I've given you, you can start untangling its history. We can't undertake that search for you—unless you give us the painting to sell. Get the papers, and I'll get you the price."

"I've told you before, I don't care to sell it. I just want to find out how it came into my possession."

Scot sighed. "I understand. But we should both keep in mind that the Hungarian government can always declare the painting a national treasure and demand its return."

"After the Nazis and the Communists . . . let 'em try."

At LAX, Adam changed his ticket so he could stop in Denver on his return journey to New Orleans. He called Rachel to tell her of his change of plans, and he booked a hotel for one night in the Mile High City. The wild buffeting that the plane experienced on its approach to Stapleton Airport no doubt had to do with the proximity of the mountains and the warm and cold wind currents colliding. Glad to exit the airport, he happily discovered that the city stood just a short distance away. The meter on the cab read a little over ten dollars. He tipped the cabby and entered the Brown Palace Hotel. Pausing to admire the skylight and impressive cathedral effect of the main lobby, he checked in and took the elevator to his fourth-floor room.

After studying the Yellow Pages, he called a bureau that advertised itself as tracking Colorado families. Called Lost and Found, the service had an office not far from his hotel. The next morning, Adam talked to a short, bald, muscular man with spiked teeth, Charles Langdon, who ran the agency. His fingers and teeth bore the nicotine stains of a chain-smoker. Adam, who disliked cigarettes intensely, asked Mr. Langdon to refrain from smoking for the duration of their interview.

"What did you say?"

"Please, I don't like the smell of cigarette smoke."

Mr. Langdon pondered that mystery. "You mind if I chew?"

"Go right ahead."

Removing a tin from his desk, he took a pinch and stuffed the wad inside his cheek. "Now tell me the situation. On the phone, you said something about a Hungarian family and a painting."

Adam explained everything, including his wish to discover his own roots. Langdon took copious notes, while the wad presumably burned the lining in his cheek.

"I trust," said Adam, looking around at the austerely furnished room, "that you have a good track record."

"Mr. Shaw," Langdon said, "I once made a living as a tracker in Canada. Now I hunt human prey."

"I'm not sure the word *prey* captures what I have in mind."

"Just a figure of speech." He leaned back in his swivel chair and chuckled with immense satisfaction. "A pretty lady recently hired me to locate her deadbeat husband. I tracked that loser from Denver to Dallas to Miami to Quito to Santiago to Patagonia, where I found him living on a hacienda with a lady from Wales." Langdon chuckled. "He paid up."

"With whose money, I wonder."

"Didn't matter to me or his former wife. Then another time I tracked a Frenchie from Denver to Reno to LA to Vegas to Phoenix. Another deadbeat, but this one had left with his ex's fur coat and family dog."

"So you're saying . . . ?"

"Langdon, like the Royal Canadian Mounted Police, always gets his man."

Adam left behind a check for five hundred dollars and a signed contract agreeing to ante up another five hundred if Lost and Found actually located the family in question. He left three numbers with Langdon: home, work, and mobile. His question—whether a train ran from downtown Denver to Stapleton—elicited a burst of explosive laughter that caused the wad to shoot out of Langdon's mouth and land on his green desk blotter. Sweeping up the mess, Langdon apologized for his "uncouth manners" and explained that mass transportation never crossed the minds of Colorado legislators, who, for the most part, did the bidding of the energy industry.

"Sounds like the US Congress."

"Same mugs."

The two men shook hands, and Adam left feeling reassured that the man he had hired, notwithstanding his filthy nicotine habit, had the experience to accomplish the task.

The medical report forwarded from Panama City, Panama, said that Ori was having trouble breathing, running a high temperature, and likely to die unless transported to a hospital specializing in tropical diseases. She had been flown to the United States on a military aircraft—a mission of mercy—accompanied by her parents, Naso Teribe Indians from the Panamanian rain forest. By the time Adam arrived, Mrs. May had put Zoe Hildreth in charge of the parents, who insisted on sleeping in the same room as their daughter. Zoe had provided the parents with cots and arranged for meals; she served as a translator, but had little luck persuading the Indians to allow their daughter to receive the treatment recommended by the medical staff. Initially thought to have contracted a tropical disease, Ori had been misdiagnosed. Had her family known in advance that surgery would be the recommended treatment, they never would have left Panama. Her wheezing and "noisy breathing" and sleeplessness issued not from a jungle malady, but from a subglottic hemangioma, a benign vascular tumor of the throat that consists of dense clusters of blood vessels. Otherwise a completely normal baby, born full term with no complications, doctors had originally diagnosed her problem as epiglottitis. Dr. Shapiro found her tumor with an X-ray and discovered that it occluded 90 percent of her trachea; hence he wanted the surgeon to immediately perform a tracheostomy. But the parents refused, fearing that an incision would permit evil spirits to enter her body.

Zoe tried to explain the alternatives to the parents: surgery, a temporary "trach," or death. The parents said no to surgery, convinced that even if malevolent spirits did not enter her body through the incision, the bleeding would kill her. A trach they likewise vetoed, saying that her infant body could not stand the strain of the procedure. They wanted medicine. An impasse ensued.

Maurice concluded that barring surgery, without a trach, the child would in the next five weeks more than likely suffocate. He explained the situation to Adam in the latter's office.

"Adam, believe me. One or the other. Surgery or a tracheostomy."

"No other alternatives?"

"Absolutely none."

"Have we ever performed one on a child so young?"

"We, no. But Tulane, yes. We can send them there."

Adam, deeply concerned about lawsuits and Moss's reputation, said, "I'd want to go along, since the Army medical corps first sent her to us."

"One of the Tulane doctors could come here. Then we wouldn't have to move her and scare the parents any further."

"What happens with a hemangioma?"

"They'll place a tube through the neck into the trachea, below the level of the tumor. The trach will allow her to breathe."

"The risk?"

"With a trach in place, I can guarantee you the child will not suffer respiratory arrest. A tracheostomy is a fairly low-risk procedure. Our medical staff believe that the child could easily tolerate it without complication."

Weighing the consequences of fitting a jungle child with a high-tech instrument, Adam said, "How long will she need to live with it?"

Maurice knew he had arrived at the hard part. "These tumors tend to grow for a few years and then, generally, decrease in size, sometimes disappearing altogether. Therefore . . ." He paused, well aware that his next statement would ring financial alarm bells, "The trach would most likely need to remain in place for at least a couple of years."

Before Adam could reply, Maurice quickly added, "But then it could be removed and the child would live a completely normal life."

"Come on, Maurice, she can't go back to Panama with a trach in her neck!"

"Then this discussion, Adam, is meaningless. The family will not permit the child to have surgery."

"So the infant dies."

"Yes," said Maurice glumly.

"What did Stalin quip, 'One death is a tragedy, millions a statistic'? Millions of children die every day, but this one child is in our trust. She came to us on a military transport. I want this case to go to the ethics committee. It's not a decision that one person should have to make."

Adam told Zoe that the case would be heard by a group of doctors and the Moss Hospital ethicist, and that she should not let the family out of her sight. He feared that the parents would take the infant and run; and given their impoverished state, wherever they landed would be less hygienic, less salubrious, less caring than Moss.

Adam decided that for the next few days he would not return to Hungamon; rather he would use the private basement apartment in the hospital, the well-appointed space usually occupied by visiting physicians. Rachel said she understood completely and would visit him in two days, once the ladies' auxiliary of the First Baptist Church had held their annual meeting with the ladies of Mt. Moriah. She wanted to persuade others to support her attempt to see Manny buried in the city cemetery.

Zoe, who had reluctantly asked a friend to look after Wayne, had been sleeping on a rollaway bed in the room off the main nurses' quarters. She got up regularly during the night to make Ori and her parents comfortable. The night nurse had promised Zoe that she'd pay special attention to room 172. That first night, Adam joined Zoe in the cafeteria for dinner and then sat with her at the side of the parents and infant.

Occasionally the Indians would say a few words to Zoe and then lapse into silence. Adam's inquiries always brought the same response.

"They are worried about her 'noisy breathing.'"

The longer Adam sat in room 172, the stronger his conviction became that somehow his staff would have to rescue this baby. Baby Ori led him to a new knowledge, one that doctors know well: The science of medicine fosters faith, not in vapid prayer, but in the power to cure. Feeling that power, Adam decided that even if the ethics committee voted in favor of the parents, he would, in his capacity as director of Moss, find some means to see that she received treatment. The problem, over the long term, lacked a solution. Once in place the trach would require maintenance: suctioning, cleaning, and changing.

All of these necessitated a modern machine. To suction a trach one needed to place a plastic tube into the hole in the neck, turn on the machine, and suction out the secretions. Even if the parents stayed in the United States, these activities would require their cooperation for several years. If they returned to the rain forest, who would suction this child and how? Placing the trach, therefore, was only half the battle; should the parents permit the procedure and then choose to leave, the child would still be condemned to death.

To Zoe's question, would they rather the child died than have the trach, the parents replied, "If the forest spirits will it, our daughter will live with them."

"Not very helpful," muttered Adam.

Zoe, fearing that her question might have frightened the parents, remained in their room. Adam dragged a lounge chair from the waiting area and joined her vigil. They spoke, as people will, of their lives and other accidents. He told her about his adoptive parents, at least what he could remember, since they had died before his sixth birthday, and his foster home, where he had learned, like Oliver Twist, never to ask for more. Sorrowfully, he recounted a childhood in which he had been taught to subdue his appetites, but readily admitted a love of the beautiful, whether in women or art, perhaps because of the one possession his real mother and father had passed on to him, a painting.

Shortly after midnight, Ori's parents, lying in adjoining cots, fell off to sleep. The only sound came from Ori's labored breathing. Besides the child's hemangioma, Adam instinctively felt something amiss. No, not the antiseptic white walls and linoleum and coverlets and sheets. Room 172 lacked an item, an object of meaning. Baby Ori had no dolls, no playthings, not even a mobile to attract her attention. Adam excused himself, skipped down one flight of stairs, and used his pass key to enter the gift shop. On his return, he wordlessly placed a fluffy doll next to Ori's cheek. Back in his lounge chair, he found the silence unsettling and turned to Zoe. Tears trickled down her face.

"One Christmas," she said, "the Tarpers, who didn't believe in exchanging gifts—they thought it commercialized the holiday—let me buy a doll from a street merchant. I called her Suzie. Several days later my father wished to punish me for some infraction and tried to take away my doll. I clung to Suzie. He reached for the doll, caught hold of her left arm, and pulled. Suzie's arm came off. For weeks after I felt like my own left arm had been amputated." She wiped her face with a Kleenex. "Did you ever fight with your parents, or anyone else, to keep something dear?"

"No, I learned early to acquiesce, to follow the path of least resistance."

"To say what people want to hear."

Her comment, phrased not as a question but as a declarative statement, annoyed him. "Don't we all, at one time or another?"

"It depends on the situation, doesn't it?"

Adam remembered a professor speaking of self-preservation as a moral imperative. Collaborators in wartime often had little or no choice. Rat or die. But what constituted collaboration in peacetime? He could think only of martial examples, not of personal ones.

During the night, Ori's parents awoke. Zoe spoke to them softly. Whether or not they had been thinking of decamping, Zoe's gentle persuasions made them visibly relax and fall back to sleep.

Adam and Zoe talked well into the new day. After much soul baring, they had sundered the veil between them, but not so completely as to keep Zoe from migrating toward the subject that Adam had hoped wouldn't surface: his posture after the trial, standing on the courthouse steps expounding on justice.

"If each of us," Adam said, "is allowed one cowardly mistake in his life, that was mine. I can only be grateful that it has left me enough time to make amends. My wife and I have talked it over. We would like to pay for Wayne's college education, as well as singing lessons."

Zoe sank into an uncomfortable silence. Her response, when it came, caught him off guard. "If you had no money, how would you do penance? The rich always buy forgiveness for their sins. But what if you were poor? What then?"

The answers that Adam wanted to give would have debased the moment. Fighting off her electric appeal and resisting the urge to embrace her fondly, he said simply, "I would be like a father to your son—if he needed me—and a faithful friend to you."

She gave him an undeserved absolution, saying, "I accept your terms: an education for my son and comradeship."

The word *comradeship* brought to mind distasteful political associations, leading Adam to think of bloody revolution, purges, plots, and betrayals. Having satisfied his college history requirement with a class in the Russian Revolution, he no longer trusted the word and those who used it. "What's wrong with faithful friend?" he asked, adding, "I'm not a communist."

"No, I don't suppose so. But tell me, Adam, what *are* you? I've never known a married man as unmarried as you. A Northerner in the South. An agnostic married to a Baptist lady. A man in search of his beginnings, hoping that a painting will bring him home. What you need is a backbone, not a family tree. You say the right things, like wanting to save this infant here, but when the chips are down, will you fight? I'm sure you know about the road to hell and how it's paved."

He replied bravely, "I want to learn courage."

"Which kind, physical or moral?" Her question seemed to mock him. "Moral's the more difficult."

"Yes," he hesitated, "that's a lesson I'm slowly learning."

Suddenly, without realizing it, he found himself apologizing for his weakness and gripping his chair in preparation for leaving the room.

"Sit down," she said, "I have a lot more to tell you."

"Morally," the judge mused, "we should make every effort to see Manny buried in the Hungamon Cemetery." Rachel smiled, feeling she had come to the right person to help with her crusade."And as you say, money greases the palm. A long time ago, while presiding over a court case, I learned the unabridged implications of bribery. To my utter amazement, the defense lawyer tried to mitigate the crime on the grounds that we all practice it."

"Perhaps not all," said Rachel defensively, well aware that her offer to build a children's center constituted a form of bribery.

"Surely, money can be used for good or ill."

Judge Waters had agreed to meet her at the courthouse cafeteria, a tasteless room with puke-green walls, metal tables and chairs, and food offerings that ranged from iceberg lettuce salads to a chili made with peppers so hot that the menu warned the unwary about the bite of the sauce. The judge had settled for something more tame, a ham sandwich on white bread, while Rachel protected her stomach with a banana and hot tea.

The judge seemed to relish the chance to relate the incident to which he had just alluded. "I even remember the name of the defense lawyer, Martin Yewsufruct. A company had been bestowing gifts on an employee from a rival company for insider information. Accused of bribery, the gift-giving company hired a clever lawyer who tried to distinguish between bribery and barter or swaps or favors. He argued that we all engage daily in various kinds of bribery. If we want to subvert someone's judgment or ingratiate ourselves, we frequently proffer our integrity, our honesty, our decency. Thus, in effect, we try to bribe a jury one way and a lover another. The fellow even admitted that as a defense attorney he often had to make deals he found unsavory. Alluding to women, he asked, before I could gavel him out of order: Don't they sweeten the pot with salves and powders, dyes, and combs to suit the circumstances?"

"Are you saying that all of life involves us in a continual round of bribery?"

The judge rubbed his jaw and said he hated to admit the truth that preferment, justice, influence—the whole of them—depend on bribery, to some degree or other. One person offers the plumber a beer to save a buck, another tells the boss how good he looks in his cheap suit. To earn the good regard of others, we fawn and flatter and play the fool. All for the same end: to influence another person, to obtain a favorable decision, to corrupt a person's judgment. To Rachel's great annoyance, he became personal and observed that she, like everyone else, offered bribes.

"As you are doing now," he observed. "You tell me that my reputation in the white community won't suffer if I stand up for Manny, and that my standing in the black community will soar. Aren't you trying to bribe me to say yes?" Before Rachel could answer, the judge remarked that church matters always left a bad taste in his mouth, and denied her request for moral support. Having been lectured and rebuffed, Rachel drove away feeling poisoned from the fare the judge had dished out.

Enjoying crawfish étouffée served over steaming rice with crusty French bread, and white wine, at a small Cajun restaurant, Adam told Zoe that the hospital ethics committee had voted for surgery. They thought a trach impractical. The report forcefully argued that the Moss medical staff could not sit by and watch the child choke to death.

"The committee directed me to get a court order for surgery," he said. "I'll be asking a judge to override the parents' decision to refuse consent." Zoe looked at him skeptically. "The parents will just have to stay in the country until she has fully recovered and can travel again."

"They've threatened to take the baby out of the hospital."

"Maurice said that any cold or congestion will completely occlude the airway and the child will suffocate."

"What if Ori goes into respiratory distress while you're waiting to get the court order? Will the doctors do an emergency trach?"

"If the family tries to leave, I'll call the police and the Department of Children's Services. In that case, the child will probably be taken from the parents."

"We are talking about a loving family."

"Any ideas?"

Zoe could imagine the parents eventually spiriting the child out of the hospital, but not making their way back to Panama. So where would they go? Even if some kindhearted soul offered to house the family for five years, the immigration authorities would have more than a little to say about such an arrangement. "Adoption," she said aloud, but quickly thought better of it. "No, the family would never hear of it. In a nursing home, the questions are easier. When it comes to children, the moral issues can drive a soul crazy."

They continued their meal in silence. After Adam paid the bill, they sat facing one another, each trying to guess the other's thoughts. Adam tipped his hand by reaching across the table and touching Zoe's arm. "Can we be friends now?"

"We already are."

"Close friends."

She smiled as if quieting a child beseeching a favor. "Give it time, Adam. It's too soon."

As they drove back to the hospital, Adam consoled himself with the fact that she hadn't said no.

---

When Adam returned to the hospital, he heard that a Mr. Langdon from Denver, Colorado had been trying to reach him, but Adam's mobile phone didn't respond. He had left it in the car, wishing to have lunch without interruption. Adam retreated into his office and telephoned the investigator, who coughed his smoker's hack into the phone.

"Foreigners aren't always the easiest people to trace. I ran up a helluva telephone bill. Colorado Springs, Pueblo, Santa Fe, Albuquerque, Grand Junction, Aspen—"

Adam interrupted. "Mr. Langdon, I don't wish to sound rude, but I have a meeting to attend. Just give me the conclusion."

"It's important that my clients appreciate—"

"I do."

Mr. Langdon's voice dropped from excitement to dullness. "I located a Lawrence Weiss in Madison, Wisconsin. He teaches physics at the university. I'm sure I've got the right person. The family briefly lived in Denver before moving to Chicago."

"You actually spoke to him?"

"Even asked him if the family name had ever been White. No, they changed it to Weiss. The parents are dead, and his sister Alice lives in New York, on the west side. Both of them are married. Her name is now Posner. I can give you her address. It's 201 West Seventieth Street. He said to reach him just call his office at the university."

Langdon gave him the number and said he would be forwarding a bill to cover the successful conclusion of his search. Adam thanked him and suggested he call Scot Marco at Butterfields in Los Angeles and use his name. Butterfields occasionally conducted nationwide searches. Perhaps they'd use him.

A minute later Adam dialed Lawrence Weiss's number. A secretary answered and said that Professor Weiss could be reached in the lab and forwarded his call. Adam doodled on his notepad, writing the name *Zoe* and then adding the letter *l* after the letter *o* and making the *e* an *a*, to produce *Zola*, a writer he had read in a required intro to literature course at Vanderbilt. He strained to remember the title of the book, but the "Yes?" on the other end of the phone interrupted his cerebrations.

After explaining his quest, Adam was excited to learn that in Hungary the Weiss family had indeed traveled in art collecting circles, and yes the parents had left behind letters and documents from the old country, all stored in a bank near Professor Weiss's summer cottage in Northern Wisconsin. Adam just naturally assumed that the professor knew Hungarian, but asked anyway. His affirmative reply completed Adam's happiness.

Could Professor Weiss be induced to spend a weekend at the cottage in Three Lakes, although now mid-October? Adam would be glad to come to Madison and pay for a flight to the closest airport, which the professor identified as Rhinelander. They settled on the following weekend and hoped that some of the fall colors might still linger. Adam wrote down the directions and agreed to meet Professor Weiss a week from Thursday at his university office. He would fly through Chicago and take a commuter flight to Madison. Mrs. Weiss would not join them, because she had to look after the school-age children. They could rent a car in Rhinelander. Adam volunteered to make all the arrangements.

After telling Zoe that he would have to leave town on business, and that he would call regularly to check on baby Ori, he drove home to find a dismayed wife, who told him that the ladies from First Baptist and Mount Moriah treated what she called her "Manny proposal" hostilely.

# Ah Bartleby! Ah Humanity!

ADAM CAUGHT A SIX O'CLOCK FLIGHT TO CHICAGO, BUT NOT BEFORE calling the hospital to determine the well-being of Ori. After his arrival, he telephoned Rachel. He apologized for his sudden departure and hoped that his absence would not inconvenience her.

"There's so much about my own family I don't know," she said, "and wish I did. You're doing the right thing."

She truly felt his need. To this day she wondered about her grandfather's portrait, hanging in her father's house, with its cryptic title *Kinsman* and its unknown origins. As a child she had made up stories about the painting, bizarre wonderful tales in which celestial hands appeared at night to capture on canvas her grandpa's regal bearing. She wanted to believe that she had issued from royalty or from some magical isle. Adam's wish to know his forebears made perfect sense. Why not, she thought, use the local library—that very day—to discover the provenance of the painting?

With the breakfast dishes put away, Rachel drove to the Washington Parish Library to read government and state documents bearing on the history of Hungamon. Surprised to find a drably dressed, pale, freckled woman in charge instead of the prim Mr. William Gruning, with his starched white shirt and bow tie that moved in unison with his prominent Adam's apple, she asked about him.

"He couldn't be here this morning. His mother, you know, she's been ill. I'm just a substitute. Normally I'm a cataloguer."

The punctilious Mr. Gruning had never, in Rachel's memory, missed a day, and he took special pride in helping her father amass documents bearing on the 1930s underworld.

"He said he'd be gone just an hour or two. Your name, please?"

"Mrs. Rachel French Shaw. My father is a benefactor of this library . . . Mr. Montgomery French."

"Really?" she gasped with delight. "So good to meet you. I'm Mrs. Dolores Ellsworth." She extended her hand. "I guess you're here to get the key to your father's special collections."

"Collections? What does he have besides Bonnie and Clyde?"

"Oh, he has been perfectly wonderful, donating gangster material assembled from other parishes, and also personal files. Which ones do you wish to see?"

"Neither. I'm here to learn about local painters. Does the library have any files on Hungamon artists?"

"You'd have to ask Mr. Gruning. That's not my area."

Rachel said she'd wait, but thought twice. "As long as I'm here, it might be interesting to see the sources father uses for his occasional pieces about Washington Parish."

"We all love to read his articles. I don't think my husband's ever missed a one." Mrs. Ellsworth suddenly seemed distraught. "You do know," she said, "that the special collections aren't housed here but in the old library on the other side of the underpass. We keep the building locked. I hope you don't mind if I ask you for identification."

Rachel produced a driver's license that bore both her maiden and married names. She had always liked the name French, but had actually kept it to honor her family. Mrs. Ellsworth produced a key attached to a wooden board. "The key," said Mrs. Ellsworth, "will open both the front and back doors. It's musty in that building, but the lights still work. You do realize, honey, that the boxed items can't leave the room. But we have a table you can use. It has a lamp."

In all the years since the new library had been built, Rachel had never returned to the old one. But she remembered it well enough, the wooden bungalow. Who would have guessed it currently housed the historical archives of Washington Parish and her father's personal papers? He had never shared that information with her.

Mrs. Ellsworth, having relinquished the key to the bungalow, now felt uneasy. She summoned a volunteer to watch the desk and told Rachel that she would accompany her to the old library. They drove in separate cars. When they arrived, Mrs. Ellsworth pointed out a stack of crated documents.

"Those belong to your father." Rachel thanked her. "Bring the key back," she said, and left.

Rustling through a number of boxes, Rachel found a strange mélange of old newspaper clippings—from the Hungamon *Daily News*, the Baton Rouge *Morning Advocate* and *State-Times*, the New Orleans *Times-Picayune*, and the *Jacksonville Courier*. Also in the box were private communications, including parish and state documents; confidential letters between the governor and the mayor and between the mayor and the local police; as well as letters, supportive and threatening, from local and rural residents. Without stopping to read through them, she noted police surveillance reports, correspondence between the sawmill and the authorities regarding the hiring of black women, several internal city memos about the Congress for Racial Equality (CORE), a cache of letters between the Ku Klux Klans in Louisiana and Mississippi, and, not least, Klan files confiscated in a police raid in Varnado, near Hungamon.

As she began to read, she discovered that the stories her father recounted in his articles either omitted specific names or used pseudonyms, no doubt for the sake of propriety. By comparing newspaper accounts and referencing her father's personal papers, she easily unearthed the real names of those engaged in the integration struggles of the 1960s, many of the people now dead or decrepit. But some still remained active—and still served as church elders. She began to wonder if her father, who deplored racism, could have been part of those benighted times. Libby, her devoted nanny, and Samantha, the judge's cook, had over the years faithfully worked for both families and to this day were treated by her father as kin. But some facts couldn't be denied—for example, the faces in the photographs, like Judge Emory Waters's.

She took pains not to rearrange the material, but just as she began to grasp the outline of the racial unrest, Mr. Gruning, thin-lipped and pale, briskly entered the building, acting like a schoolmaster intent on punishing an errant student. He told her that he had designated the integration files, except for the newspapers, as "off-limits." While he hastily re-boxed the materials, she argued her right, as Mr. French's daughter, to see them. Mumbling his apologies, he told her that she would have to leave, because the documents had been placed under court order. No other city in Louisiana, she felt certain, would have the valuable documents that Mr. Gruning had somehow amassed for the Washington Parish Library.

"Who issued the court order?" she asked.

"Judge Waters."

"At whose request?"

"Mr. French's."

Turning on her seductive charms, she slightly simpered, "How long have we known each other? Ever since my childhood. All these years I have always admired your good sense. You know I can access the newspapers at the New Orleans Public Library, but not my father's personal papers, which are important to me."

Mr. Gruning, not a man for all seasons, preferred the quiet and unruffled life. Like all unimaginative people, he took refuge in rules.

"I wish I could help, but the law's the law. I'm afraid you'll have to vacate the premises."

She threatened to sue. Mr. Gruning looked around the room, as if hoping to find a friend in the shadows, but seeing no relief, whispered that the integration files belonged to Mr. Montgomery French, and reserved for him in recognition of all his contributions to the library. She could speak to her father about the conditions that Mr. French had outlined when he offered the library not only a generous endowment, but also his gangster collection. In return, he wanted exclusive viewing rights for his lifetime to the integration and lynching files.

"Lynching?" Rachel repeated softly, out of deference to the librarian. "Thank you, Mr. Gruning, I wouldn't have thought to ask about such material. You have been a great help."

Mr. Gruning's ruddy lips metamorphosed into bloodless labial folds, and his face reminded her of the cadavers she had seen one summer in the church catacombs outside Kiev. "I beg you," he muttered, "don't breathe a word of this to your father. Please! He has been such a liberal patron of the library. If he resigned from the board, I would," he tried to swallow, but his constricted throat muscles caused him to rasp, "I would be dismissed from my job."

"I promise," she murmured, "*if* you allow me access to both collections . . . after hours. So no one will know."

At that moment, Mr. Gruning looked as if his neck rested in the collar of a guillotine, waiting for the metallic whisper of the falling blade. He led Rachel outside the building, locked the door, and asked her to follow him back to the new library, where they could talk in private. She noted his old and rusted white Ford, mentally comparing it to her new, sleek black Audi. Although his office walls stood bare except for a single framed picture bearing the inscription, "Hungamon Paper Company, 1918," every flat surface, including the floor, held papers and books.

He stood behind his desk, clearly terrified. His hands shook. "My God, do you know what you're asking? To do what you want would be to deceive Mr. French—your own father. I can't break a promise. My word is my bond."

Rachel said nothing. She looked around at the clutter, which reminded her of the old library. Turning her back to the librarian, she studied the picture and then, slowly and purposefully, remarked, "I have other means. The library board, the City Council, a suit, an interview with the editor of the *Daily News*."

Mr. Gruning choked, "Oh, my God!"

For a moment Rachel felt sorry for the poor man. She knew that librarians ranked among the worst-paid professionals in the United States, probably even worse off than public school teachers. But Rachel would not be gainsaid. Her tenacity, like her father's, ran in her blood and nourished her coruscating intelligence.

"I repeat: No one need know."

"Your father has an eye like a hawk. If I move even one piece of paper from the file, he asks me about it."

Rachel began to pace. He watched. Sitting down, she leaned her elbows on Mr. Gruning's desk, cradled her chin, and said deliberately, "I suggest the following. Photocopy the files for me. I will pay for the prints—and then some. To forestall any suspicions, copy the pages in the exact order you find them. I'll collect them at your convenience—and never utter a word."

Rachel could hear Mr. Gruning hyperventilating. He had suffered a heart attack a few years before, and she did not want to cause another. She stood and took both his hands in hers. "Will a check for a thousand dollars help the history collection?" His breathing immediately improved. But when she added, "Be sure to copy the lynching file," he tried, between aspirations, to explain, but finally exhaled in defeat.

"Just make the check out to the Washington Parish Library."

On the shuttle flight to Madison, Adam buried himself in Langdon's report, dated September 27, 1988, and received two weeks before. The investigator had learned that Lawrence Weiss had graduated with a degree in physics from Carleton College, matriculated at the University of Colorado in Boulder for graduate school, and studied for a PhD with Carl Wieman, who had helped him secure an assistant professorship at the University of Wisconsin, where he had earned a reputation as a first-rate scientist.

Adam took a gypsy cab from Dane County Regional Airport to the university, asking the driver to drop him off at a point on Lakeshore Drive within walking distance to Sterling Hall. He tipped the driver and stopped to admire Lake Mendota, even though he could feel the autumn chill blowing off the water. As he slowly made his way to the building that housed the physics department at 475 North Charter Street, he mentally compared the immensity of this campus to the university he had attended, and the stature of Wisconsin's president to the buffoonery of Vanderbilt's. Madison shone for its research, Vandy for turning out ladies and gentlemen. Even the students looked different. He remembered with a tinge of regret why he had chosen Vanderbilt. Mr. and Mrs. Dexter, his foster parents, had pronounced Adam "rough around the edges." Their goddaughter, Claudine Grant, a professor there in classics, had pulled strings to get Adam a partial scholarship. Although his good grades had gained him admission to Wisconsin, Berkeley, and UCLA, those schools could not give him any financial support. Also he knew that he wanted to distance himself from the Dexters. For all their kindness, he felt that between them and him existed a world of difference. Before graduating from Vanderbilt, he legally changed his last name to Shaw, to laud Artie Shaw, who played the meanest clarinet he'd ever heard.

As he approached Sterling Hall, where physicists busied themselves tracking the origins of the universe back to within seconds after the Big Bang, he wished that his own attempts to look into the past proved as successful, not just in the matter of the painting's provenance, but in the atavistic sense of a paradise lost, a family expelled. He had made the trip in the hope of learning from whence he had come. Making his way up the stairs to the narrow doors with their large glass panes, he hoped that his findings would explode the erroneous stories he felt sure the Dexters had purveyed.

A student pointed him in the direction of Lawrence Weiss's lab. As Adam slowly walked up the stairs, he noted in the passing students their focused demeanors. His own feckless undergraduate days came to mind, leaving him feeling somewhat abashed. Halfway down the hall he found the lab—actually a series of connecting rooms. Timidly he entered through a door marked "Physicists Know All Their Atoms" and asked for Professor Weiss, who sat at the rear of the lab in a cubbyhole just large enough for a small table and stool. Poring over papers covered with numbers and charts, he leaped to his feet and greeted Adam warmly. At Vandy, Adam had always tried to avoid seeing professors during their office hours, owing to their posturing and polysyllabic language. With few exceptions he had regarded his professors as stiffs. The man sitting in front of him with long disheveled salt-and-pepper hair that fell over the collar of his shirt and across his forehead looked more like a hippie than an academic. He needed a shave and could lose ten pounds. His jowly face, with its lifelines of thought etched into his skin, exuded a certain stature. His remarkably striking dark-blue eyes fixed Adam with a warm gaze that seemed to say that he welcomed Adam's presence.

After a handshake and the usual polite throwaway comments, Professor Weiss—who insisted on being called Larry, even by his students—rose to his full six feet and gave Adam a quick tour of the lab; but before they could decamp for the parking lot and the ride to the airport, Larry explained he had to have a quick word with one of the university apparatchiks, Vice-Chancellor Piers Speyers.

As if on cue, the administrator entered the lab briskly, on tiptoes, feet splayed. A hand at once went to his black mustache, as if preparing for a photograph. Without so much as a nod at Adam, Piers Speyers expostulated, "Your grant application to the National Science Foundation, which I have been reviewing, includes a request to add another graduate student to your group."

"Yes, Andrea Stein. She's quite gifted in string theory."

"That's another issue. I fear you'll jeopardize your grant by asking for more money than the last time."

"The NSF liked the application."

"That's another issue. What they praised before may currently be out of their price range."

"I can telephone the agency and inquire."

"That's another issue. The NSF expects us to make reasoned judgments and not ask them to do our homework."

"Well, Piers, thanks for calling to my attention what you regard as a problem. I would appreciate your sending the application forward. If it encounters any difficulties, I'll take full responsibility." Just as Speyers prepared to reach for his stock line, Larry anticipated it and said, "Yes, I know that's another issue. Good day."

The two men then swept out of the lab and left Piers Speyers, no longer on his toes, with only a mustache to cover his nakedness. Driving directly to the airport, Larry left his car in long-term parking. Adam had booked them a late-afternoon flight to Rhinelander. The single-engine plane seated ten people and once off the ground felt like a bobbing kite, a toy in the autumn breezes out of the Canadian North, a portent of the coming winter. They spoke little. The propeller droned and strained in the wind, and the small aircraft dropped and rose as if the pilot had difficulty controlling the elevator flaps. Outside the plane, the gray clouds obstructed any view of the ground. An occasional flash of light splintered the gossamer mist, bringing a smile to Adam, who recalled the first time he had visited the National Gallery in London and beheld the later paintings of William Turner, with their radical experiments in light. That experience had enhanced his appreciation of Turner and given him a new understanding of abstract painting. Coming in for a landing, the Cessna fell through a series of air pockets, and the flimsy wings looked as if they'd give up the ghost.

The airport waiting area, small but neatly efficient, provided views in every direction. While Adam waited at the car rental desk, he looked at the overcast day and wondered how people this far north endured winters without sun. On their way east to Three Lakes, Larry pointed out a new hospital, which looked state of the art, and all the fast-food restaurants and bars in Rhinelander. Adam stared out the window and concluded that a good time in this part of the world involved eating at McDonald's or Arby's, or drinking at one of the local bars. Larry drove to a supermarket to buy enough groceries for the weekend. Inside the spacious store Adam saw the fattest people he had ever seen, except perhaps for those he encountered in North Carolina's Outer Banks, where every person seemed to weigh more than three hundred pounds. Larry must have noticed Adam's expression, because he remarked: "They have little else to do but eat."

The customers' shopping carts, loaded with potato chips and soft drinks and candy and cakes and tins of Spam and lard, bespoke an America hell-bent on dietary destruction.

"Cardiac bypass surgeons must have a booming practice in this part of the world."

Larry's laughter gave way to sobriety. "The unhappy truth is that in December, January, and February, domestic abuse soars. So do suicide rates. Strange place. Once we're back on the road, you'll see the billboards are antiabortion, antitax, patriotic flag-waving expressions of the right-wing mentality. Years ago George Wallace carried Vilas County, which explains why some of us call it the vile county. Yes, I know, why would anyone want to spend time among Philistines? Simple: the lakes and bogs and woods."

And, indeed, just as Larry had promised, they drove past advertisements promoting the American Legion, the Armed Forces, the right to bear arms, the wrongness of evolution and the truth of "the Holy Bible," the sin of flag burning, the virtue of church attendance, the power of prayer. Adam, politically neutral, observed that northern Wisconsin had much in common with Louisiana. "They have the same billboards there."

They skirted Three Lakes, essentially a one-street town, and continued east for three miles until they reached O'Neill Road. Larry turned south and continued to the end, turning right on Hull Road. The names posted on mailboxes reflected the original German and Polish settlers. Nosing the car into a dirt track, Larry went about twenty-five yards and stopped next to a blond log cabin with a porch facing Planting Ground Lake, about a hundred feet distant. The property also held a modest boathouse. On either side of the cabin, the homes stood boarded up for the winter. Apparently only two or three families lived year-round on Hull Road. To Adam's query about the appalling isolation, Larry replied that once snow covered the ground, snowmobilers frequently came through the area, and that Eagle River to the east billed itself as the snowmobile capital of the world.

"Do you own one?" asked Adam.

Grimacing, the professor said, "Not a chance."

Larry had called ahead to his winter caretaker to turn on the electricity and water, open the propane gas stored in a large bomb-like canister outside the house, plug in the refrigerator and other appliances, and ignite the pilot light to the wall heater and the hot-water tank. The caretaker had even stacked a pile of logs next to the fireplace at the end of the room. Larry expertly laid a fire and then turned on the wall heater. Suddenly the cabin smelled of burning dust, as summer homes do when families return for the season and first use the thermostat.

"Give it a few minutes," said Larry, "I'll open some windows."

The windows lacked sashes and required sticks to stay up. Adam felt the cabin could have used a good dusting and vacuuming. The place had two bedrooms and two bathrooms, as well as a finished study in the attic, reached by a ladder. To move around in the attic meant bending at the waist. The headroom measured just five feet. Larry had installed an inexpensive desk, a Dell computer, and a Hewlett-Packard printer. Freestanding bookshelves held not only various volumes, but also piles of papers: drafts of manuscripts.

"How did you ever find this place?" asked Adam. "It's so damn isolated. What's in the boathouse?"

"A sailboat, a canoe, and a small World War II landing craft, an aluminum Aero Craft powered by a fifteen-horsepower outboard engine. It just putters."

"Fishing gear?"

"Some. I prefer swimming to sitting in a boat waiting for a bite. If you'd like, you're welcome to use what I have."

Adam, in fact, liked to fish, but he had made this journey for other reasons and refused to waver from his mission.

Larry took the room with twin beds, leaving Adam to enjoy the large bed in the other room. After they had both unpacked their few belongings, they sat in front of the fireplace and shared a glass of smoky Irish whiskey, which Larry always kept stocked in one of the cupboards. They drank it straight, having neglected to buy ice cubes at the supermarket.

"It's tastier this way," said Larry, "the ice neuters it."

Watching the flames dance in the disembodied air and dart over the logs, Adam wanted to ask immediately about the family papers, but the moment felt social, not ripe for business. Larry's expression of contentment, as he sipped the whiskey, said as much.

"So tell me, how *did* you find this property?"

Larry looked amused. "I celebrated Hanukkah with a gentile friend, Winthrop Bone, a collector of rare things. He admired my nine-branched silver menorah, in the form of the seven-candled menorah seen in Titus's gate in Rome. It had come from Poland and was attributed to Eliyahu Hanavi, a Jewish silversmith and master of his craft. I suggested an even exchange, the menorah for the cabin. We agreed on a price—fifteen thousand dollars—and he walked off with the menorah, and I took possession of the cabin."

"It sounds to me as if you got much the better deal."

"Some collectors would disagree." He then explained that in Poland the fashioning of menorahs, a greatly skilled craft, remained tantamount to a religious act. "It must be cast by a gifted silversmith, a devout individual, specially trained in the laws governing medieval metallurgy. I don't think that even now we have discovered all the old secrets of the artisans and apothecaries."

"And Winthrop?"

"Old Boney went to live with his sister in Florida." Larry said they exchanged greeting cards at the start of each year.

"How did Mr. Bone know that the menorah dated from eighteenth-century Poland? Did he authenticate it?"

"Good collectors don't take chances. He knew." Sipping his drink and staring at the mesmeric flames, Larry said, "Tell me about yourself. Background. We all have stories."

"You really want to hear?"

"Given my own family history, I'm intrigued to learn about yours."

"I arrived in America as Adam Vadas in 1955, with an official certificate that listed my birthplace as Budapest, Hungary. Year: 1954. My adoptive parents, Berta and Fulop Vadas, had among their belongings a painting bearing an exit permit from the Hungarian communist government, which had stamped the painting the work of an amateur. My distinct memories of childhood begin around my fourth or fifth year."

Adam went on to say that he vaguely associated the name Vadas with a middle-aged couple that often spoke words that he understood then but had mostly forgotten. Those that had stayed with him counted few: *nem* (no), *igen* (yes), *kérem* (please), *tolni* (push), *húzni* (pull), *reggeli* (breakfast), *ebéd* (lunch), *vacsora* (dinner), *bocsánat* (excuse me). In his fifth year, 1959, the Vadas family returned to Hungary, finding the English language too difficult to pronounce and the job market inhospitable. They originally immigrated to America because Fulop had an unmarried older brother, János, working in Hartford, Connecticut; but János had gone to the United States in the 1930s, early enough in his life to learn English. In fact he spoke it so well that the US Army employed him as a translator during World War II.

Adam and his adoptive parents also lived in Hartford. The first year was difficult for the couple, but János's presence mitigated the hardships. Unfortunately, his health began to fail. Diagnosed with lung cancer, János, a heavy smoker, lingered for about six months and then died. Utterly at a loss, Fulop and Berta decided to return to Hungary and leave an "Americanized" Adam in the United States. The only agency willing to help the family, one with a shady reputation for foreign adoptions and foster care, recommended a childless couple in Newark, New Jersey, Ethan and Beverly Dexter, who, for reasons having to do with inheritance and the stringent conditions of a trust, chose not to adopt but to foster him. After their deaths, the Dexter estate went equally to a nephew and a niece.

Even so, the Dexters treated Adam to many of the benefits of an upper-middle-class family. They clothed and fed him well, enrolled him in their church (Congregationalist), encouraged him to read good books and use English correctly, screened his friends to keep out the riffraff, and occasionally took him into New York City to visit the museums. His favorite, the Metropolitan, had a bookstore that he regarded as one of the wonders of the world. He saved his pocket money to buy catalogs and reproductions, purchases that quickly exhausted his allowance. Invariably Adam would ask for something else, perhaps a second catalog, and invariably the Dexters refused, lest they spoil him. They exhibited similar behavior about toys, but proffered a different explanation: Too many toys would stunt his imagination. He could never quite comprehend their cramped goodness.

In contrast, his dim memories of the Vadas couple centered on their openhandedness, on their taking him to the corner candy store, treating him to the carousel, buying him a small sled for winter excursions in the park. Those fond remembrances had more than once led him to ask the Dexters to tell him all they knew about Fulop and Berta; but the Dexters insisted that their contact with the couple was limited, their knowledge scant. From their three meetings with the Vadases, they could see that Fulop and Berta had never overcome the language barrier, making Fulop essentially unemployable. From Berta they learned that she felt alone and estranged, and that she found the burden of raising a young child on few resources greater than they could manage. For these reasons they put Adam in a foster home. As to family records, Ethan and Beverly were given only what the agency had sent along; and those papers Adam knew by heart. When the Dexters applied, on his behalf, for citizenship, they encountered a great deal of red tape, because according to immigration laws, Adam, as a foster child, should have returned to Hungary with the Vadases. To the credit of the Dexters, when it looked as if Adam might be sent back to Hungary, they hired a lawyer and footed the hefty bills that eventually led to Adam receiving a hardship dispensation—and finally citizenship. Given this history, Adam felt it wrong of him to resent their small parsimonies. By reminding himself of their tenacity in fighting for him to remain in America, he had learned to suppress his annoyance and show his appreciation. But he never lost the hope of one day discovering the names of his real parents and their reason for giving him up for adoption.

Larry seemed moved. He patted Adam on the shoulder and said, "We'll get started early. I keep the stuff in a safe-deposit box seven miles from here, in Eagle River. You're no doubt wondering why. For tax reasons. If the paintings I have in my Madison house were known to be originals, I couldn't afford the insurance to keep them on my walls. All incriminating evidence I keep up here, in Peoples State Bank on East Wall Street."

---

That night, Adam lay in bed and listened to the loons. A steady rain began to pelt the cabin. In the moonlight he could see the water streaking his bedroom window. When he fell off to sleep, he dreamed that Lawrence Weiss's safe-deposit box resembled a jeweled Fabergé loon, and that the professor had lost the key to it. How could they possibly destroy such a valued object to open it? Better to just let it be. Once pried open, he feared that it could never be repaired. Suddenly he found himself sitting with a child on a linoleum-covered floor, reciting, "Humpty-Dumpty sat on a wall. Humpty-Dumpty had a great fall. All the king's horses and all the king's men couldn't put Humpty-Dumpty back together again."

"The English call them bangers," said Larry bending over the stove making sausages. "How do you like your eggs?"

Adam watched the rain dripping from the cedars and oaks and white birches. The corrugated lake had attracted one boat, holding a lone fisherman, who seemed oblivious to the inclement conditions. Several ducks paddled by close to shore. The colors had begun to fade from the trees, leaving a rusty tinge. So far Adam had said nothing of the Mihály Munkácsy painting on sale at Butterfields that once belonged to Larry's family and debated with himself when to broach the subject.

The drive into Eagle River took only a few minutes. Larry went directly to the desk in charge of the safe-deposit boxes, presented his identification, removed his key, disappeared with the woman through a barred door, and returned carrying a large metal container. Evidently Professor Weiss had rented the largest drawer on offer. He carried it into a side room and carefully took out several ledgers and numerous manila envelopes, each one meticulously marked with names and dates. Putting in his briefcase everything bearing dates from the 1940s and 1950s, he returned all the other written matter to the box. Larry thanked the woman and told her he'd be back the next day, Saturday. He wanted to secure all his important documents before flying back to Madison late Sunday night.

With his briefcase resting on the backseat of the rented car and his ignition key in his hand, Larry turned to Adam and asked, "It's none of my business, but are you Jewish?"

The idea had not escaped Adam. When he thought about his past and the rumors and murky events he could extricate from his childhood memories, he had weighed the possibility that he had been spirited out of Hungary because of communist persecution.

"Why do you ask?"

"Perhaps it's just a coincidence, but hardly a day passes when the newspapers don't run a story about artworks and valuables being returned to their original Jewish owners. Swiss banks are finally being asked to open their records and empty their vaults of stolen Nazi loot."

"One reason for my learning about your family's friends is that I'm hoping it will lead to my own parents."

Larry drove silently in the rain until they turned off at O'Neill Road. "My father would never talk about the war years, even though he seemed to keep every scrap of paper bearing on the fascists. He must have believed there'd be a reckoning, and he wanted to have the facts at his fingertips. He lived in memory. The present and future hardly mattered. My mother wanted to make a new life in America. Not my dad. His scraps of paper, his letters, his yellowed diaries, one for each year until 1945, they consumed his life."

"Then you've read through them?"

"Selectively. It's too painful. My parents had wealth. They lived on a hillside in Buda with a beautiful view of the Danube. They could see all the Jews shot on the riverbanks and shoved into the river. During late 1944 the weather had turned brutally cold. Snow and ice everywhere. My father described how the Hungarian Arrow Cross marched naked Jews down to the Danube. He swore that the Hungarian fascists behaved worse than the Nazis."

At the cabin Larry cleared a large table and neatly laid out the documents, virtually all of them in Hungarian. As he translated from his father's papers, he looked visibly touched. Those events that Adam hoped would prove useful to him, he recorded on a yellow legal pad. The process proved tedious, because to determine the importance of each document, Larry first had to read it. Occasionally, when his Hungarian vocabulary failed him, he had to look up words. Frequent interruptions made the minutes become hours, as Adam asked Larry to provide background information for the different papers. One letter seemed particularly revealing. Dated Sunday, 20 December 1953, it had been sent to Simon Weisz and signed by a Mordekhai Rashi.

*Dear Sir:*

*As we discussed, I am willing to sell all my paintings except the Munkácsy. My son and his wife may need it to bribe their way across the border.*

*I must say, though, I admire your good taste. Your comment that the subject matter reminded you of Herman Melville's "Bartleby" sent me back to reread it. Such a fine story—and a reminder of how much more we all ought to do for our fellow man.*

*Wishing you a safe journey, I am*
*Gratefully yours,*
*Etc.*

Adam read the letter several times, weighing every word. At last, a clue. Simon Weisz had tried to buy a Munkácsy from a Mordekhai Rashi. At least now he had the name of a fellow collector. The Melville allusion escaped both men, neither of them having read the story. Perhaps the Eagle River library was open on Saturdays, in which case, while Larry returned the family papers to the safe-deposit box, Adam could find out more about this "Bartleby." Eventually Larry told him to write down all his questions, and they could go over them later; otherwise the work would carry on through the night.

Agreeing to have a hefty drink when the task reached its end, they ate a Spartan dinner of soup, bread spread with mustard, and canned sardines. They finished shortly before eleven, and Larry suggested they open the boathouse doors facing the lake, remove two fishing rods from the rafters, and do some fly casting while fortifying themselves with schnapps. But as much as Adam liked to fish, he wanted answers even more. Larry could talk and fish at the same time, but Adam needed to take notes.

"I'll watch," said Adam, "and tomorrow morning, if we have time, go after the walleye and musky and northern pike you've told me about."

They dressed warmly. Fortunately the boathouse had electricity. Larry brought along a small floor heater and an arc lamp by which Adam could read his notes and take additional ones. The rain had stopped and a mist rose off the lake. It reminded Adam of a Pre-Raphaelite painting. Had a canoe with a beautiful lady trailing golden hair appeared in the distance, Adam would have thought her arrival fitting. Larry pulled up a crate and put down a bottle of Austrian schnapps and two shot glasses. He carefully filled them both. Holding his up, he said "L'chaim!" Adam clinked his glass against Larry's and responded, "Long life!"

In two gulps, Larry finished his schnapps and refilled his glass. Adam merely sipped his, impatient to get started. Larry removed one fishing rod and then, as he reached for the second, said "Are you sure?" Adam said yes. As Larry let out his fishing line, Adam could tell in an instant that the professor lacked the finesse of a skilled spin caster.

"Let the weight of the line carry the fly to the fish," said Adam, the only advice that he offered. Though sorely tempted to lecture Larry about casting arcs, he needed to stay focused.

In the dim light Adam squinted at his notes, pencil poised. "Your parents came to America from Israel?"

"Actually, Palestine, in 1947. The state of Israel dates from '48."

"Why didn't they come directly to the United States?"

"They couldn't. The war hadn't ended. They fled to Switzerland and then Palestine."

"How did they get out?"

"Do you know the word *Zionism*?"

"Yes, but if you asked me for a meaning, I'd be stumped."

"Simply, the Zionists wanted to move Jews from Europe, and even other parts of the world, to Palestine in order to create a Jewish state, namely, Israel."

"I see. Your parents were Zionists."

"No, my father, a linguistics professor, opposed the idea of creating national states based on religion. He believed in all people, all religions, living together in peace."

"But he went to Palestine."

Larry reeled in his line, stood the pole in a corner, and took up his glass. "I'd better explain." He sat and threw back another shot. "It's a dark story."

A seasoned university lecturer, Larry fell into the easy cadences of a teacher filling in the background to the day's lesson. He told Adam about Joel Brand's attempt to save Hungary's Jews by trading trucks and other war matériel for people, and Brand's imprisonment in Egypt by the English, none too eager to see their Palestine Protectorate, mostly occupied by Arabs, overrun by Jews. When others tried to follow in Brand's footsteps and barter for Jewish lives, the Allies blocked their efforts, fearing that such trades would merely assist the German war effort. Desperate, some Zionist leaders entered into an agreement with the Nazis, in particular, Adolf Eichmann, the man responsible for the deportation of the Hungarian Jews, most of whom knew nothing about the death camps. Eichmann feared that if the existence of the camps became widely known, the Jews would fiercely resist or escape over the border to Romania, which by that time had refused to hand over Jews to the Nazis. Eichmann and the Zionists therefore entered into an agreement: One trainload of Jews would be allowed free passage across Europe to Switzerland, and from there they would be allowed to immigrate to Palestine. In return, the Hungarian Zionists would remain silent about Auschwitz and discourage their brethren from fleeing across the Rumanian border.

One of the major planners, Zionist Rudolf (Rezsö) Kastner, subsequently faced trial in Israel. Found guilty, he appealed. The authorities released him for mitigating circumstances.

Larry sadly explained that though many American Jews would rather not know about this black chapter in Zionist history, the facts remain undeniable. The Zionists not only suppressed rumors about death trains headed for Auschwitz, but also persuaded masses of Jews from Hungary's ghettos to regard the cattle cars as an escape to Kenyermezo, a presumed safe haven. Of course Kastner's friends and relatives boarded the train to Switzerland, along with young and healthy Jews needed to populate Palestine. Eichmann himself told the story in 1955 to a Dutch-Nazi journalist, and *Life* magazine had carried the article in 1960.

Rezsö Kastner was a young man at the time. Eichmann described him as an ice-cold lawyer and a fanatical Zionist, so steely that he agreed to help keep the Jews from resisting deportation and to keep order in the collection camps. Eichmann thought it a good bargain, a few thousand young Jews for hundreds of thousands. He said Kastner could have passed for an SS officer. He drew a picture of a man taking aromatic cigarettes from a silver case and lighting them with a little silver lighter, nonchalantly smoking one after another, as though relaxing in a coffeehouse. Eichmann was not alone in thinking that Kastner would have sacrificed untold numbers of Jews to achieve his political goal. And because Kastner rendered the Nazis a great service by helping keep the deportation camps peaceful, they let his chosen ones escape. "Think about it. A *shanda*. A scandal," said Larry. "Even though *Life* magazine ran the story, to this day very few people know about it."

Adam thought deeply about what he'd just heard, downed his schnapps, and tentatively asked, "How did your parents survive?"

Larry, too, reached for the bottle, paused, and put it down, as if to say, *I'll risk this statement without whiskey*. "My parents bribed their way onto that train."

"Bribed Kastner or the Zionists?"

"Kastner didn't want them because of their anti-Zionism. He told my father he'd be better off dead. So my father bribed a German official."

"With paintings? Money?"

"Although a number of paintings and sketches from my parents' collection had been confiscated, they had managed to hide dozens of smaller works with a gentile friend, an honest man who returned them after the war." The mist had parted enough for shafts of moonlight to slice the lake diagonally. "Cash. All they had. They arrived in Palestine destitute."

"If Kastner spied them on the train, he must have been awfully surprised."

"He threatened to have them expelled. My father swore he'd tell every person on the train about Kastner's villainy. Kastner immediately shut up—he knew that all of the escaping Jews had left behind relatives and friends sentenced to death by the Zionists' silence. When they arrived in Palestine, my father, among others, pressured the authorities to put Kastner on trial."

Both Larry and Adam found sleep evasive. Rather than toss in their beds, they sat in front of a log fire that Larry laid. For a long time both men remained lost in thought.

"The depths to which people descend," said Larry, ostensibly referring to Kastner and his ilk. "And more often than not, they're religious people."

"My wife says we need a new Dante to describe the twentieth century."

"She's not wrong. Rule by the rich. Government by big business. The Italian fascists knew all about it. They even gave it a name: corporatism." Angrily, Larry poked the ashes, sending a stream of fire flakes up the flue. "And soon we all shall sleep beneath the soil / We who would not let each other live above it."

"What's that?"

"Lines from Marina Tsvetaeva, a Russian poet my father used to quote. She committed suicide in her forties."

"My wife would know the name. Frankly, except for my interest in art, I don't keep up. In college I had the sense that some people lived for art and books and music and culture. I suppose there are more of those kinds of people in Europe than in America. My wife writes poetry. I don't even read what she writes. I sometimes think a wall separates us. While she talks about the sound of words, my ear is tuned to the needs of patients—and the cash register. Do you know what I mean?"

"In Europe the intellectual and cultural constitute part and parcel of everyday life. Not in America. We have a long tradition here of anti-intellectualism, even though we also have a record of incredibly brilliant accomplishments. A strange place, America."

"Where I live—"

Larry interrupted. "I've lectured at Tulane and LSU and other Southern schools. To me the South is a foreign country."

"My interest in art . . . sometimes I feel like I'm weird. I mean, the way people look at me. So I mostly keep it to myself."

"That's how we promote conformity. We make the 'other' a pariah—as the Germans did to the Jews."

Adam walked to the picture window, leaning his forehead against the glass and watching the incipient sunrise erode the shroud of darkness. A light mist still remained on the lake. "I'm not an idiot," he remarked without provocation, "although I sometimes feel like one." He paused. "In my whole life, I've never had a conversation like the one we're having."

"Your wife sounds like a very interesting person. Talk to her."

"I can't."

"Why?"

"I've been trying to answer that question since the day I married her. There's something between us. Like I said, a wall." Adam started to pace and laughed nervously. "If we weren't here in this cabin by ourselves, talking man-to-man, I don't think I'd ever say what I've just told you. Do you see?"

"Not exactly."

"I sometimes think of myself as the accidental Adam, a man who wandered into the Garden of Eden, where he found a rich and pretty maiden. I know, it sounds like the stuff of fairy tales. But that's exactly the point. I'm living a make-believe life, when I want to live one of different flavors and colors, from uninhibited sex and dungarees to high-class restaurants and art galleries. From Mozart one day to oozy jazz the next. Do you understand or am I just rambling and sputtering nonsense?" Before Larry could respond, Adam went on to explain that he had never belonged at Vanderbilt. He didn't fit in. The young men and women all seemed to act like debutantes at a coming-out ball. Sorority parties, of which he had attended many, made him think of young adults trying to act like grown-ups, but imitating all the wrong clothes, gestures, turns of phrase, and attitudes. He felt more at home on the football field, with the smells of sweat and sod. In moving to Hungamon, he had jumped from the frying pan into the fire. Besides the black-white split, with the former still behaving deferentially to the latter, he had fallen in among church people, who spoke an entirely different language from his own. The gagging sentimentality and social mores, the assumptions of morality, the provincialism all take place in a humid crystal palace infused with the scents of bougainvillea and camellias and gardenias and eucalyptus and peach blossoms, creating a bouquet of temptation. The palace lacks only a serpent; but instead of a snake, kudzu coils and climbs and clings, greening the garden and slowly choking the plant and tree life to death.

Adam abruptly stopped and seemed to change course. "She's damn smart, probably a lot smarter than me. But it's as if our lives are at odds. Don't get me wrong, it's not because of what she says, or what I say, but because we want different things. For example, a young black man recently drowned in the lake behind our house. A kid, eleven, also black, saw it happen and shouted for help. My wife and I, horrified, ran to the dock. She even jumped into the water to try to help. I couldn't move, not from fear. I kept thinking of the little kid—and his needs. You see, I identified with him, overcome by the strangest sensation: that I didn't belong there, that I stood in a strange place, far away from home. But home, where is that? I didn't know. By the time I collected my wits, the rescue squad had arrived and Rachel and I led the boy to the house. Then Rachel left for church, and for some reason I felt perfectly at home with that black child, comfortable and at ease, a feeling I hadn't known in a long time. And when his mother arrived, I thought someone had shoved my finger into a light socket. I nearly lit up from the charge. Sure, she was pretty, but so is Rachel. That night I lay awake asking myself, *What is happening to you, Adam*?" He raised his hands as if in surrender. "I know all of this must sound crazy to you. I apologize. It must be the lack of sleep and the excitement that came from your translating all those documents."

Larry cooked breakfast. When they finished eating, the clock read 6:47 a.m. They cleaned the dishes, put on Wellingtons, and followed Hull Road to the lake. Standing in knee-high reeds, they watched the ducks glide through the swamp, while fish rings, like pebbles thrown in a pond, widened their circles. A large northern pike leaped a foot in the air and disappeared beneath the murky waters.

"Lousy eating," said Larry. "They have a million little bones."

"I once caught a bluefish off Cape May," said Adam aimlessly.

"What took you there?"

"I don't know."

"Let's see what we can find in the Eagle River library."

Their first stop that morning, the bank, saw Larry redeposit his family's papers. Adam sat in the car thinking how dreary the main street looked, another Hungamon *sans* the flora. Why did most small towns in America have the same squashed, gray appearance, the same stores, the same weary obese people getting in and out of cars, performing mind-numbing chores? Larry opened the door, turned over the engine, and drove around the corner a few blocks to the Walter E. Olson Memorial Library, a handsome, modern stone building utterly out of character in a neighborhood of one-story bungalows perched on narrow lots.

Greeted warmly by a woman behind the circulation desk who pointed them to the modest Melville collection, the two men easily found what they wanted in the open stacks. Larry removed an anthology of Melville short stories. He peered at the table of contents for what seemed an unusually long time.

"Something wrong?" Adam asked.

"Does the word *scrivener* mean what I think it does?"

Adam's face brightened. Conjoining the words *scribe* and *scrivener*, he said, "At the front door I saw a stand with a large dictionary."

"Let's be sure," said Larry.

Adam thumbed through the *Merriam-Webster Unabridged Dictionary* until he found the word. "A scribe, copyist, or clerk. A notary."

He excitedly said, "The painting that Mr. Rashi refused to sell your father is my painting. I'm sure of it. How could it not be? Is there a bookstore in town?" Larry nodded. "I have to read 'Bartleby the Scrivener,' but not here."

Returning the anthology to the shelf, he joined Larry in thanking the librarian and left. Rather than move the car, they wordlessly walked the three blocks to East Wall Street and to Book World. At the front door Adam asked anxiously, "What if they don't have it?"

"Don't worry, there's always the university."

Yes, the bookstore had a paperback of three stories by Melville, including "Bartleby the Scrivener." While Adam paid for the book, Larry picked up a hardback novel, *Chin Music.*

"What the hell does the title mean?" asked Adam.

"No idea, but I understand it will soon be a movie."

As Adam tucked the book under his jacket to keep it dry, his reserve changed to garrulity, as if he had just stumbled on the Rosetta Stone. "Who would believe it? The name Bartleby in the letter. Now the story . . . about a scrivener. A scribe. I just know we're on to something. I've never before felt so close to the truth. God!" he yelled, "won't Rachel be surprised."

With Adam buried in his book, Larry said nothing as he drove back to Hull Road. Both men ran through the rain into the cabin. While Larry built a fire, Adam sank into a chair and couldn't be roused, even when his host, an hour later, suggested that they don ponchos and launch the landing craft to go fishing.

"I want to think about what I've just read. To tell you the truth, I'm not sure I understand the story. Rachel could."

Larry teasingly replied, "Sounds to me like you need her."

Adam looked at him vacantly and then forced a smile.

After lunch they did go fishing, and Adam finally had his chance to show Larry the fine art of fly casting. The landing craft, a flat-bottomed metal boat with shark teeth painted in red on the bow, drifted in the wind. The two men sat under umbrellas and trolled the waters for dinner. Overhead an eagle swooped and made a perfect dive, coming up with a squirming fish in its claws. Retreating to the top limb of a dead tree, the eagle perched proudly, as if expecting the world to admire it.

"That bird's a lot better fisherman than I am," said Larry.

"Just wait. We'll bring in a walleye or two. I can feel nibbling at the fly now."

But the men caught nothing and retreated for dinner to the Black Forest Inn, a favorite restaurant in Three Lakes. Ordering walleyes and foot-high lily-shaped glasses of Hacker-Pschorr beer, they agreed that someone else's cooking eclipsed their own. In the next room a pinball machine sounded and some electronic games buzzed. The one pool table held the attention of two men enveloped in cigarette smoke. In the dining room the man-size fireplace crackled and the logs released the pleasant aroma of cedar.

Adam felt torn. If he told Larry about the picture that Scot Marco sold, he would be making Scot's life difficult. But he owed Larry a favor for all the trouble he'd gone to on his behalf. He produced the article he had clipped from the *New York Times* specifically for Larry. It would provide an introduction to what needed to be said. The article confirmed what Scot Marco had told him about stolen Hungarian artworks.

Reading silently, Larry looked incredulous. "Unbelievable! Our own army." As if to convince himself of the article's veracity, he read aloud. "U.S. to pay Hungarian Jews in 1945 looting. Gold, silver, paintings, statuary, and furs had been stolen from Jews, some of whom had been sent to internment and death camps by the Nazis." He asked, "May I keep it?"

"Of course."

Larry folded the article and put it in his shirt pocket. "I wouldn't be the least bit surprised . . ." He speared a piece of fish on his fork, started to raise it to his mouth, but then dropped his hand. "Some people have no shame. If I knew the name of the soldier who bought my family's paintings . . ." Again he interrupted himself and fell silent, his face etched in anger.

The time had come for Adam to tell Larry about the family in Long Beach. Detailing the antecedents, Adam explained that Larry's gain meant Gabor Molnar's loss, and also Scot Marco's. Larry listened intently and scribbled some notes. Suddenly he rose from the table and wordlessly hugged Adam, as if to say this discovery was worth more than money. He then said: "I'll see to it that fairness prevails."

# Shell Shock

Samuel Hildreth's story, being played out every day in America, had little resonance in Louisiana, where post-traumatic stress disorder, or PTSD, sufferers received only rationed medical help. After all, the shock of war, like the fog of war, comes with the territory. So why complain? Horrific dreams, insomnia, suicidal impulses, dependence on booze to get through the day—these provided no excuse for Samuel quitting his job in Hungamon and drifting into dealing drugs. The year: 1984. He maintained his personal pride by not using drugs himself, not heroin, not cocaine, not marijuana, not even glue. But he found that two or three sales a month brought him more cash than a week of working in a stockroom. Although he had tried to join the Hungamon police force—he had earned the rank of marksman in the Marines and knew all about firearms—he could not pass the psychological test. For good reason the local constabulary worried about his state of mind, in particular, his delayed PTSD.

Samuel grew up a military brat. Both parents died—his father from disappointment and despair, his mother from cancer. His brother, Isaac, lived in France. Samuel trained for the Special Forces and was inducted into their exclusive fraternity. Sent to Panama to help prepare an undercover team for a possible US invasion of Nicaragua, he met Zoe quite by accident. A tropical storm had damaged a great many buildings, including the Baptist church that the Tarpers attended. Samuel volunteered to help clear the debris and rebuild the building. Zoe and her family brought sandwiches and soft drinks to the volunteers.

As a child, Samuel moved from one military base to another, in this country and abroad. He especially liked living in Germany. He even visited Berlin to see the wall and stood on a raised platform that looked into East Berlin, where he could see the boarded windows of those buildings facing west. Once in Ramstein, accosted by half a dozen skinheads, he made short work of the racists, owing in particular to his martial training. Grabbing two skinheads at once, he clapped each one under an arm in a headlock, and then slammed their heads together in a bloody collision that left them barely conscious. The other skinheads fled at the sight of this mayhem. Rumor quickly circulated through Ramstein: Don't bully Samuel. He learned fortitude and patience growing up in a military family; he also learned that a staple of the human condition is waiting. We wait for births, christenings, birthdays, weddings, graduations, holidays, orders, buses, trams, meals, appointments, and perhaps even for the one we fancy most. So when he met Zoe, he would have waited until her parents agreed to their courtship, but in light of their religious scruples, which made him persona non grata, he saw her on the sly and, at the right moment, eloped.

Shortly after he and Zoe separated, he found himself sleeping on the Louisiana wharves, which provided him with an unparalleled view of drug runners, buyers, and dealers, including one in particular—a well-dressed, smooth-talking Louisiana lawyer. Samuel moved into the trade when he noticed that a particular fishing boat unloaded not fish but cotton bales. No fool, Samuel knew that the days of cotton bales had passed with the paddle wheelers. Something smelled fishy. To discover whether he had sniffed out skulduggery, he approached the Coast Guard, told them he knew of a boat bringing in contraband—though he knew no such thing—and said he would identify the craft if the Coast Guard allowed him to tag along as they trailed the *Happy Susan*, the boat in question. The Coast Guard in this part of the country, definitely part of the old-boy network, ate well and drank better. What the hell did it matter to them if some darkie wanted to go along for a ride; after all, they had blacks working in the Coast Guard, though not on this government boat. "Sure," said Captain Jack "the Spider," his sobriquet, and Samuel joined the crew for a trip to Tampico, where the *Happy Susan* docked and loaded what the manifest called cotton bales, and the Coast Guard, cocaine. Samuel had a yen to work with the Coast Guard, but he knew that he'd have to reenlist, train, pass tests, and take whatever posting he received. So when the Coast Guard prepared to leave Tampico, he chose to stay behind, illegally, in Mexico. Not averse to nights in cantinas, sipping tequila and enjoying the company of welcoming women, he figured better broke in Mexico than in the States.

On his first night in Mexico, the barkeeper put the bill on the tab; on the second, a lovely dark-haired lady paid. On the third, a young girl, no more than eleven or twelve, perhaps younger, offered, in good English, to show him the "sights." Happily, she had in mind not sex, but smuggling. Her parents had died, and she supported herself on the streets. Samuel instinctively treated her as a daughter. Her face looked as if it had been hewed from stone, with accentuated cheekbones and small lips. Her dark eyes and hair contrasted with her white teeth. She would one day undoubtedly grow into the body of a beautiful woman. Lidia, whose last name never surfaced, had seen him arrive by boat and assumed he had access to that same craft or another. She told him a fortune lay in smuggling drugs to America. She also told him that the Mexican gangs, killing each other in the cities and streets of the country, were so consumed with power and territory they'd never notice a few missing crumbs, enough to make a modest man—and young girl—rich, not beyond the dreams of Croesus, but within the reach of an ordinary mortal. He listened as she sipped a Coca-Cola and he tequila. She knew the country towns outside of Tampico like her navel, which seemed like an eye peering out from below her shrunken shirt.

Nothing escaped her attention, not the brothels, not the butcher boys (the hit men for the gangs), not border agents and police on the take, and not the gang *tumbadores*, who stole from other gangs.

"I know a tumbadore. He would sell to you. He says the best way to move drugs is by water."

"If I had a boat."

Lidia smiled, well aware that the police had confiscated dozens of drug boats and sold them illegally for a pittance. "Let's go talk to Pepé. He knows everyone in the business."

Pepé Ramos, a local bartender and ex-prizefighter, short in stature and long in muscle, agreed that for a percentage he would buy a boat from the cops. Samuel could then motor the drugs across the Gulf waters to Louisiana, where he could find any number of eager customers.

The former tumbadore, Fernando Gomez, owned a small farm outside the city limits. He supported himself by stealing bricks of cocaine from other tumbadores and from law officials and then reselling them.

"The cops," said Lidia, "grab maybe five hundred pounds," but they report only three hundred fifty. They sell the difference to Fernando. He's what you call a fence."

"I don't have the money to buy from Fernando or anyone else."

"No, but Pepé does."

A few days later Pepé arrived at a Tampico dock with a motorboat, sporting a 1,200-horsepower motor in place of the original 800-horsepower. Samuel and Lidia boarded, and Pepé sped off to a secluded beach, where he and Fernando, a dwarfish man with a big cigar stuck in the middle of his face, loaded the plastic-wrapped blocks onto the boat. Pepé handed Samuel the keys and said, "Good luck, partner. I'll collect on your next trip to Tampico." Pepé departed with Fernando in a white Toyota pickup, leaving Lidia and Samuel alone.

"Where can I drop you off?" he asked Lidia.

"I'm going with you."

"Impossible. You have no papers."

"I'll go overboard at some beach and swim to shore."

"Not yet. Later. For now I need you to act as my middleman, my contact with Pepé and Fernando. When the time is right, I'll bring you to the States. I promise. In the meantime Pepé will see that you have enough money and a good place to stay. We talked it over."

In no time, given Lidia's enterprise in Mexico and Samuel's in New Orleans, he made regular weekly night runs from Tampico to the shrimp docks off New Orleans, where the same smooth-talking Louisiana lawyer, having bribed the coastal authorities, bought the blocks of cocaine from Samuel and used a cadre of young boys to run the stuff. The boys knew the dapper fellow, David V. Dozier, only as DVD. They suspected that he formed part of a larger drug ring being financed by some kingpin, but none of his runners, if asked, could have supplied names. One of his runners, Manny Crenshaw, had made himself invaluable to the operation. Having grown up in eastern Louisiana, Manny knew the landscape and quickly discovered those who had a drug habit. Samuel met him through DVD and invited both men to dinner at Tujaque's, an exclusive New Orleans restaurant. Samuel felt a man could live on Cajun cooking for only so long; eventually he had to try European cuisine.

Over the next several months, Samuel took a liking to Manny Crenshaw, whom he treated like a son, and he often accompanied him on "deliveries" to towns along the Mississippi border, including Hungamon, where he left Manny to his own devices while he visited Wayne and Zoe. On one of Manny's trips to Washington Parish, with Samuel in Mexico, the police stopped the boy in his shiny new Toyota pickup, which had caught the eye of the cops. Under the hood, they found a brick of cocaine, and hauled the lad before Judge Emory Waters. Samuel never did learn what transpired between the two, but the judge, citing leniency for first offenders, set the boy free. According to Manny, his release came with a stern warning to behave. In January 1986, the police accused Manny of shooting DVD, the Hungamon lawyer, and jailed him. Manny was found in the house at the time of the murder and his fingerprints were identified on a jimmied window. Hearing the news, Samuel returned immediately to Hungamon, where he found himself summoned to serve on the jury. With the community clamoring for justice, the trial and sentencing took place in under three months. The district attorney made much of Manny's dealing drugs and taking the life of a white man, a prominent citizen of the town. But although the DA charged Manny with murder in the first degree, the defense attorney requested the judge allow for a "lesser included offense." The judge agreed and explained to the jury that in murder cases, where a convicted defendant may face capital punishment, the court, at the request of the defense, *must* instruct the jury that they may find the defendant guilty of a lesser included offense, such as voluntary manslaughter. Judge Waters clarified the point: "The reasoning behind this rule is that jurors are often inclined to sentence a murderer to death lest he be set free." The sequestered jury, which included Samuel, seemed to agree in their deliberations on first-degree murder, but every time they held a secret ballot, at the judge's direction, they came up with a vote of 10–1–1. The town grew restless, and whispers surfaced about a lynching. The miasma of menace did not lift with the verdict of manslaughter and the judge's sentence of fifteen years, with a mandatory minimum of ten.

"The kid'll get out after five or six years. You'll see," said an outraged Vincent Dozier, the victim's son. "It's a miscarriage of justice."

"Judge Waters musta had a good reason," said a member of the local constabulary. "Maybe he's countin' on the kid to reduce his time in prison by spillin' the beans about where the drugs come from. A dead kid can't talk. The judge's no fool."

David V. Dozier, attorney-at-law and grand marshal of the Hungamon Mardi Gras celebrations, organized by the Rougarou Club, had initially been close friends with Montgomery French. Their fathers had been fraternal brothers, members of Rotary and the same country club and, through their friends in local government, privy to the secrets of 1930s segregated Hungamon. The only time Rachel could remember their disagreeing in her presence concerned a packet of letters and a few photographs that she assumed bore on her father's interest in Bonnie and Clyde. Several years earlier French had asked Dozier to sell him the collection. But he refused. After Dozier's murder, French approached Dozier's son, Vincent, with an offer to buy the lot. Rachel knew about this meeting because her dad had crowed that Vincent sold it to him for a song.

"The boy had been drinking. A ne'er-do-well. You could sell that boy Lake Pontchartrain, he's so gullible."

But either Vincent or his father had removed two letters and a photograph from the original lot. Perhaps Vincent had not been a fool.

Once the trial concluded, the federal drug authorities wanted to discover Manny Crenshaw's source. The paper wrapper and the shape—a partial brick—told them that the cocaine had come from abroad, probably Colombia by way of Mexico. How Manny obtained a brick, worth thousands, led to numerous interviews with him in Monroe, Louisiana. But the young man clammed up the moment the feds raised the subject of his sources. Did he think the people he protected would have the means to persuade the parole board to grant him early release? If so, the police told him to forget it. No matter the angle or the tack they took, the police could not persuade Manny to talk. Even when they bugged his cell and interviewed his cellmate, they learned nothing of value. If the flow of drugs to eastern Louisiana had stopped with Manny's arrest, the police would have quickly lost interest; but the traffic not only continued, it increased. The distributors who had been told to leave the territory exclusively to Manny now moved in with the rapacity of maggots. The number of drug-related murders increased, as did the number of ODs, catching the eye of the governor and other state officials, who thought nothing of puffing on a reefer themselves but in public inveighed against the danger of drugs.

In a downpour and with traffic slowed to a crawl, Samuel made the trek to Monroe and the correctional center. After enduring the usual security checks, he found himself sitting across from Manny Crenshaw. Both men knew better than to discuss the business of drugs, given the jail's omnipresent surveillance. Samuel condoled with Manny and asked: "What took you to Dozier's house?"

"The man owed me for yard work. But he didn't act like a gentleman."

The word *gentleman* functioned as a code for *fairness* among Louisiana drug dealers. When Manny called Mr. Dozier ungentlemanly, he meant the old man had been shorting him. Samuel looked at the stoic guard leaning against the wall. What did such a job pay? Surely not enough.

"You pleaded innocent and said you didn't shoot him."

"Like I said in court, when I got to his house, I rang the bell. No one answered, so I looked through a window and saw the old guy on the floor. I jimmied a window and went in. A minute later, cops came from everywhere and accused me of shooting him. I never carried a rod in my life. And the cops couldn't find the murder weapon."

"Who do you think shot him?"

Manny shrugged. "No idea."

"If we could find out—"

"Then I could get out of this hellhole," he responded feverishly.

Samuel saw in Manny an image of himself: a kid enlisting in an "army" that promised regular work, meals, and a bed. He promised Manny to put all his efforts into seeing him freed.

"I'll speak to Judge Waters about an early parole."

Manny smiled appreciatively. "The judge saved my life."

Samuel nodded knowingly. "Mine too."

Lapsing into silence, Samuel wondered how far Dozier's operation extended and the source of Dozier's seed money. He could imagine Dozier getting shot for shorting someone, but who? What had he missed? In a gesture of solidarity, Samuel raised his right hand. Manny did the same. "Take care of yourself, bro," said Samuel. "I'll be back."

# The Sweet Song of Justice

Manny's death became the catalyst for Samuel to store his motorboat and quit his runs to Mexico. But before he put the boat in dry dock, he would bring Lidia back to New Orleans. Perhaps she could help him with the investigation he'd decided to undertake. His drug sales had earned enough to keep him comfortable for the rest of his life.

To bring Lidia into the States legally would have taken months, perhaps years. Samuel knew not to deal with consulates and immigration authorities. He always turned off the speedboat's running lights when he entered US waters. Never stopped before, he ran out of luck. The Coast Guard signaled him to cut his engine. Lidia immediately went overboard with a scuba mask and air pipe to wait until the authorities had checked his papers, which he always kept in order. Rebuked for sailing without lights, he used the excuse that he had turned them off in preparation to repair some electrical lines. The Guard thoroughly searched the boat for contraband and then gave him leave to continue, but not until one of the coastguardsmen asked him to open his bags. Clothes for a child? They belonged to his daughter, now dead. He wanted her mother in the States to have them. He even listed Zoe's home address, should they wish to check his story. After the Coast Guard had left—fortunately they had not told him to leave before them—Lidia swam back to the boat and climbed aboard, cold and scared but unscarred. Samuel piloted the motorboat into a dark bayou, unloaded Lidia on a spit of land among the moss-laden trees, pointed out one of the innumerable fisherman's shacks dotting the landscape, and told her to wait for him there while he found a safe place to leave the boat. He gave her a blanket for warmth.

On his return, he heard voices. Peering in the window, he saw a drunk Cajun brandishing a bottle of homemade hooch in one hand and a gun in the other. His incoherent ranting about religion, race, and sex carried beyond the shack.

"The Good Lord said to procreate. He didn't make no difference between women and children, though he did put down as sin men doing it with men. He had no time for queers. But man-woman, that God approved."

Samuel listened a moment and then entered. Lidia was huddled in a corner, terrified. Ever after, Samuel regretted not coming up behind the man and disarming him, as he easily could have done. His military training had equipped him for just such encounters. Instead he tried to reason with the man, asking him to put away the gun. But the filthy smelling, teeth-rotted drifter took a swig and turned the revolver on Samuel.

"You get smart with me, nigger, and you dead. I think I'll make you dead anyway."

But the man, having trouble cocking his gun with one hand, put his bottle on the floor, enabling Samuel to spring and wrestle him for the weapon, which discharged. The Cajun looked into Samuel's eyes as if to say, "How could you?" and then slumped to the floor, a bundle of soiled rags. The pistol remained in the man's hand. Samuel had never touched it; he had merely twisted the man's wrist inward as it fired.

"Let's get out of here," said Samuel, grabbing Lidia by the arm and leading her through the spongy bayou until they reached a small country store. Samuel asked the owner if he could use the telephone. The man, sucking on a toothpick, seemed pained by the request.

"You're black, she's brown. How do I know you ain't up to some impiety?"

The shelves, stocked with locally made white lightning, inspired Samuel to slap some bills on the counter and ask for a bottle. The sale seemed to relax the man, who allowed Samuel to call a friend, Joe-Boy, to ask for a ride to the town of Franklin, where Joe-Boy lived. Twenty minutes later the three of them headed toward Franklin. As the car reached the town, Lidia remarked that the place felt like a watery cave. She preferred the sun and sand of Mexico. The mossy trees depressed her, and the people looked as poor in their way as the campesinos.

"Who would live here?" she asked.

"They got a lotta churches," said Joe-Boy. "And they got some nice old houses. Just look around. The English settled Franklin, and the folks in this town make much of that fact. Not sure why, though, 'cause the English treated the locals as bad as the French. But that's people for you."

Joe-Boy, a former carpenter, had gnarled hands and leathery skin. His rasping cough, from a lifetime of smoking, regularly racked his body. But Lidia liked his soft laugh and friendly eyes. She instinctively felt his kindness. Although years of hard labor had bowed him, he never complained.

"Didya hurt your back?" Lidia asked.

"Arthritis," he explained, "but complainin' won't make it better. If it did, I'd yowl all over the place."

Joe-Boy had built himself a comfortable house. Functional without architectural charm, it had three bedrooms, one of which housed his hunting trophies: stuffed fish, deer antlers, a stuffed wild hog, the jaws of an alligator, and other miscellany. As he showed his guests around, he reveled in the success of the New Orleans Saints football team. For love of the game, he had purchased a large television set.

"When I watch a game, I wanna be right in the action," he explained.

After dinner, which Joe-Boy expertly cooked himself, Samuel offered him a couple of C notes to put his motorboat in dry dock. Jimmie agreed, and Samuel handed him the keys.

"You through takin' fishermen out for marlin?" Joe-Boy asked.

"I got some business in Hungamon needs takin' care of," replied Samuel, glancing at Lidia, who kept her composure and silence about their previous ventures.

"You said you want to place the kid," nodding toward Lidia, "with a family out there?"

"With my wife and our boy, Wayne."

Referring to Lidia, Joe-Boy asked, "She got papers? I can see she's already got the language."

Ignoring the question, Samuel replied, "She can get a job and earn some money to send to her parents in Mexico."

Joe-Boy nodded and agreed. "Yeah, a lot of them folks need help."

That night, Joe-Boy drove Samuel and Lidia to Hungamon.

The black old-timers smiled to see Samuel back in town, to say nothing of Zoe's astonishment. She had been trying for several months to contact him, but to no avail. Now, suddenly, he appeared knocking on her door and asking her to house Lidia, a waif from Mexico. He would rent a furnished trailer he had seen advertised. On those days that Zoe wished to have the house to herself or that Samuel needed Lidia's help, she could stay with him.

"Where you been all this time?" asked Zoe.

"Mexico. I started a small business there. I'm thinking of maybe expanding to Hungamon."

"And your head . . . problems?"

"Come and go. I find bein' on the water, on my boat, helps."

"You got a boat?"

"Yeah."

Zoe looked at him incredulously. How could Samuel, who lived in a rooming house, afford a boat? She looked at Lidia and wondered whether to ask Samuel a compromising question. But Zoe concluded that since the child had not spoken, she knew little or no English. She therefore addressed the child in Spanish. Lidia answered in English.

"If you think we stole it, we didn't."

"I got it at an auction for abandoned boats," said Samuel. "The price bein' so low I guess you could say I stole it."

"What's your business in Mexico?" she asked, looking hard at Lidia, implying that Samuel trafficked in child prostitution.

He read her meaning at once. "She's like a daughter. She helps me in my brick business."

"Since when did you become a mason?"

Samuel tried to turn her question into a joke. "I never joined the Masons. Not my kind."

"Bricklaying. Who taught you about mortar and sand and cement? I thought you hated that kind of work."

"I apprenticed in . . ." He nearly said New Orleans but realized that she could easily check. "Mexico. A man by the name of Pelé taught me. We don't lay bricks, we make them."

"From clay and then bake them?"

Samuel's lie about bricks had just about run its course. He had no more rope to play with. Thank goodness, Lidia chose this moment to speak.

"We make ceramic bricks. The clay comes from a special lime pit. And our ovens . . . all German-made."

Zoe, astonished that the child knew English so well, felt compelled to sound clever. "German ovens. It figures."

After several seconds, during which no one spoke, Wayne materialized from inside the house, shouted Samuel's name, and gave him a hug. Wayne's effusive greeting broke the spell. Zoe invited Samuel and Lidia into the living room and asked them to stay for dinner. Within the first few minutes it became apparent to Zoe that her son took to Lidia, who clearly embodied Aztec and Spanish blood. Wayne, having been spoiled by the good looks of his mother, knew handsomeness when he saw it. Once he learned that Samuel wanted to leave Lidia with Zoe and him, he insisted that she should take his bedroom and that he would remove himself to the basement, where they kept the television and sofa bed. He assured his mother that he would be comfortable "downstairs."

Dinner proceeded swimmingly. It had been years since Zoe had seen Samuel so relaxed. Lidia, she concluded, had a calming effect on him, though she didn't know why. After the children repaired to the basement to watch television, Zoe asked, "Does she have papers?"

"No."

"Then how do we enroll her in school?"

"She'll work with me and learn on the streets."

"Rubbish! She needs a good education. Maybe Ben Lumpkin can teach other subjects besides music. I haven't seen you in so long, I haven't had a chance to tell you that Ben is giving Wayne singing lessons. The Shaw family, as promised, is paying."

"The guy can hardly stand," said Samuel. "I thought he retired." Ben Lumpkin, a former music-school teacher, suffered from spinal stenosis, which bowed his back and caused him to shuffle like a turtle with his head protruding forward and upward. Although his specialty had not been choir or singing, but rather wind instruments, he knew enough about voice training to introduce Wayne to vocal scales, correct breathing techniques, proper mouth position, rhythm, diction, timbre, phrasing, and expression. He had him sing both loudly and softly, and he taught him to breathe in the right "gaps" or "rests."

Shortly after Lidia took up residence in Zoe's house and moved into Wayne's former bedroom, she began to accompany him to music lessons. Like most children, her attention span ran from short to shorter. So she began to explore the wind instruments that Ben had on the premises. She particularly liked the shining brass French horn, but

Mr. Lumpkin observed, "Too difficult to play." He directed her instead to the clarinet, which she blew into and actually produced a reasonable sound. Mr. Lumpkin offered to give her a few simple lessons for free. Before long she found that she could, without knowing how to read music, accompany Wayne. In short order, she joined him in a black church for Sunday services and played while he sang. Her attendance and skill quickly endeared her to the black community. But as an illegal alien, she had to live a different life from Wayne's. She worked with Samuel Hildreth on what had now become his sole pursuit in life: finding the person who murdered David V. Dozier and clearing Manny Crenshaw's name.

Although Samuel had money enough for a good life, he made it a point not to spend ostentatiously, lest he draw attention to himself and invite questions about how he managed to live without working. Over the course of several months, Samuel insinuated himself into the local drug community, having learned from Manny the names of the users. A man will appear less threatening or be less likely to get himself shot if he shows up with a child in tow. Lidia served that purpose. From a person's behavior or marks on his arm, she could tell the drug that he fancied, and she had an unerring sense of who could or could not be trusted. Little by little, Samuel assembled a mosaic of information that enabled him to map most of the drug scene in Hungamon, except for one missing piece: the banker.

Mr. Dozier's house had been sealed since being vandalized. The police declared the crime scene polluted, and yet continued to comb through the house, a procedure that seemed to take months. Rumors abounded that eventually the FBI would arrive to investigate. In the meantime, a yellow tape surrounded the home, warning people not to trespass. Samuel hated rules. Even in boot camp and in war zones, he behaved according to his own moral orbit, not the military's. He decided that he wanted to enter Mr. Dozier's house and have a look for himself, but he had no intention of breaking a window or jimmying a door.

After casing it, he decided that the small oval window under the peaked eaves in front offered the easiest entry. Such windows often had no locks. He waited for an overcast night to hoist Lidia onto the pitched roof. Wayne, he had decided, lacked a yen for larceny; moreover, the lad was *his* son. Lidia positioned herself with one leg on the roof and one hanging down, which she used like a pendulum against the top of the window frame. The latch popped and the hinged window fell open and inward. Now she would have to hang from the roof and vault through the opening without landing on the window. Samuel held his breath as the acrobatic Lidia, like a trapeze artist, arched her body and swung through the aperture and into the attic. A minute later she eased open the front door and Samuel entered the dusty, airless house. They both wore gloves. He immediately stood to one side and peeked around the closed curtains to see if any neighbor might have observed him. No lights appeared in the closest house, situated at least six hundred feet distant. At that moment he remembered that some neighbors, plural, had heard a shot the night Dozier died and called the police, who discovered Manny in the house. He pondered the word *neighbors*. Did the police mean several people from the same house, or did they mean several houses? The latter seemed impossible. He would have to find out.

The police had found Mr. Dozier's body in the den, where a bearskin rug displayed a rust-colored stain. Samuel reasoned that the killer had been invited into the house; otherwise the shooting would have taken place at the front door or in the living room. Why retreat to the den at the back of the house? Or did the killer try to position Mr. Dozier as far away from the front door as possible? With nothing but a stand of woods behind the house, the den would have been the safest place to kill the lawyer. But again Samuel wondered about the gunshot having been heard by the neighbors. From the back of the house, it appeared unlikely that anyone other than someone in the woods could have heard the shot.

Two brandy snifters had been found on the coffee table. They had long since been sent to the lab. Perhaps a cabinet holding after-dinner liqueurs stood near at hand. If Mr. Dozier's "guest" had taken the liberty of pouring himself or herself a second drink, the person's fingerprints would be on the bottle. Lifting the window seat, he found the liquor store, including a bottle of B & B brandy and one of Kahlua. A fingerprint analysis of the bottles might lift the veil of unknowing.

While Samuel looked in the cabinets and cupboards, Lidia admired the antique musical instruments exhibited over the fireplace: a French horn, a cornet, and a shawm. Lidia struck gold when she aimlessly reached her hand into the bulb of the French horn and withdrew a small packet that contained two letters and a photograph. Samuel squatted on the floor, lest he be seen, to read the letters and study the photograph, both yellow with age. The two letters had dates: May 7, 1933 and July 21, 1936. The photograph, undated, showed a group of mostly well-dressed men sitting on horseback, followed on foot by some hooded men. All the riders wore fedoras or driving caps, but the man in front, wearing a wide-brimmed hat, which put half his granite features in shadow, made Samuel want to study the photo more closely. He kept a magnifying glass in his trailer.

Samuel slept poorly that night. Rising early, he wrote an anonymous letter to the police suggesting that they carefully remove the brandy and liqueur from Dozier's window seat and test the bottles for fingerprints. Although the local police took their time about acting on the tip, when thcy finally ran tests, they found only Mr. Dozier's prints.

In the meantime, Samuel had the mysterious letters and photograph to unravel.

Zoe had mixed feelings about Samuel's return and her current houseguest. He seemed in perpetual motion, and Lidia no less so, returning home at all hours of the night. But she liked the girl because Lidia adored Wayne; in fact, when some unruly youths had made fun of Wayne for taking voice lessons and called him a "fag," Lidia weighed into the boys with flailing fists and sent them scurrying home. A tigress who had been taught to wield her bare knuckles by a professional lightweight fighter, Pepé Ramos, she soon had no need to defend Wayne from bullies, owing to Dame Fortune. Wayne's school had recently entered a statewide singing contest. The winners would earn a spring appearance in Baton Rouge at the Shaver Theatre across the street from LSU's College of Music and Dramatic Arts. Although the chorus lost early in the competition, Wayne made it to the final round. Each of the half-dozen finalists had to sing a different piece from the one that had earned them an appearance. At first Wayne could think of only some spirituals. Lidia, who had often listened to canteen music in Mexico, suggested he select a Maná song with a lilting, longing melody about love lost and regained. Mr. Lumpkin advised him to sing Gluck's "Che faró senza Euridice" ("What will I do without Euridice") from *Orfeo.* Wayne agreed, but had difficulty with the Italian pronunciation of Eurydice. Lidia, accustomed to rolling her r's, schooled him in the proper sounds: *ay-ooh-ree-dee-chay.* They practiced together so often that he heard the name echoing in his sleep.

Samuel drove the family to Baton Rouge in his Honda SUV, the car he had long wanted to own and could afford only when he started bringing cocaine into the country. Wayne sat up front and Lidia and Zoe in back. From the rearview mirror hung a few assorted brass and silvered Milagro charms that had come from Lidia and that Samuel attributed to his not having been arrested for drug running. The charms, in the form of animals and people, had attracted Wayne's attention from the first, but only now did he ask about them.

Lidia replied, "*Milagro* means 'miracle.' Your mom can tell you that. Charms bring blessings into our lives, like you going to the finals."

Zoe leaned back and wondered whether miracles or hard work—in a word, discipline—led to success. In Wayne's case, the explanation lay in the latter; in Samuel's case . . . what?

The Shaver Theatre's splendid old marble staircase and the wall designs of the balcony made up for the unimposing lobby. Official policy allowed only one person to accompany a performer backstage. Normally, Mr. Lumpkin would have had that privilege, but when his wife fell ill and he had to stay behind in Hungamon, Zoe assured him that she would take his place and steady her son.

Of the six finalists, three black and three white, four tenors and two baritones, no bass had made the cut. The judges, two black and two white, came from different parts of the state, east, west, north, and south. In the past, regionalism had caused disharmony, but ever since the committee introduced the idea of representing each part of the compass, the contest had run smoothly.

Before sliding out of the front seat of the SUV, Wayne had removed the Milagro charms, which he found himself fingering now that his turn to sing arrived. He looked into the wings, smiled at his mother, and began. When he reached the last repeat of the lines "*Che faró senza Euridice*," he sang "*Che faró senza Li-Lid-di-di-a*"—and pointed to the balcony. As Lidia stood and waved, the judges swiveled in their seats and noted the young bronze beauty. Normally such a liberty would have cost a singer—any singer—the contest, but when the judges subsequently convened in private to make their selections, they agreed to overlook the violation of protocol.

In the male category two singers received the most points, Wayne and a lad from New Orleans, Thaddeus Blakemore. Instead of the judges giving both boys the gold medal, they invited them to sing their songs again; and again at the end, Wayne replaced Euridice with Lidia. But having forgiven him once, the judges saw no reason to countenance his misbehavior twice.

"Mr. Hildreth," said the head judge. "You tested our patience the first time. A second time constitutes rudeness."

Thaddeus received the gold prize, and Wayne took home the silver. Although Zoe felt desolate that her son had a second time substituted names, Wayne looked ecstatically happy. He had honored his voluble friend and loyal companion, the girl who had socked boys in the nose to defend him. Miss Lidia, as Zoe called her, glowed from the recognition and, as well, from Wayne's show of courage.

His classmates, hearing of his second-place finish and guts to change the words of the song, now treated him with respect. He and Lidia found themselves invited to parties and dances by people who had treated them as pariahs. Ironically Wayne's celebrity—the New Orleans Opera had invited him to sing in their youth concert—reformed the bigots. Wanting to share in his fame and bask in his glory, they suddenly disavowed the prejudices of the past and saw the future in a new light. His schoolmates declared that they would accompany him to New Orleans for the concert, even though hardly a one of them, if asked, could have brought to mind the title of an opera. But in all fairness to his peers, some of them had exceptionally good voices, and had they not been born in this part of Louisiana, they might have had the opportunity to train for the operatic stage rather than for a place in the paper mill.

Rachel had a special interest in Wayne, since she and Adam were footing the bills for Wayne's voice lessons. To celebrate his achievement, she hosted a party at her house, inviting the first families of Hungamon, church friends, neighbors, Wayne's peers, and of course Judge Waters, Samantha, Libby, Zoe, Samuel, and Lidia. The caterers set up tables on the lawn and strung lights in the trees. A trio played popular and light classical music, while forest frogs sang an accompaniment. Her father and Libby arrived in his famous car. The Hildreths and Lidia pulled up in Samuel's SUV. And last but certainly not least,

Judge Waters and Samantha drove into the driveway in a Lincoln Continental, which he leased new every year.

With all the guests settled, Rachel stepped forth and announced that Wayne would sing the Gluck that had earned him second prize. This time, however, he stuck to the original Italian and asked, "What shall I do without Euridice?" When Irma Wallace requested a translation, Rachel mentioned the myth, to which her Baptist friend replied: "I never heard of a woman being called Euridice."

Rachel explained the meaning of Euridice's name—"don't follow"—and Orpheus's love for her and his mistake in looking back.

Irma shook her head disapprovingly. "It sounds un-Christian to me."

Eight days after the party, Wayne sang at the First Baptist Church's Sunday service. The congregation, normally white, included a large number of blacks, to the discomfort of Judge Waters. Like the slave owners of old, the judge had an eye for a pretty woman, like Samantha, but could not accord blacks the same rights as whites. (Integration had come too far too fast.) Yes, he recognized equality under the laws of country and state, but he did not have to include "those people" in his social circle or in his church—yet. The Baptists had "their own" black congregation down the way. Samantha and the judge had always attended different churches, even though both adhered to the Baptist persuasion. She knew better than to transgress in traditional areas, which over time had become ossified. Did she not rule his house and kitchen? Some said she also shared his bed, but those rumors could never be proved. On this day, Samantha and Libby attended the First Baptist Church with the judge, though he felt awkward with Samantha at his side. Cooking his food and cleaning his house did not, to his mind, justify her sitting with him in a church pew. What would people think?

Wayne sang gloriously, combining spirituals and classical arias. The minister felt moved to say that the congregation ought to invite Wayne to sing regularly at First Baptist. But except for a slight ripple of clapping to indicate agreement, most of the congregants sat on their hands. In the womblike room, shaped like a bowl, the architects had hoped the faithful would feel they reposed in the bosom of Abraham. As Wayne's sponsor, Adam attended the service; Samantha and Libby wanted to hear the music; and Rachel sat beaming with pride, wishing she could say aloud, "This comes of generosity." Mr. French, of course, did not attend. He busied himself trying to prove police perfidy in the killing of Bonnie and Clyde. Judge Waters sat stiffly up front, brimming with self-importance.

After the service, people filed out of church, shook the pastor's hand, and dispersed down the walk to their cars. Judge Waters paused on the sparse lawn, which he likened to a moth-eaten coat, and dilated on the enjoyments that his father, long since deceased, took from good music. Rachel and Adam listened patiently, though Samantha and Libby strolled to the adjacent building to observe the children in Sunday school.

"My daddy always regarded blacks as uncommonly handsome and gifted in the ways of song," said the judge.

"Wayne sang gloriously," added Rachel, shifting from one foot to another because her new shoes pinched. She could have kicked herself for letting the saleswoman talk her into buying shoes a half-size smaller than usual.

"The boy acquitted himself splendidly," declared the judge, "but Pastor Rominy has some peculiar ideas. To go from the horrors of Soviet children taught to denounce their parents to truths that all of us suppress at the risk of our souls constitutes a bit of a leap. I sometimes wonder what motivates that man."

The judge broke off as he saw the pastor walking toward them. Everyone shook hands, and Rachel praised the sermon. Judge Waters looked away, a gesture of annoyance that encouraged the imp in Rachel to continue. She asked the pastor to expand on what he meant by "those secrets that erode our souls."

Pastor Rominy looked up at the scudding clouds and replied, "Our Catholic brethren, hundreds of years ago, stumbled on a truth: that people need a means to confess their sins, a way to unburden themselves and wipe the slate clean. Of course the confessional booth has often been abused, and some priests send the faithful away not relieved of sin but weighed down with guilt. By which I mean, good things can always be corrupted. But confession serves a useful purpose. It serves as the psychiatry of the church. Why suffer when help is at hand?"

The judge turned and said pointedly, "You mean your parishioners should confide in you?"

Pastor Rominy, familiar with Judge Waters's self-appointed position as the town's resident intellectual and legal expert, gently touched his shoulder and said, "I am no Freud, but I can help."

"The sins of the past," said the judge, "can of course be repeated, and I have no doubt that to prevent them from happening again we ought to own up to them. But let us not lose sight of the mistake we make by judging the past by contemporary standards." He even confessed that his own opinions had changed, and that he would not like anyone judging him now by statements he made years before. "We owe our forebears," he opined, "the decency of not disinterring their bones or their beliefs."

On the way home from church, Adam wondered aloud about the judge's reflections, and Rachel dismissed them as characteristic of a man who had a need for an audience.

"He gets restless when he has to listen," said Rachel. "Even for Daddy, he won't sit still. I think that happens because he's so used to expressing his ideas from the bench and being revered."

That same afternoon, Adam telephoned the judge to ask if he could see him. He apologized for calling on the weekend but said he wished to discuss a matter of importance. Judge Waters generously replied that he had an ample supply of Wild Turkey and Chivas Regal.

A punctilious man of predictable habit, the judge arrived at the courthouse, Monday through Thursday, at eight, took lunch at noon, and left at 4:30 p.m. From five to seven he entertained visitors at home, in his study, where he shared sipping whiskey or sherry. To see the judge, one need not make an appointment; the petitioner had only to show up. Whites and blacks arrived, equally welcome, except on Friday, when he heard cases in Slidell, and on the weekend, which he reserved for himself, spending untold hours alone in his garden cottage, a kind of miniature guesthouse. The main manse, facing Founders Drive, had been constructed in the antebellum style, with white pillars and a circular pebbled drive out front. When his high-born neighbor, the beautiful and rich Hattie Lee, whom the judge swore drove her husband to an early grave with her demands, put her house up for sale, the judge bought and razed it, built the guest cottage, and planted an acre of trees. Hattie, outraged that the house she had lived in since childhood had been so rudely treated, called the judge a barbarian and said that if she had known his plans for the house, she would never have sold it. She moved in with a widower who owned a smaller but tasteful house on the outskirts of town. Hardly a day passed when she didn't drive slowly past the judge's house in her antique Bentley, hoping to catch a glimpse of him. On the few occasions she found him outside, she stopped, brandished her ubiquitous parasol, and berated him for his vulgar display of wealth and his "keeping" a black woman.

"I lived next door to you long enough, Emory Waters, to know about you and Samantha Larkin. Many's the day I saw you brush your hand across her derriere. You might fool the others in town, but you can't fool me."

The judge just laughed and said, "Always good to see you, Hattie."

Adam liked Founders Drive. Its beautiful homes and winding street always made him feel surrounded by good taste. Even if most of the homeowners held conservative views at odds with his own, he relished the sense of stability, no doubt owing to his own opaque provenance. He thumped the porpoise brass knocker on the front door, and Samantha appeared. She gave him a great hug—family deserved no less—and led him into the den. Once inside the house, she put a pipe in her mouth and the judge's top hat on her head. The gloves she ignored. He could never understand the ritual, but he assumed it must have originated in Africa and entered her genes. Adam could not help but notice that Samantha still remained a handsome woman, strong and healthy, unwrinkled, and firm bosomed. In fact she enlivened the aging, pale-skinned judge, energizing him and, strange to say, giving him color. Around her his vellum cheeks took on a pink hue, and his spidery hands sprouted blue worms. She disappeared as quickly as she had materialized, leaving the two men to their business.

"A deucedly fine woman," said the judge.

"Very decent," added Adam.

"Like her daughter."

"Amen."

The judge poured some Bayou booze for himself and asked Adam his preference, knowing that the young man from the East had no taste for Samantha's firewater. When Adam replied "Scotch," the judge filled half a cut-glass tumbler with Chivas Regal. Never parsimonious with liquor, the judge put the bottle down next to Adam and told him to take a "patch" whenever he wished. The men sat side-by-side in matching plaid parlor chairs that reclined. Putting their feet on the footrests, they sipped their drinks in silence. At last the judge sighed and said: "Well, out with it, boy. You didn't come here to drink my Scotch. I know a worried face when I see one."

"Manny Crenshaw—"

The judge interrupted. "A sweet boy who got involved in drugs. I tried to do what I could."

"I visited him once in Monroe."

Judge Waters put down his glass, wiped his mouth with his monogrammed handkerchief, and remarked, "Not the sort to whine, right?"

"He didn't."

"I wouldn't have thought so." Pause. "Did he say anything that made you take note?"

"No."

"Too bad. If he had only shared with the court his information about where the drugs originated and their numerous destinations, I might have been able to do more for him."

"You treated him kindly."

The judge, bowing his head like a good penitent, said, "I tried. God knows, I tried."

"Maybe Manny didn't know as much as people thought."

The judge silently nodded.

Adam had come to seek absolution for his foolish words on the courthouse steps. But now, sitting across from the judge, he wondered what the old man could do for him. He looked around the fashionably decorated house, at the poor reproductions of famous paintings, like Van Gogh's *Irises*, and wished he could excuse himself and leave. But the judge's gaze riveted him to his chair. Adam took a "patch."

"At dinner one night, at our place, you said Samuel Hildreth had come to see you."

The judge immediately short-circuited that transmission line. "Legal business."

Adam nodded in agreement. "I don't expect you to violate a trust. It's about me I want to talk—or rather about me and Samuel and the Crenshaw trial. You see," he paused, inhaled, and then, on a rush of breath, said, "We voted by secret ballot, as you wished. I have no idea how Samuel voted, though most people agree he opposed murder one. I abstained. So now you know."

At first the judge looked as if he had not heard or comprehended. He shook the ice cubes in his tumbler and started to raise the glass to his lips. But before the glass reached his mouth, he stopped, placed the drink on the end table next to his chair, and ran a finger along the rim of the tumbler. "Let me be sure I understand you, son." The judge breathed heavily. "You cast your lot for leniency."

"We had the choice between breaking and entering on the one hand and murder on the other."

"The defense requested it. But they hardly weigh the same."

A bewildered Adam, emotionally confused, felt more than ever like an immigrant trying to understand the native language. "Would you have preferred a different outcome?"

The judge sat lost in thought: "Poor Samuel Hildreth! He's suffered a great deal, wrongly." The judge spoke slowly and carefully. "You wouldn't know it, but a few of my closest friends questioned my judgment in arranging for him to sit on that jury. They said his war experiences made it impossible for him to think clearly."

The judge seemed to suggest he had put Samuel on the panel to vote a particular way. Adam wanted to ask, but knew his question exceeded the limits of propriety.

"As I said that night at dinner: You should have put me in the slammer. I spoke out of turn and made things worse for everyone."

Judge Waters, as if taking his cue from the fading light in the western sky, fell into a state of enervation. He said nothing, refilling his glass and sipping his homemade "likker." Then he sighed, checked his pocket watch against the hall clock chiming six, picked at his nails, and bit off an offending cuticle.

At last he roused himself. "What you have said, sir, troubles me. I advise you to let the matter drop."

The judge rose from his chair and extended a hand to Adam. Having been called "sir," which hinted at the judge's displeasure, had caused a rush of blood to Adam's forehead and a consequent vertigo. He knew not to unsettle the judge, lest he invite his wrath. Adam drove home in the dying light, which he treated as an omen. Annoyed with himself for wishing to absolve his troubled conscience, he could barely answer when Rachel asked him about his meeting.

"Are you drunk?" she asked.

"In a way, yes, but not from alcohol."

She smiled that ironic smile of hers that always preceded some unfamiliar literary lines that made him feel unread. "I see. You tasted a liquor never brewed."

"Not now, Rachel. I have a headache." And he went off to bed.

# Silent Words, Secret Words

IN COLLUSION WITH THE LIBRARIAN MR. WILLIAM GRUNING, Rachel made late-afternoon trips to the new library building to collect her photocopies of the integration and lynching material that her father had requested be kept from the public. Once Mr. Gruning had agreed to copy the files, she had purchased a steel-gray four-drawer filing cabinet with a lock. The cabinet would soon be full to overflowing. She had more material than she could digest, more pages than she had time to read, given her social commitments. If only Adam would leave for a few weeks, then she could cloister herself in the house to slowly make her way through the papers. For the first time she understood why writers and scholars seek solitude. When alone and free to study the historical records, any interruption offended her. At times she wanted to cut the telephone lines and disconnect the front doorbell.

Rustling through the hundreds of pages of letters and memoranda and newspaper articles and decrees and ordinances and photographs, she found few surprises. Integration in Louisiana had been greeted with the same demonstrations and discourtesies as everywhere else in America. Blacks attended separate schools; they could shop in some stores but not eat in most restaurants; they received long sentences for minor crimes; they suffered broken heads and bones from police clubs; they had their rallies broken up by fire hoses, horse charges, tear gas, and arrests; they risked loss of their employment, to say nothing of their lives. The KKK night riders bombed the homes of "troublemakers" and even kidnapped and tortured the more effective black leaders. She found frequent references to Judge Emory Waters. His statements nearly always struck the same note and used the same metaphor. He promoted a separate-but-equal society. He argued the rightness of the one-drop rule, and rhetorically asked his audiences if they had ever seen a lion (presumably a white) and a zebra mate? Rachel pondered why the judge would instance a black-and-white animal, the zebra, intermarrying. What might he have in mind?

Montgomery French's articles, as she had initially noted, tended to cut corners. White misbehavior, for example, he never condemned outright, but rather warned that anarchy and gangsterism marched hand-in-hand. Rachel couldn't be sure whom he blamed for the civil disturbances, white or black. Occasionally he editorialized, urging the black community to enter its own floats in the Hungamon Mardi Gras celebration and to select its own queen of the carnival. The few times his picture appeared in the paper, he stood between Miss Ellen and Libby. Rachel scrutinized those photographs with her magnifying glass. She didn't want to miss a single detail. From the first she had decided that Libby, an uncommonly handsome woman, eclipsed even her mother, Miss Ellen, who looked frail and consumptive. On this particular day, while yet again looking at her father and the two women, she noticed that in one of the photographs, her father's right arm rested on Miss Ellen's shoulder, and his left arm circled Libby's waist. But in fact his left arm actually fell below waist level, suggesting that his left hand might be resting on her rear. Did he intend this pose as some kind of joke? She could hardly ask him without revealing that she had access to his personal files.

Among the latest documents she had collected, some dated from the 1930s, were several racist ordinances, the kind that authorities mimeographed and posted in city halls, post offices, and other government buildings. The one that had caught her eye included the following preamble, signed by a Montgomery X. French.

*The whites of Hungamon must teach their children from infancy that the Negro cannot be allowed to associate with them. To allow such association would assure contamination of the whites. The white child must be taught at home and in school that Negroes have no rights that a white man is bound to respect, that Negroes are not fit to travel with white people, eat with them, gather with them, work with them. Negroes are inherently inferior to white people, unfit to vote, lazy, corrupt, and violent, with no aim other than to gratify their passions. The white people of our fair state must understand that it is our high mission in life to protect the purity of white womanhood, and that we must stand ready to play our part in a separate-but-equal society.*

Rachel had always been taught that her grandfather harbored no bigotry, but behaved like a gentleman, a knight, like the man on horseback in the oil painting. The word *pentimento* crossed her mind. She had heard Adam use it innumerable times, and she had taken two art history courses, one in European Medieval painting and sculpture and one in Italian Renaissance art. She felt certain she knew the meaning of the word, but looked it up anyway.

**pentimento:** *The emergence of lines, images, etc. in a painting that become visible as oil paint grows transparent with age, thus revealing the artist's earlier ideas; an undertext.*

She suddenly had a desire to inspect the oil painting of her grandfather, identify the artist, and x-ray the canvas. An involuntary laugh escaped her full and lovely lips. Like her husband, she had become obsessed by a painting and its provenance. If the artist had been supported by FDR's Federal Art Project, the Louisiana State Archives would have records of his work. And if the State Archives had been purged, as periodically took place for political purposes, she could always find the information in the Library of Congress. Again she laughed. She and Adam had undertaken similar tasks, but she told herself that she would reach her goal before he attained his. Her records, after all, stood near at hand, while his remained buried somewhere in the libraries of Budapest or perhaps even Moscow, where the communists had removed many Hungarian archives.

Not long after Adam's return from Wisconsin, Rachel told him, over dinner, how much she liked doing "genealogical studies," and how she could now understand his own passion for "getting to the root of things." His response surprised her.

"All those telephone calls between me and Larry Weiss?" She smiled politely. "The two of us plan to fly to Budapest—over Thanksgiving."

"We always have Daddy and Miss Libby to dinner on that day. I know I just said that I appreciate the search you've undertaken, but can't you make it after the holiday?"

Adam tried to make light of her concern by saying that his absence would just make her heart grow fonder. "I'm sorry I didn't say anything sooner. The travel agency has my tickets. Larry and I already made plans."

She raised her eyebrows, as she often did, to show her social disapproval. "Surely if Professor Weiss has unearthed information that bears on your family, it can wait a week or two longer."

Lawrence Weiss had flown to Los Angeles and met with both the art dealer Scot Marco and the man trying to sell the Munkácsy, Gabor Molnar. He paid Scot a commission for the money he would have made had he sold the Munkácsy. To recompense Gabor for relinquishing his painting, very likely stolen, Larry gave him another painting, though probably worth less; but Mr. Molnar stood to lose his Munkácsy without any return if it proved to have been stolen from a Jewish family. In addition, Larry recommended that the Simon

Weisenthal Center bestow on Gabor a special commendation for his candid admission that his father had not only worked in a Budapest warehouse tending stored stolen property, but also used some of those paintings to gain entry to the United States.

"My papa told me the story on his deathbed," Gabor confided to Larry. "After he admitted the theft, I wanted to sell the painting because I regarded it as tainted."

With Gabor Molnar's disclosures, Larry could now write the Hungarian archives and put his questions about Mordekhai Rashi and his family in a precise context. Larry had therefore suggested that he and Adam fly to Budapest. Adam paid a special fee to receive his passport immediately, and made arrangements at the hospital for his absence. Rachel would just have to understand.

In the days leading up to Adam's departure, Rachel felt despondent, not about Adam's trip but about what she had discovered in her father's papers. To put her mind at ease, she sought out Libby, her guardian angel. Rachel knew that Libby and Samantha regularly met for a good laugh and tête-à-tête at the judge's house on Friday afternoon, when he presided out of town. She drove to the house and started for the front door. But hearing raucous music, she circled around to the back door and entered, unnoticed. Samantha played a washtub bass, pushing and pulling on a stick to change the tension to adjust the pitch; and Libby piped a kazoo, adding a timbrel quality. Samantha periodically took a sip from the homemade brew at her elbow, but Libby stuck to white wine. The two women, in their element, played and sang the blues, which sounded to Rachel like a mournful keening. Their laughter rose like smoke, filling the room with a cackling that had probably echoed in some plantation slave houses more than a hundred years before. The combination of music and laughter sounded eerily primitive. It suggested another continent, a place where dancing and clapping, and music and laughter, attended rituals. Rachel stood entranced. The two women, clearly tribal kin, engaged in a musical pas de deux. At the end of the riff, Libby fell into her mother's arms, as the two of them hugged and swayed to an invisible rhythm.

Feeling that she had violated a deeply private moment, with ceremonial overtones, Rachel eased out of the house, returned to her car, and drove off. But the music remained in her head. The haunting and lugubrious tones made her think of Louisiana's dark history of lynchings, rape, segregation, and, of course, the stigma of miscegenation. If, at that moment, she had doubts about her own roots, she quickly dismissed the thought. After all, if you went back far enough, probably most people in Louisiana had some degree of black blood coursing through their veins. She knew Libby's mother, Samantha, but Libby's father? Might he have been a white man, a mulatto, an octoroon, a quintroon; if a white European, which country had he or his forebears come from? Although light-skinned enough to "pass," Libby chose not to. She knew others not so proud of their roots. She forced herself to stop thinking about race, the ever-present subject just below the surface in Louisiana society. Upbraiding herself for neglecting the Crenshaws' request after the judge's rejection, she drove directly to the First Baptist Church.

Adam met Larry in Chicago, and they flew to London, where they stayed overnight before continuing on an early morning flight to Budapest. During the short plane ride, Adam asked Larry which possible escapes sounded the most plausible: hiding, trying to cross into Romania, converting to Christianity, bribing local officials to turn a blind eye, obtaining forged documents and moving to another city in Hungary, or something else. Larry pondered the question in light of his family's own experiences.

"Hide where?" he asked rhetorically. "In a private house? Too dangerous. In the countryside? Everyone knows everyone else. In an embassy? Unlikely. No country wanted Jewish refugees. To reach Romania would have required traveling by foot. The Nazis searched trains, and stopped cars and buses at roadblocks. They guarded the border. Some churches promised protection in return for conversion. Bribery worked for my family, but for poor Jews? False documents, if one had the money, offered the only hope. I can tell you that the demand for forged passports turned many an artist and printer into a forger, but some forgers denounced the very people who had engaged them. To answer your question: I think the Catholic, Lutheran, and Scottish Presbyterian Churches offered the best chance of escape, but the fascists frequently scanned their membership rolls for Jews."

"Do you think we can gain access to church records?"

"We'll certainly try."

From the airport they went directly to Bécsi kapu square, the Hungarian National Archives, an imposing building constructed in the historical-romantic style, decorated with stone statues. Larry, speaking Hungarian, asked an assistant for the head archivist. The assistant led the Americans into a waiting room tastefully appointed in a nineteenth-century style, with leather chairs and red linen wallpaper. A window looked down on the wood-paneled reading room, richly ornamented with frescoes and a vaulted ceiling, gilded with tiles.

The head archivist, Mr. Bela Baranyi, bore a striking resemblance to Woodrow Wilson. His scholarly mien would have fit in nicely at Princeton. He likewise had perched on the end of his nose pince-nez glasses. A gold chain hung from the spectacles and attached to the lapel of his jacket. To punctuate important statements, he would screw up his nose, causing the glasses to drop and dangle from the chain. He would then, as if pouring tea, fastidiously use two fingers to daintily reposition the pince-nez.

"You can hardly blame them," he said sympathetically in perfect English. Larry had asked about Jewish converts to Christianity.

"Numerous Jewish families tried to save their lives through conversion, and a great many churches happily complied."

Perhaps the Rashi family had used this escape route, and if they had survived . . .

"How?" asked Mr. Baranyi, clearly knowing the question had no answer. "The Zionists, well, you know about Rudolf Kastner. In your letter, you said that your family rode on that infamous train. Before you leave Budapest, I would appreciate taping an interview with you—for our archives."

Larry readily agreed and steered Mr. Baranyi back to the question of conversions. "Which precise churches, and do you have the church records here on the premises?"

Mr. Baranyi made a further adjustment to his pince-nez and continued. "As you indicated in one of your letters, you already know that the Scottish Mission in Budapest, a Calvinist group, wished to convert Jews. But I will say in their defense that in those difficult days their headquarters at 49-51 Vorosmarty utca welcomed everyone. In fact, Jane Marianne Haining, the mission's leader, welcomed so many outcasts that the Gestapo arrested her for issuing false baptismal certificates and hiding people." Mr. Baranyi sighed. "Despite the intercession of Bishop Ravasz, they put her on a train and gassed her at Auschwitz.

"You also mentioned another mission, run by the Norwegian Lutheran Church in Zugló, at 14 Gyarmat utca. They had been trying to gain converts since 1902. But the Jews who sought help there mostly accepted Jesus as the Messiah, though they rarely converted. By the time Eichmann arrived in Budapest, the Lutheran Church had been ordered by Bishop Sándor Raffay to convert only those Jews in danger of losing their lives."

"Except for the Zionists and their friends, who could escape?" asked Larry.

Mr. Baranyi turned up his palms. "The bishop's order allowed for a broad interpretation. Conversion could occur in cases of serious illness, threat of deportation, or a church member's recommendation. Some could pay, some couldn't. Some made it across the border to Romania, some did not. Need I say that church members feared lending their names to their Jewish friends lest they taint themselves?"

Larry opened his briefcase and removed a manila folder. Thumbing through it, he withdrew a sheet of paper. "These are the families I wrote you about."

Mr. Baranyi peered at the paper, nodded, and then excused himself, disappearing into an elevator that led to the vastness of the stacks. In Mr. Baranyi's absence, Adam thought about people whose politics, religion, or ethnicity served as a pretext for governments to make them disappear. He wondered whether all mention of them in print disappeared also. He'd know soon enough.

Thanksgiving dinner at the Shaw house was unlike any before. Rachel entertained not only her father and Miss Libby, but also Zoe, Wayne, and the irrepressible Lidia. Over soup, Lidia asked Mr. French about Paris. Rachel had mentioned that her father and mother had spent 1953 to 1954 honeymooning there, her place of birth, which had earned her French and American citizenship. Mr. French mumbled about Ellen's frail health and the unseasonable rains. Asked about the Eiffel Tower, Mr. French mentioned its grandeur, and Libby, who had sat silently through the conversation and perhaps wished to register her presence, softly added, "C'est magnifique."

At the same moment, Rachel and Lidia said, "You saw the Eiffel Tower?"

Before Libby could respond, Rachel asked, "When? I didn't know you even visited France. Before or after Sophie Newcomb? Tell us about it. I've never been, though Adam and I visited Budapest and London."

An embarrassed Libby seemed to regret having spoken. She replied shyly, "I took a two-week tour . . . nothing special."

"But," cried Lidia, "you just called the Eiffel Tower wonderful."

Without raising her eyes, Libby explained, "I went to the top, but not by the steps. I felt in no condition for that. When the man said '1,652 steps,' I just laughed—and took the elevator. The tower is like an eighty-one-story building."

Lidia looked disappointed. "That ain't very tall nowadays."

The guests laughed.

Raising her head and conspicuously sniffing the air, Libby said, "I can smell the turkey." She excused herself and left the table.

"She insisted on cooking the bird," said Rachel.

"A Bourbon Red Heritage turkey," said Mr. French proudly. "I drove twenty miles to get it. You do know, don't you," he asked rhetorically, fully aware that his disclosure would be new to all the guests, "with turkeys, space and cannibalism cause problems. Not enough space and turkeys will kill themselves or eat other birds. They also dislike too much light, heat, and crowding. Damn sensitive, but they sure do taste good."

As Libby returned through the swinging door that separated the kitchen from the dining room, she added, "And so will the beans and sprouts and sweet potatoes and cranberries and garlic bread. I promise." She stood behind Lidia and stroked her hair. "Sorry, no Mexican food today." Then she cleared the soup bowls from the table.

Wayne and Zoe, silently witnessing the unfolding family dynamic, winked at one another. "Wayne used to keep a turkey as a pet," said Zoe. "Raised him from a poult. Wayne named him—"

"Hector," her son keenly added.

Mr. French roared, "What kind of name is that?"

"Ever read the *Iliad*?" asked Wayne.

"In high school. If it'd been me, I woulda picked Achilles."

"Hector was Wayne's uncle on his daddy's side. He died young," said Zoe sadly.

"How come?" asked Lidia.

Zoe ran a hand down her party dress, a silver-and-white floral print top and black pleated skirt. She obviously wished to gain time to say something important. "A shooting."

Wayne mumbled one word. "Klansmen."

After a disconcerting silence, Montgomery French said, "Those things happened in different times. Hell, just look at Bonnie and Clyde and their treatment."

Zoe softly replied, "To my way of thinking, all those people acted like gangsters, every last one of them."

Libby left the room to collect the turkey and side dishes. Zoe elbowed her son, who immediately jumped up and said he would help. The guests said little over dinner, as they knew better than to talk with a full mouth, and given the tastiness of the food, they hardly paused in their eating. When dinner ended, Wayne remarked that he wished Adam had joined them, and that he liked talking about paintings and playing golf.

"He told me he wanted to find out about the painting over the fireplace. I guess it has something to do with his folks."

Uncomfortable with talk about Adam's roots, though she prided herself on her own, Rachel volunteered that in her estimation Adam's trip to Budapest constituted "a lost cause."

Zoe soberly riposted that knowing your ancestors made good medical sense, because their genes, their inherited diseases, and their environment could all prove helpful when illness struck. For example, to know that your parents lived in close proximity to dangerous chemicals could be an important detail. Her explanation deflected the conversation, which lost its through line, becoming fragmentary and stichomythic.

"Wonderful bird, Mr. French."

"Delicious."

"Everything."

"Thank you, Mrs. Shaw."

"Don't thank me, thank Libby—and my daddy."

Rachel sat down with Pastor Rominy in the vestry, handsomely paneled with a cloakroom, holding all manner of paraphernalia. Two windows faced the children's yard. His church robe hung from a hanger behind the door, a disembodied reminder of the power of ceremonial garb. In his business suit he looked like everyman, undistinguished and ordinary. She wondered if vested in the robe lay the power to grant her wish. If so, she would gladly step aside for him to change. He smiled and waited for her to speak. Although unmarried, he wore a wedding band on his right hand. Did the right hand indicate a European custom or symbolic wedding to the church? Perhaps neither.

"Excuse my forwardness, but is there or was there a Mrs. Rominy?"

"Once," he said gravely.

"You have my sympathies."

"She died in 1945. Ravensbrück."

Rachel blinked. The pastor could not have been much more than forty years old. "The concentration camp?"

"For women. My mother died there, two years after giving birth."

"But why . . ."

"Did they intern her?"

"Yes."

"Roma."

A mystified Rachel told herself she must have misheard. She tried to dispel her confusion by remarking, "Aren't they—"

"My father married a gypsy. They killed her. I never married. This wedding band belonged to my father. I wear it in her memory."

The sad silence that overcame them both seemed interminable. Finally Rachel nerved herself to say, "I've come on an errand of mercy." After telling the pastor about the Crenshaws' wish to see their son buried in the city cemetery, and her family's willingness to build a children's center for the church, she studied his face for a positive sign.

After resting his head in his hands in an attitude of contemplation, he rose and donned his clerical robe.

"The boy took his own life," he said.

"Driven to despair."

"According to our faith, only God has the right to give and take life. Ravensbrück functioned as a death camp . . . run by murderers."

"Are you saying that Manny Crenshaw engaged in self-murder?"

"Just another name for suicide, isn't it?"

"Then you oppose—"

"Any kind of murder, whether by the state or one's own hand." Adjusting his collar, he said, "I'll have to meet with the church elders."

"May I be present?"

He opened the door for her to leave. She stood and waited. He looked away and spoke into the emptiness, "I have no objections, but others may."

As she passed him at the door, she said, "One never really recovers from the death of a parent. It leaves scars."

---

Sitting in his trailer, which he shared with brown recluse spiders, Samuel pushed aside the letters and the photograph and studied his notes: same writer. Same signing initial: F. Same stationery: ivory colored. Same postmark: Hungamon. Same postage stamp prices: 1933 and 1936, three cents. Different messages. The first letter read,

> *Greetings GC,*
>
> *We will need to have a party soon. One of the local darkies is strutting around. It sends the wrong message to the others. You'd think by this time they'd know their place, but these boys are so thick-headed even a pickaxe can't dent them. The only cure for what ails them is a good necktie party next to the Pearl River and the gators.*

*I regret to say that some people never learn, so from time to time it's necessary to learn them. You folks in V never seem to have any trouble. I guess you learned them good and final. That's what we need to do here. When's the best day for you? I'm free almost any night of the week. Just send me a note with a date.*

*F*

Unfortunately, Samuel did not have the reply from GC. So he wrote himself a note in capital letters: CHECK THE NEWSPAPERS. He might find mention of a lynching around May 7, 1933.

The second letter, although different in tone, struck the same chord.

*Greetings GC,*

*The protectors of white womanhood are goddammed angry. An incident took place in town the other day. A darkie tried to photograph a white woman coming from the market. He wanted to make a few pennies and offered to paint her from the picture. His uppityness so shocked her, she dropped her groceries and ran. Then she told her husband what happened. Though he ain't one of our members, we agreed to settle matters for him. He expressed his gratitude. So it's time for another party.*

*If you would kindly bring your brethren here sometime next week, I'll arrange that the boy is on hand. These smokes seem to think that just because we got a communist in the White House, they can get away with corrupting white blood. Send me a note, and as usual I'll have my people ready.*

*F*

Regarding the second letter, Samuel thought, as before, that the local newspaper files for the period around July 21, 1936 would have reported a lynching, if one had taken place along the Pearl River. Now if he could decipher GC and F, he might get a glimmer of who killed David Dozier and why.

At the end of the four-day Thanksgiving holiday, Samuel went to the *Daily News* and requested back issues of the paper. Shown to a long table, he waited ten minutes to receive bound copies of the newspaper for the years 1933 and 1936. At first he chuckled at the dated advertisements. The men's and women's clothing, the furniture, the automobiles . . . they gave him an odd feeling, of a place and time that his parents had described as desperate and dangerous. Hell, most of his teenage years he had grown up with the very clothes and furniture featured in the papers. Cars? Hardly a black family could afford one. Eventually he found what had brought him: reported lynchings that corresponded to the dates of his letters. He took in every word and then had a library assistant Xerox them.

> *May 9, 1933, p. 3: Two fishermen recovered from the Pearl River the body of Ned McLaren, originally from Chicago and a veteran of World War I. Alligators had devoured much of the torso. Two Negro witnesses, unseen in the woods, gave evidence that Mr. McLaren had been lynched. They identified four of the men, all of whom confessed to being present at the hanging. According to the four, they put McLaren, who had gone to buy groceries, into a car and drove to the river. The sheriff has detained the four men and said that only a trial could determine their guilt. One will likely take place in several weeks. The four men have hired the law firm of Waters and Clark to represent them.*

Samuel looked at later issues of the paper to follow the trial proceedings. The four men, contending that they had confessed while drunk, went free, found not guilty of murder. Their retracted confessions had met no objection from the district attorney. The defense had argued bias on the part of the witnesses. Judge Smithers agreed to release the four men on the condition that they "man up" and pay their defense lawyers for their legal fees.

*July 27, 1936, p. 4: Seven men took Godwin Rush, a local artist, from the local jail. Mr. Rush, sentenced for stealing paint supplies, had denied the theft. His body, found hanging from an oak tree a few feet from the Pearl River, and that of a dead young woman dragged from the river, had both been burned. The jail's inmates said the jailer gave the lynchers the keys. All seven men produced alibis. When a* Daily News *reporter tried to question the jailer, J. T. Albert, he told our reporter that "he best mind his own business unless he wanted the same."*

The all-white, all-male jury found the seven men innocent for reasons of tainted evidence; namely, how could the word of other inmates be trusted? Godwin Rush's mother became hysterical and was helped from the courtroom. The jubilant seven invited all their friends to a local tavern to celebrate what one of their attorneys called "the triumph of truth over 'black calumny.'"

Returning the bound volumes to the newspaper desk, Samuel left the building and looked at his wristwatch: 3:31 p.m. Zoe had asked him to collect Wayne at school and drive him to the house of Montgomery French. Rachel would meet him there to take Wayne to an evening recital in Baton Rouge. As usual, she had been tidying up for her father and thought it easier for Samuel to come to her father's house than to her own, on the outskirts of town. Mr. French, given his preference for routine over randomness, had removed himself to visit Libby Larkin, in her nearby cottage. When Samuel reached the high school, Wayne paced impatiently out in front. Samuel apologized for his tardiness and darted down the road toward Mr. French's house.

"Watch where you're driving! Geez, you nearly clipped that old lady crossing the street."

"Sorry. I got a lot on my mind."

Samuel could not help thinking about the initials GC and F. Two lynchings requested by F had been carried out, at least in part, by GC. Had the other men involved come from Hungamon; or did they hail mostly from Varnado, or perhaps from Mississippi, just across the river? If any of them still lived, they'd be in their seventies or eighties, but could he find them and would they talk about what had happened in the 1930s along the Pearl River?

Rachel met them at the front door, hugging Wayne and shaking Samuel's hand. Wanting to start for Baton Rouge immediately, she worried that if she invited Samuel to stay for a cup of coffee, she'd be late. Her quandary ended when Wayne said to his father: "You oughta see Mr. French's collection of gangster letters and Most Wanted fliers for Dillinger and Baby Face Nelson and Pretty Boy Floyd. Neat stuff!"

Given no choice, Rachel asked Samuel into the house. Passing through the narrow hallway and small parlor, they entered a large room, formerly used for dining, where Mr. French kept his papers and files. The painting that had long ago captured Rachel's imagination looked down from the wall. Samuel stopped in his tracks—and stared. The painting seemed based on the photograph that he now had in his possession. Or might it be a photograph of the painting?

"Miss Rachel," said Samuel, "I don't wish to act forward, but that painting there—" He pointed.

"Yes?"

"May I ask who that is?"

Taken aback, Rachel sweetly—perhaps too sweetly—answered, "*That*, as you call it, is my grandfather, Montgomery X. French."

The wide-brimmed hat, the beard, the bottom half of his stone face, the jodhpurs, the riding boots, the crop, the horse . . . all the same, so too the woods in the background, and the men who looked cowled or hooded. A silver belt buckle engraved 1933 added an element absent from the photograph, suggesting a later addition. The painting revealed more of the subject's face, whereas in the photograph, only part of the nose, the mouth, the chin, and the beard could be seen. Even with the slight differences, Samuel knew that it captured the same person and scene.

"I sure would appreciate knowing who painted it. And where and why."

"Do you mind giving me your reasons?"

"Ghosts," he said enigmatically.

"It sounds mysterious. Perhaps I can help."

They sat at the table covered with Montgomery's gangster lore, an auspicious setting.

"I think this painting has a story to tell. Can you say anything more about it?" prodded Samuel.

She found his tone too forward for her tastes, but maintained her Southern graciousness, answering politely, "The painting is unsigned, though titled. I gather that the artist painted it in 1933 or shortly thereafter."

Samuel ran a hand over his day-old beard. "You think," he said tentatively, "the picture oughta be called 'Klansmen' and not 'Kinsman?'"

Rachel now regretted admitting Samuel into the house. She remarked tartly, "Why's that?"

Samuel, attuned to her diction and voice, replied deferentially, "Miss Rachel, I gotta hunch that man is leading a lynching party."

"Nonsense!" she replied.

Ignoring her response, he asked, "Any idea who painted it?"

She felt that his questions could lead only to mischief, and nothing about them pleased her. "I think you've made yourself painfully clear, and I would prefer not to continue this conversation."

He forced a smile and replied, "From my own research, I would guess a black artist painted it." To her astonishment, he added, "And I think I know his name, Godwin Rush."

Rachel sat speechless. Had she not seen the papers in her father's private holdings, locked in the library, she might have been inclined to protest what she heard. Instead she reversed herself and asked Samuel to explain himself.

The tale that Samuel told corresponded to the papers confiscated from the Original Knights of the Ku Klux Klan and Hungamon's own Sons of Dixie. "Your granddaddy had a snake in his veins. Anyone cross him and he struck. I seen some things—private letters—and checked them out in the newspapers. They're all true."

The muscles in Rachel's neck visibly tightened. She noticed Wayne standing transfixed at the kitchen door. Samuel's information, unsuited for a child, prompted her to reach for her pocketbook, remove a few bills, and ask him to run around the corner to the convenience store and bring back some cupcakes and a few small boxes of raisins. "Just in case you want a snack tonight." Reluctantly Wayne took the money and left. "You were saying . . ." Rachel continued.

"I need to talk to some of the old-timers, black folk who were here then. A few still live in town. If my supposin' is right, two men riled your granddaddy, one a World War I vet, Ned McLaren. Probably after fightin' for his country and livin' in Chicago, he came here feelin' he had rights, and the locals didn't like that. They called him uppity. Accordin' to the papers, Ned got lynched in 1933, the year etched on *his* belt buckle." Samuel gestured over his shoulder to the painting. "The second man, Godwin Rush, also got the rope treatment. I'd bet my bottom dollar he made that picture."

Unsettling thoughts coursed through Rachel's mind. Although familiar with racial attitudes in Hungamon, she had never heard of the city being a hotbed of KKK activity in the 1930s. The 1960s presented a different story. Her own father had been questioned in 1965 about the shooting death of Sheriff Deputy Oneal Moore and the wounding of his partner David Creed Rogers, who had lost an eye in the drive-by hail of bullets. But she had no knowledge of local lynchings in the 1930s. Other cities in Louisiana, yes; Hungamon, no. Her daddy's papers, as far as she'd read, did not touch on his father. Perhaps the letters that her daddy and Mr. Dozier had fought over concerned that period. Her daddy had never said, and she had never asked. But why, she thought, would her grandfather lynch the very man who painted his picture? It made no sense.

When Wayne returned, Samuel wished the lad well and left. Rachel collected the treats and drove the boy to the recital in Baton Rouge. Later, she could not remember hearing a single note, preoccupied with what Samuel had told her. She could hardly wait to get back to her daddy's papers. The librarian, Mr. William Gruning, could not photocopy them fast enough. Then a troubling thought crossed her mind. What if Mr. Gruning copied only those papers that did not show her daddy in a bad light? After all, he could easily read them and decide which to copy and which to omit.

The next day, while Rachel drove to the building housing the newspaper, Samuel motored to the home of Jeremiah Lincoln. Now seventy-eight, he and two other black men had lived in Hungamon at the time of the lynchings. Sadly, one of the two had lost his mental faculties and now lived in a retirement home; the other feared to speak of those days. Whether Jeremiah Lincoln's memory remained unimpaired, he would soon discover.

Taking the three front steps at a bound, Samuel opened the screen door and knocked. Jeremiah's granddaughter, Marva, led him to the back of the house, where her grandfather reclined watching a television quiz show. The old man asked Marva to turn off the set, and he pulled his chair upright to face Samuel.

"Your call got me to recalling what happened back then." He shook his head. "Whatever we may think of things nowadays, those times were worse." He sighed, buttoned his white cardigan sweater to the top, and folded his arms over his chest. His face resembled chafed leather, and most of his teeth had long disappeared. The few wisps of white hair that peeked around his ears stood out like angel wings. His bald head bore several scars. Running a hand over them, Jeremiah said, "My four purple hearts. They come from police truncheons. Things got pretty bad along Border Street."

Marva brought a tray with coffee and homemade banana pudding. She whispered that her granddaddy had poor hearing.

Between sipping his coffee and licking his fingers, Samuel loudly asked Jeremiah about the two men who had been lynched.

"I have my own theories," said Samuel.

"No need for theories. I can tell you what ya need to know. Ned came back from France a new man. The Frenchies had treated him royally. He even dated French girls. White women. He also came back with a medal for bravery. In Chicago he fit in."

"Let me guess. In Hungamon, Mr. McLaren wouldn't bow and scrape anymore. He even spoke to white ladies."

"That's the long and short of it, as they say. They made an example of him so the other black folks wouldn't step out of line."

Marva brought more coffee and pudding, pleased that Samuel liked her cooking. He praised the pudding and explained that he had missed breakfast to talk to Mr. Lincoln. Wiping his mouth, Samuel leaned forward, prepared to ask the question that haunted him most.

"Why did they kill Godwin Rush? For Chrissake—" He stopped on seeing a crucifix hanging over the door. "Geez, he painted the night riders. I saw the picture in Montgomery French's house."

"I ain't never seen it, but I heard about it."

"They must've asked him. Hell, they posed for him."

"That's where you're wrong. They had no idea of their bein' photo'd—and then painted."

Samuel looked confused. Hadn't Godwin posed the group, taken their picture, and then made a painting from the photograph?

Jeremiah's furrowed face looked even more ridged than before, the ravines and wrinkles more pronounced. He took a handkerchief from inside his sweater and blew his nose. His eyes teared. "Just a child," he mumbled.

"Who?"

Jeremiah dabbed his eyes.

Marva cleared the tray and asked Samuel if he would like a bowl of hot cereal. He smiled appreciatively and said as a matter of fact he would, and repeated that he had skipped breakfast.

"No need to apologize," she said.

Looking straight ahead at the darkened screen of the television, Jeremiah seemed to see through it to the bigotry of the black beyond. "FDR and his people created the Federal Arts Project. The New Deal made it possible for writers and musicians and painters and potters and photographers to do what they do best and get paid. Godwin painted. His neighbor down the street, Mary Judd, just sixteen years old, bought a camera and took pictures. Sometime around the summer of 1933, while out in the woods snapping birds and flowers and other such things, she heard a commotion, and when she approached, she saw in the distance this group of men, mostly on horseback, with some others on foot. All of 'em members of the Sons of Dixie, hollerin' and yellin' 'bout their plan to burn a cross that night. Mary took their picture with them swearin' allegiance to God, country, and the purity of the white race. After she developed it, she showed it to Godwin Rush. He asked could he have a copy 'cause he wanted to do a paintin'. Well, you know the rest."

Not so. Returning to his cramped quarters in the trailer, Samuel stamped on a spider and peered at the photograph for the umpteenth time. What in the photograph had led Mary Judd to show it to Godwin; why had Godwin painted the scene; and why had the painting led to two murders? He needed to study the canvas more closely—and with a magnifying glass. The photograph lacked the definition found in the painting. He especially wanted to study the belt buckle bearing the date 1933. What made that year so damned important?

While perusing the files in the newspaper archives, Rachel found a notice of her father's birth, August 21, 1925. In less than two years, her daddy would turn sixty-five. At the time of her birth, June 1954, he was twenty-nine, and her mother twenty-five. Moving from 1925 to 1933, she found several articles bearing on the lynching of a Ned McLaren. One even quoted the *Times-Picayune*: "A veteran of the Great War, he had returned to a young wife in Chicago. She persuaded him to move to Hungamon, her parents' home. Out of work, he had been running errands for people in the better part of town. When he approached a white woman and offered to carry her groceries, she told her husband. A few days later, the police found the man hanged, an apparent lynching."

The Hungamon newspaper reported that among the men questioned about the crime, Montgomery X. French loudly proclaimed his innocence, claiming that he and the other men had airtight alibis. Rachel wondered why her grandfather would have been a suspect. Did anyone see him near the crime? His membership in the Sons of Dixie did not make him a murderer. She could hardly entertain the painful thought. He may have uttered some nonsense about blood, but he couldn't have really believed it. If his prejudices actually showed, his son might not have escaped the virus. But her daddy had done more than hire Miss Libby to work as a nanny, he had, after his wife's death, taken up with her, she whom he called "the lovely octoroon." Did he call her an octoroon to mitigate his seeing a black woman; did the word lessen the crime? What, she mused, would her grandfather have said?

The day after her visit to the newspaper, Rachel had invited Mr. Gruning to her home to ask him a question that only he could answer. He arrived carrying a bundle of papers, which he passed on to her. Taking no chances that her father might arrive unannounced, she put the papers in her filing cabinet and locked it. If her father should appear, she and Mr. Gruning had met to discuss the amount of her current and future contributions to the library. A memory flashed through her mind of Mrs. Neninger, her English teacher, saying that libraries will get you through times without money better than money will get you through times without libraries. She led Mr. Gruning into the kitchen to enjoy a coffee break. Handing him a cup, made of fine bone china, she filled it from a white swift-style ceramic server. He sniffed the aroma and beamed contentedly, enchanted by this invitation, no doubt because of the neglect and inadequate salaries librarians normally received.

"You agreed to copy all my daddy's papers," she said. "Tell me, do they follow some chronological order? When I looked through them, I saw that he had his own organization, by category."

She knew at once from Mr. Gruning's expression that he had been reading the material first and then deciding whether he thought it suitable for copying. "I would remind you, sir, that my gift to the library depends on my receiving copies of the papers, not just some. Do I make myself clear?"

Mr. Gruning never finished his coffee, which he liked exceedingly. For the next few minutes, he effusively apologized for trying to keep Rachel from revelations that a decent Southern lady should be spared.

"Disagreements have a way of becoming personal and ugly. Epithets get thrown around; the legitimacy of one's parents and children questioned; threats made; miscegenation charged. I couldn't imagine, Mrs. Shaw, you wanting to read such vileness."

He went on to explain that some of the documents in Mr. French's personal collection bore on his disagreement with Mr. Dozier about some letters written in the 1930s. "But the two letters that the men fought over are not in your father's collection. They seem to have disappeared."

Rachel breathed deeply. Did she, even if she could locate them, have the stomach or nerves for what they might reveal? In the silence she could hear the hall clock ticking. *Tempus fugit.* Time flies. But where does it fly to? Could it ever be recovered? She decided then that memory was a homecoming, worth the pain. Putting her hand on Mr. Gruning's wrist, she hazarded: "From what you can tell, did the letters concern lynchings in Hungamon?"

# Budapest

Putting several files on his desk, a wheezing Mr. Baranyi wiped his forehead and asked Larry and Adam if they would object to his smoking a cigarette. "The rules forbid it—the library, you know, valuable papers—but we all have our little sins."

Adam weighed whether to object or not. But since the man had volunteered to help him, he bit his tongue. Larry seemed indifferent.

Treating silence as consent, Mr. Baranyi lit a Turkish cigarette, which he held between his index finger and thumb, and inhaled deeply. From Mr. Baranyi's dour expression, his two visitors concluded that he bore bad news. He opened one of the files and removed several carbon copies of a report.

"We think Mordekhai and Sára Rashi died in Auschwitz, early 1945. Their son, József, and his wife, Abagail, may have converted to Catholicism and taken refuge in the Majk Monastery, seventy kilometers west of here. At war's end, like others, they may have resumed their Jewish identities. I would guess they're now dead, but much of this, you understand, is unconfirmed. The art gallery that Mordekhai—"

Larry interrupted. "Which art gallery? I never knew that the Rashi family owned one."

"By the end of the war, the gallery . . ." He thumbed through some more papers. "belonged to a Vilmos Kovács, who had been Mr. Rashi's partner before the war."

Larry and Adam stared at one another.

"One puzzle solved," said Larry. Turning to Mr. Baranyi, he said, "I don't suppose he's still alive."

"Unlikely. The communist records indicate that the government confiscated the gallery and turned it into a youth center."

"And the paintings?"

Mr. Baranyi extinguished his cigarette against the sole of his shoe and put the butt in his pocket. "Who knows? They could be hanging now in some German houses or Russian dachas. They could have been sold or buried in some attic." Mr. Baranyi crossed his arms and leaned forward on his desk. "Or," he said, clearing his throat, "they could be the property of some Americans. I trust you know about the train they stopped that was carrying stolen paintings." Larry and Adam nodded. "Then you know the artworks had been warehoused near Salzburg, and your own people looted much of the treasure."

"Yes," said Larry glumly.

Straightening up in his chair, Mr. Baranyi ran a hand through his thinning hair. "I could have cried when I learned that the American officers in charge refused to do anything to prevent the thefts or confiscate the artworks from the wrongdoers. They dismissed the crime as 'the spoils of war.'"

Many of the soldiers, who had little appreciation for art, returned to the States and sold the "spoils." When they came on the market, art collectors, slow to realize the implications of their buying such goods, only years later returned them to their rightful families or heirs. The Jews of both Europe and America had employed lawyers to recover stolen property, but those recoveries required hours of work to establish provenance and rightful ownership.

Not for the first time, Adam wondered whether his painting by Mihály Munkácsy had come to him through some illicit channel. Surely, Fulop and Berta Vadas could not afford such a painting, and their explanation that the canvas had come from his parents began to ring false.

"Mr. Baranyi, how comprehensive are your genealogical archives?"

"Like any such records, Mr. Shaw, ours have gaps. But what in particular do you want to know?"

"Anything you can tell me about József and Abagail Rashi."

"Such a search could take weeks or months, and then there's no guarantee . . ."

Adam removed five hundred dollars from his wallet.

"Keep searching."

Samuel decided to approach Mr. Dozier's son, Vincent, and suggest that the neighbors could not have heard the shot that killed his father, and that Vincent ought to request a police investigation. Unbeknownst to Samuel, Vincent Dozier lacked his father's acumen and cunning. David Dozier had always been ruled by one passion: money. Hence he had no reluctance, in pursuit of cold cash, to employ Manny Crenshaw and other blacks. Vincent always acted cautiously. Frail from birth, he had been protected from his father's abuse by his mother, who eventually took the boy away and divorced his father. In his teens the lad decided that if he blended into the background, he would be treated like a sensible, conservative man with a purpose in life. Instead he was laughed at and eventually married an overbearing woman. He trained to work as an accountant, fancying numbers, but he couldn't pass the state CPA accreditation exam. So he balanced the books for a local car dealer, earning a modest but livable salary, until the sale of his father's estate left him unexpectedly well-off. Rhoda, his wife, an obese virago, loved nothing more than to drive to New Orleans and shop. Childless, she dedicated her newfound money to self-adornment and pretension.

When Vincent told his wife about Samuel's request, she immediately grew wary. "He must be involved. Otherwise, why care? I don't want you messing with his kind."

True to his nature, Vincent equivocated. "I think there's some value in what you say," he told Samuel, "but my wife thinks it's a wild-goose chase."

Samuel shrugged and remarked, "The killer may have made off with a bundle. But if you don't want to recover the money, that's fine with me."

On hearing the story and the word *money*, Rhoda told Vincent to forget her previous advice and, instead, go directly to the police. Coming from a white man, the request to investigate received prompt action. To the police's surprise, but not Samuel's, the neighbors all said the same: They had heard no gunshots. Then which neighbors had called to report them? At the time of the murder, the police studied the telephone records and discovered two calls made to their station. One came from a telephone booth in a small shopping mall, and the other from a drugstore housed in the mall. The police had tried unsuccessfully to follow these leads. No one could remember seeing the callers. They gladly shared this information with Vincent Dozier, but had Samuel requested it, he likely would have been refused.

"As far as the police go," Samuel said, "this case is settled. They got their man, Manny Crenshaw. From their standpoint, what's gained lookin' any deeper, 'specially if they found a white man did the shootin'?"

Vincent agreed. The two men met at Samuel's trailer. Vincent brought a six-pack of bottled beers. He had already been drinking. Samuel could smell hard liquor on his breath. "Do you have any idea," asked Samuel, "why your old man and Mr. French got in a dogfight over some letters?"

"Not for sure, but I got a few guesses."

"Whoever wrote them—"

Vincent, approaching inebriation, which always made him happy, loudly laughed and slapped Samuel on the arm. "Hell, that's easy. You don't need any 'whoever.' Montgomery Xavier French wrote them.

The old bastard himself. The high and mighty father of Montgomery junior. My old man said that much."

Samuel put his bottle down and told himself to remain sober. If necessary, he would take mouthfuls of beer and then void them into the potted orange tree at his elbow. Vincent would never notice.

"The letters are addressed to someone whose initials are GC. Do you know who that is?"

Vincent guffawed, thinking himself much smarter than Samuel. "Damned if you don't have a thick, wooly head. GC stands for Grand Cyclops." He laughed until tears ran down his cheeks. "Hell, anyone knows *that*."

Samuel smiled, well aware that the Grand Cyclops for each KKK group served as the enforcer, the hit man. The lyncher.

"How come your daddy got mixed up with them kind?"

An incredulous Vincent said, "Back then, all the important people belonged to the Klan."

Samuel's mind raced. Were Vincent and Montgomery trying to paper over the crimes of their fathers? With all the current concern among blacks about civil rights and revisiting old wrongs, if these letters became public knowledge, the sons could no longer pretend that their fathers had been innocent of crimes committed in the 1930s. And the man who owned the letters could always blackmail the other or at least sully the reputation of the other's father. Samuel knew that in the South, you can never underestimate the importance of Big Daddy, the overseer of every family. Montgomery *fils* would not have his father defamed, or so Rachel had implied. Samuel speculated: Might Montgomery have killed David Dozier to get the letters? Or was David Dozier killed for another reason?

"I assume," said Samuel, "that you know what's in the letters."Vincent, having trouble keeping his head up, wanted to doze. "I read them," he slurred, "but that stuff is dead-and-gone history."

"Three people murdered."

"Terrible! But what can we do? Sure, Louisiana had a reputation as a hotbed of lynching. Some people even called us the rope capital of the world, what with all that strange fruit hanging from trees."

"Your granddaddy—"

Vincent cut him off. "By no means the worst of them. Hell, he told my daddy, who told me, that he tried to save that painter man and the girl with the camera, but the elder Montgomery wouldn't hear of it."

Samuel took a swig of beer, turned his head, and spit it out. "I can't help but wonder, why?"

"Why my granddaddy tried to save those people?"

"No, why the old man wanted them strung up."

Wiping his mouth with his sleeve, Vincent drooled, "Easy. The KKK swore everyone to secrecy. And a picture's worth a thousand words."

"The riots of 1965 . . . you suppose your father or Montgomery French took part?"

"Hell, on both sides, the Montgomerys and the Doziers, fathers and sons got involved. You couldn't stay neutral, what with Hungamon at war. As the deputy sheriff said, niggers ain't gonna run this town."

"Child," Libby said, "why are you looking so sad?"

Illuminating one's past, Rachel now realized, runs the risk of revealing unsavory details. Recent events and Adam's absence had left her scared. The large empty house didn't help. Libby had agreed to stay with her for a few days, and had just met Mr. Gruning coming out the front door as she entered. Rachel had been struck dumb at the mention of the word *miscegenation*. In the South the word often functioned as nitroglycerin. It could destroy families and undermine dynasties; it could drive people to leave home in shame. Libby could see the upset in Rachel's face.

"Honey, why so blue? Anything to do with the man I passed coming in?"

"William Gruning," said Rachel and then lapsed into silence.

"William Gruning . . . William Gruning," Libby repeated. "Can't say I know . . ." She paused. "Of course, the librarian."

Rachel sniffled, related rummaging through her father's papers and finding "things," and then entered the enfolding arms of Libby Larkin. How many times since childhood had those strong limbs supported her? Whether unhappy over a scraped knee or a bruised ego, Rachel knew where to find comfort: in the bosom of Libby Larkin.

"Now, now, child. It can't be all that bad. How come you can be strong when alone, but as soon as I show up, so do the tears?"

"Because no one understands me like you."

"No one's trying to hurt you."

"I need protection from the past."

Not knowing how to treat Rachel's comment, Libby said nothing.

Adam landed at Louis Armstrong airport around dinnertime, genuinely delighted to see Rachel waiting behind the barrier. From a distance, he could not help but admire her handsome looks, which he told himself would remain with her into old age. "Good genes," he thought, dropped his bags, and embraced her. She, equally glad to see him, rested her head on his shoulder. Adam's fond endearments could now replace Libby's comfort. She actually looked forward, as she had the night the phone rang, to lovemaking. As they walked to Rachel's car, Adam talked about his trip but not about his family. He feared that voicing what he'd heard would make it true, and hoped for a less painful verdict. She asked about Budapest: the city, the archive, the accommodations. Did he like the hotel, the room, the location? Did he and Larry share a room or did he have a single? Adam mistakenly interpreted her last question to mean: Had he taken some maid to bed? He teased her by saying the archivist had won the Miss Universe Beauty Contest and had asked him to remain with her in Budapest. For some reason, she didn't smile.

"What is it, Rachel? You seem troubled."

She failed to reply, until inside the car. He could see her struggling to say something important. Had she taken a lover? Received bad news? Attended a funeral? Had the First Baptist Church objected to Manny Crenshaw being buried in the city cemetery?

"No, no, no, no! Something worse. You know the word *miscegenation*?"

"Why do you ask?"

"What if you discovered that someone you loved or someone very close to you turned out . . ."

She couldn't finish her sentence.

"Turned out what?"

Opening the car door, she exited from the driver's side, leaving the keys in the ignition, and circled to the passenger side. "You drive," she said. "I nearly had an accident on the causeway. My hands are still shaking."

After he changed places with her and slipped behind the wheel, Adam asked, "What's the matter, Rachel? First you mention miscegenation and then a near accident."

"They're connected in my mind, in more ways than one."

For a moment Adam digested that idea. "You mean the first would be tantamount to the second?"

"Something like that."

"You're not being clear, Rachel. You tell me to say what I mean. Now you're skirting the subject."

"Skirting! A good word. It makes me think of womanizing."

Taken aback, Adam replied, "The archivist in Budapest . . . you didn't believe—"

"Of course not."

He leaned over and kissed her hair, a gesture that elicited a torrent of tears.

"We're not leaving here until you tell me what's torturing you."

"Torturing," she sobbed. "That's a good word. In fact, the right word. I'm tortured."

~

Libby decided that Pastor Matthew Williams would be the right person to speak to. Except for Manny Crenshaw's memorial service, he had no connection to any of her friends or relations. She felt, based on his sermon, that he could be trusted; she would therefore make an appointment to see him. Instead of calling, she drove to the church and left a note for him:

*Dear Pastor Williams,*

*I need your advice. I heard what you said at the service for Immanuel Crenshaw, and I think you can help me.*

She signed the note "Miss Libby Larkin" and listed her home phone number.

Several days passed and, hearing nothing, she called the church. The receptionist said that the pastor's father had died, and that Pastor Williams had returned to Alabama to console the family. He would return in ten days. In the meantime, Libby would speak to her mother, Samantha Larkin. She drove to Judge Waters's house and found her mother making Bayou booze, which she periodically tasted with a ladle to determine the right texture and strength of the brew. It smelled noxious, but no worse than what came from the mill.

The two women entered the house and went to Samantha's bedroom. One look and anyone could tell that the bed hadn't been slept in for ages. Apparently her mama and the judge still cuddled in his room. Samantha used her bedroom for sewing, or writing letters, or reading, or praying, or lucubrating. The judge had taught her the meaning of that last word: "working, studying, or writing laboriously late at night." She liked the sound of the syllables.

"We can lucubrate here."

Libby walked over to her mother's dressing table and pinched the bulb on her perfume bottle, spraying herself with a lilac scent.

"I always liked that smell," Libby said, "it reminds me of you."

"Just let me slip out of these overalls." She quickly changed into a dress. After admiring herself in the wall mirror, she sat next to her daughter. "You have something on your mind, honey. I can always tell."

Without any soft transition, she asked, "Who is my daddy, really?"

Startled, Samantha suggested that they sip some of her homemade liquor in order "to work their way into the subject."

"Just answer me soberly: Who is my daddy?"

"I told you years ago. Why do you ask?"

"Because of Rachel."

"What about her?"

"We had a talk about family skeletons."

"Religion, money, sex . . . they're always dangerous. I try to stay clear of those confabs."

For a moment the air, vacant of sound, supported only the lilac perfume.

Samantha sighed and murmured, "Child, I think you already know. It began years ago, in Vermilion Parish, before the judge's wife died."

"I just wanted confirmation, and you just gave it to me."

"You have your regrets, I have mine. And let me tell you: I learned a long time ago to live in secret happiness rather than in regrets."

---

Zoe and Libby had met through the Shaws. They liked each other; in fact they had hit it off splendidly on first meeting. Both came from a culture of taking in strays, of extending a hand to the needy. Zoe, trying to decide whether to house Ori and her parents, knew she'd need help. Libby immediately came to mind. They met over coffee in Libby's shingled white cottage, with its street-facing porch and well-tended rear garden. She had tastefully furnished the small but comfortable house, with its one bedroom downstairs and finished attic. Her kitchen, unlike so many of her neighbors', had been designed to accommodate a table and a large work space. Most cooking areas in the South resembled coffins, but not hers. As in Italian and Jewish homes, friends and guests gathered in the kitchen. Here Zoe told Libby about Ori, the child recovering from surgery who had come from the Naso Teribe Indians in the Panamanian rain forest.

"If she goes back right now, she has no chance of surviving. I'm willing to keep the family at my house, but only if I can find a temporary home for Wayne and Lidia."

"You asking me whether the kids can stay with me?"

"They're well behaved. You could be their surrogate grandma. I'll pay," said Zoe.

"It's not the money. It's just that . . . a male friend comes here often."

Surprised by Libby's admission, Zoe struggled for words. "A caller here . . . awkward. The children . . . on those days . . . maybe Wayne and Lidia could be with me."

"I never know, until the last minute, when he plans to visit."

Such a strange arrangement, thought Zoe. Why would Libby allow it? Perhaps she lived as a kept woman. Everyone said that of her mama. Hmm. The apple never falls far from the tree.

Libby studied her coffee cup and strained for another solution to the problem of space. After a prolonged silence, she said: "Let me talk to Rachel."

"Rachel Shaw? Given her social circles, she's unlikely to want two colored kids underfoot. Now, her husband is a different story."

Always protective of Rachel, Libby immediately worried about bringing Adam and the attractive Zoe closer together; then she visibly relaxed. "Of course, you know Mr. Shaw from the hospital."

Zoe looked around the well-appointed kitchen, at the shining porcelain stove and the gleaming pots suspended from an oak beam overhead, and said, "If you thought—"

"Never you mind. The idea has already gone."

"Mr. Adams and I are just good friends—from the hospital. Nothing more than that."

"It's Rachel I'm thinking about, not Adam. She's a daughter to me. Adam, well, he's a good man, but from another place. Around him, I always feel our differences, and not because of color. I can't explain it. He seems foreign."

Zoe, warming to Libby's idea, added, "I know she likes Wayne. I think she likes Lidia, too. It would do both those kids good to see another way of life . . . at least for a short time."

"She likes 'em both, but I can tell you she's not accustomed to having kids around." She chuckled at the thought of the two children racing through Rachel's impeccable house and engaging in horseplay. If a single pillow looked out of place or had lost its puff, she descended on it like a dive bomber. "Perhaps the good Lord is thinking right now that for Rachel two rambunctious kids would be a blessing." She put a hand to her mouth and chuckled again.

In the den of Judge Waters's house, Montgomery French and his old friend huddled in front of the fireplace, saying little and watching the sorcery of fire. Each man fingered a brandy snifter. A bottle of B&B stood on an end table within reach.

"The police have been talking to Dozier's neighbors," said the judge. "Chief Jamison called to tell me."

"What about?"

"What about! The murder of course."

"How does that concern you—or me?"

The judge took a long draft of his brandy and replied, "You wanted to get those letters, and Samuel Hildreth wants to clear Manny Crenshaw's name. Even Dozier's son, that idiot Vincent, has gotten in on the act."

"Hell, I didn't kill that bastard. Do you know who did?"

"I wish, though I do admit his death has improved the social standing of Hungamon."

"If I understand you, you think for both our interests, Mr. Samuel Hildreth and Mr. Vincent Dozier ought to stop nosing around."

"The murder hardly concerns me, but I worry about the other things that might turn up. If for some reason the local investigation got out of control and the FBI stepped in . . . I'm happy to speak to Mr. Hildreth if you'll speak to Mr. Dozier."

"The worst thing about the past is that it's never past."

"That's what Faulkner said. I didn't know your read him," added the judge puckishly.

"I don't."

"Montgomery, friend, if you spent less time with Bonnie and Clyde and more with the greats . . ."

"At Ole Miss, I preferred political science studies to English."

"Would you believe that my professor in Shakespeare would actually cry when he read from the plays?"

Both men sat contemplating the idea of a teacher weeping over lines in a book. The last time Montgomery had cried was at his wife's funeral, not because of the minister's words, but in spite of them. He blamed the cold and austere ceremony on the new minister, who had hardly known Miss Ellen and spoke more of the life to come than of Ellen. Montgomery had never forgiven himself for not writing the service, as Emory Waters had done for Miss Julie, whom the judge celebrated in a eulogy that merged into autobiography.

"What do you want me to tell Vincent?"

"The same thing I plan to tell Samuel. There's a lot of things in Hungamon just under the surface that you don't want to see dug up."

"And if that dolt refuses to go along?"

"His wife loves pretty things. She'll keep Vincent in line. Samuel's a different matter."

Montgomery pondered what the judge could possibly say to Samuel to keep him quiet, and then surmised that the judge had something on Samuel. Emory seemed to have something on everyone in Hungamon, including Montgomery. To take the measure of the judge's importance, one need only look at his den walls. A framed photograph of Emory and Richard Nixon hung next to one of Emory and Ronald Reagan. In fact, pictures covered the walls with Emory and every Louisiana senator and congressman of the last thirty years. The old-boy network that Emory had created stretched from New Orleans to DC and back.

Rachel could hardly speak. In the grip of heaving sobs, she forced herself to say, "He had . . . a child . . . with a black woman."

"Who?"

"My daddy."

"How do you know?"

"Trust me, I know."

"Boy or girl?"

"Does it . . . matter?"

Adam held her close and waited until her hyperventilation subsided. He took his fine linen handkerchief from his jacket pocket and gently dabbed her tears and dripping nose. She smiled at him appreciatively, and, at his insistence, kept the handkerchief to wipe her wetted face.

"Do you know where the child is?"

"No."

"He or she would probably be around our age."

"If the person is even alive."

"Do you think your mother knew?"

"I don't know."

Taking her hand, he asked, "How did you find out?"

Rachel then revealed that she had been reading her father's private papers, being passed to her by Mr. Gruning. "I suspected he screened all the papers before showing them to me. When I asked, he admitted it."

Adam, thinking ahead, added, "And the papers he had kept from you bear on—"

"Lynching and miscegenation."

Adam softly pleaded, "Forget that last word, Rachel. Mr. Gruning told you that your father had a—"

"Bastard child."

"My dear, they say prejudices die slowly. You embody that truism."

"I can't help it. It's my upbringing. Besides, he's my father. Believe it or not, I would feel less hurt if you had a child with a black woman. You see, he and I are of one blood. You and I come from . . . different genes."

She studied his face hoping he'd understand, but she could see that he didn't. "What if you learned that your daddy had . . ."

"Had what? A black child? I don't think I'd care, but I gather you would." He shook his head and tightened his lips, affecting a look of despair. "Race, the skeleton in every Southerner's closet. I bet that if you and all your friends had a genetic test, you'd discover somewhere in your background black blood. The slaveholders had no reluctance to sleep with black women."

Rachel had run out of tears, which gave way to grievance. "I thought you'd sympathize. You can just drive us home, and spare me your lectures on race."

"That's your subject, not mine."

They drove in silence, until Adam turned off the main street through Mandeville onto Highway 21. As they passed the handsome homes set back in the trees, he asked, "Does your father explicitly say that he had a child with a black woman?"

A sullen Rachel mumbled, "No."

"Well, then, what's the fuss?"

"Mr. Gruning said that Daddy's feud with Mr. Dozier began over some missing letters about lynching and miscegenation."

"You haven't even seen the letters, but you're convinced that your daddy . . ."

Rachel gripped her hands tightly and lowered her head. "I shouldn't tell you this, but I've heard more than once that as a young man my daddy liked . . . women of another color."

Adam, trying to take the fire out of Rachel's anger, said, "Maybe Mr. Dozier's the culprit and not your father."

"I'm not a fool, Adam. I know what the man meant."

"You intend, then, to study the letters yourself."

"Just as soon as I can."

In an attempt to turn the discussion to his trip, he remarked, "The archivist thinks he may be able to tell me something about my own parents. He is going to mail Larry certain documents. I can't wait."

But Rachel had not yet recovered from her outburst. In fact her anger had turned from thoughts of bloodlines to worries about discovery. What if her friends, at church and the club, learned that she had a black relative?

Shortly after Pastor Matthew Williams returned, his secretary called Libby Larkin. They spoke in his study, a small but comfortable room attached to the church and furnished sparsely with a desk, couch, and a few chairs. On the wall behind the desk hung a framed and signed photograph of Martin Luther King Jr. The one luxury the pastor allowed himself, a Bose speaker and a CD player, he used to play operas and, in particular, the Baroque masters. At the moment of their meeting, Mozart's *Marriage of Figaro*, which had been playing in the background, arrived at Susanna's aria, *Dove Sono*. The pastor put a finger to his lips. They sat and listened.

*Where are the beautiful moments*
*Of sweetness and pleasure?*
*Where have the promises gone*
*That come from those lying lips?*

"Now," said the pastor, without turning off the music, "tell me what brings you here in such a state of upset?"

"You can tell?"

"It's my profession."

"I need to tell someone about a youthful romance."

"Yours?"

She nodded.

"There was a child."

"You know?" asked Libby.

"You are not the first."

"He came from an old family. They had money and deep roots in this community."

"A white man."

"Yes."

As the aria continued, they listened.

*Why, if all is changed for me*
*Into tears and pain,*
*Has the memory of that goodness*
*Not vanished from my breast?*

"Does the child know?"

"I've been afraid to tell her, but I have the worry she could shortly find out."

"And if she does?"

"She'd hate me for not telling her."

"Then maybe you ought to speak up."

Libby hung her head in dismay.

"And the father: still living?"

"Very much so."

"Have you broached the subject with him?"

"He won't hear of it. You see, he married a proper lady, but she couldn't have children. After he left for his honeymoon, I discovered my condition. So I wrote him, and he told me to come to him. He and his new wife would claim the baby as theirs—if the baby's skin color allowed." She laughed sardonically. "It earned me a trip to Paris."

"You're light skinned."

"The baby also, so they kept her. A real beauty."

After the birth, Libby had gone away for a year, but when she returned, her lover wanted to continue seeing her, and she, him. Even though now married, he would spend afternoons with her. His wife either didn't know or, as a well-mannered Southern lady, pretended not to. Moreover, she happily occupied herself with the baby. But not in good health, she asked Libby to help. Libby agreed. Nothing had been said at the time, and nothing since. The wife died, and Libby, without moving into the house and leaving her own, virtually became the girl's mother. Did she still love the father of her child? Yes. And still saw him?

"I've been weighed down for years with this secret, but I fear it will shortly come out."

"The 'other' mother, you said, never disclosed it, and you, of course, could never forget; and your 'gentleman,' if I may call him that, never told his daughter."

"Precisely."

"What makes you think your secret's no longer safe?"

"Years ago, my man let slip the truth to a friend. Then the two men had a falling out. I believe it concerned the sale of letters that mentioned some lynchings. When my man advised the letters be burned, the other refused. That's when miscegenation came into it. The former friend said he would tell the world about my man and me."

Pastor Williams positioned his hands in a prayerful attitude, resting his chin on his fingertips. "People don't normally go to such extremes unless they feel threatened."

Libby nodded in agreement.

The pastor stared out the window. "And the other man . . . where is he now?"

"Dead."

A surprised Pastor Williams swiveled like a weather vane. His eyes, no longer focused outside, studied Libby's face. With genuine concern, he said, "Killed?" She nodded her head yes. "I suppose, then, I know the man. David Dozier."

"Right."

The pastor puffed up his cheeks and slowly exhaled. He transited from anxiety to calm thoughtfulness. "As far as I know, the investigation is over. The case closed. So why say anything? Let sleeping dogs lie."

"Agreed. But I still don't have a solution for my problem."

"To tell her?"

"Yes. I gather she's been talking to the local librarian. Apparently she's trying to unearth something in the past. If that something exposes her roots, she'll hate me for never having told her."

"Or for telling her."

---

In no uncertain terms, Rachel informed Mr. Gruning that she wanted to see the original papers, and not selected photocopies. He suggested they meet early: at six Monday morning. As she drove up to the white bungalow, Mr. Gruning sat in his car waiting for her. He unlocked the door to the musty room and went directly to the files.

Rachel saw enough to convince her that she and her father needed to talk, and that she wanted to pursue her original desire to find out about the man who painted her grandfather. She hastily made some notes on a small pad, and put paper clips on the letters that she wanted Mr. Gruning to photocopy. One box, with green accordion folders, she hadn't even touched, but she planned in short order to start reading through that cache, especially since the box came with a red string indicating highly confidential.

That afternoon, Mr. French announced to Mr. Gruning that he wanted to move all but his Bonnie and Clyde collections to his house for safekeeping. He had cause to worry. Mrs. Ellsworth, that very morning, had inadvertently mentioned Rachel's visit to the old library. Mr. French had thought that he alone had been given permission to access the files in the building. In light of his upcoming talk with Vincent Dozier, he had two good reasons for keeping all his papers on lynching and segregation under lock and key. One could never be sure what Rachel might conclude and what Vincent, a loose cannon, might have in mind. If he knew about the collection in the bungalow, he could be dangerous.

Montgomery loaded his car with the boxes of papers and moved them to his house. On hearing what her father had done, Rachel resigned herself to defeat. Without the papers, how could she confront him or prove anything? But she did have her small pad with its notes. And she had the distinct feeling that when Samuel Hildreth first saw her grandfather's portrait, he knew more than he said and intended to discover more than he knew. Before talking to her daddy, she would stop at the *Daily News* and then speak to Samuel.

Although Adam's return had thrown her life into confusion, with unpacking and washing and cooking and hearing his account of Budapest, she took the first opportunity to drive to Samuel's rented trailer.

Proper Southern ladies did not call, unchaperoned, on black men at night. But she saw a light and threw caution overboard. Checking her skirt and her blouse, neither too tight, she secured the top button of her waist-length tweed jacket, and knocked on the door. She could hear footsteps. Samuel's face materialized in a small window at the top of the door. A slide bolt sounded. The door opened outward, forcing her to step back. Samuel stared down at her, making her feel like a child.

They sat at the small table that served him as a desk and dinette. She admired his potted orange tree, and detected the stale odor of beer. That very afternoon, Vincent Dozier had been tinning Samuel's ear with theories to explain the murder of his father. The beer bottles stood in a corner, which Rachel spotted at once. Samuel followed her eyes and remarked: "I rarely drink. A friend of mine does." Rachel looked at him skeptically. "If you'd like a lemonade, I can pour you a glass."

"No thanks."

A few seconds later, Samuel moved the beer bottles outside. "Like I said, I don't drink. If I knew you'd be calling, I'd have cleaned up the place some."

"Please, not on my account. I'm intruding, for which I apologize. But I think you may have some information I want . . . or have an interest in some of the same things I want."

Samuel pulled down all the shades in the trailer. "And what would that be?"

"A few weeks ago, I learned at the *Daily News* that you had recently asked to see some of the same newspapers I requested."

"What in particular are you lookin' for?"

"The name of the painter who drew my grandfather."

"Godwin Rush."

"The same Godwin Rush—"

Before she could finish her sentence, Samuel brutally did. "The one strung up and fed to the crocs? The same. They also killed Mary Judd, for taking a picture."

"I had been led to believe that Godwin worked for the Federal Arts Project and then moved north."

"The first is true, the second ain't."

"Why—"

Again he interrupted. "Good question."

"How did you get involved?"

"Jury duty. Same as your Adam. Manny Crenshaw, the boy found guilty of killing Mr. David Dozier—and who killed himself."

"Of course I know the case. It's cost my husband endless hours of regret."

"Well, whatever he's sufferin' ain't nothin' to what I've been through."

"I simply can't understand what took place on that jury."

Samuel's laugh sounded as rough as a crosscut saw. "Ask your husband. He knows."

Rachel found Samuel's response ominous. He seemed to suggest that Adam behaved badly.

"I thought the boy innocent from the start," said Samuel.

The many ideas that flooded Rachel's head left her dizzy. "I think I will have a lemonade." As she sat drinking from a plastic cup, she said, "Forgive my ignorance, but what does Manny Crenshaw have to do with Godwin Rush?"

Samuel clasped his hands and stared at them silently. Rachel felt as if hours passed before he spoke.

"I'm not sure I should be talkin' to you. It ain't safe."

"I'll pay."

Samuel furiously scratched his graying, wiry hair. "How come, white folks always think money can buy what they want? My mama used to say, 'Some things we don't impart, like the secrets of the heart.' Tell you what: You agree to help me get justice for Manny Crenshaw, and I'll tell you all I know about the terrible and twisted story—for free. A deal?"

She extended her hand across the table.

He then disclosed everything he had learned: in the newspaper archives, in conversations with Jeremiah Lincoln and Vincent Dozier, and, most important of all, in the letters that Lidia had found in Mr. Dozier's house. But he did omit telling her why he voted as he did in the Crenshaw case, his participation in the drug trade, and Mr. Dozier's role in Louisiana narcotics.

Over drinks in a small restaurant in Varnado, just outside of Hungamon, Montgomery French plied Vincent Dozier with plenty of liquor before he got to the point. Like Samuel Hildreth, Montgomery had concluded that Vincent must have read the letters briefly in his possession.

Slapping the table with glee, Vincent said, "Darned if Rhoda didn't guess right." He glanced around at the other diners, now eyeing him, drawn to his inebriated outburst. "What a dump," he mumbled. "Oilcloth on the tables, plastic tiles on the floor, seedy wallpaper. We should've gone to New Orleans."

"You said something about your wife . . ."

"Yeah, she guessed you wanted to talk about those old letters, and she told me not to say a word unless the price made it worth my while."

"I already paid you for the letters."

"Then what's there to talk about?"

"The content."

"Such as?"

"Lynchings."

Vincent asked for another bourbon, Jack Daniels on the rocks. His hands shook. "Your daddy and my granddaddy, you mean."

"Then you read the letters."

"I may be slow, but I'm not, as you think, incorrigibly stupid."

Montgomery nodded, but not to acknowledge, as Vincent thought, Vincent's mental capacities. "Same as you, I like big words. *Incorrigible.* Comes from the Latin, also Old French and Middle English. You'll never guess who told me that. A pretty brown lady. She characterized me as incorrigibly addicted to pretty women."

As Vincent pondered that observation, Montgomery added, "For your family's sake and my own, I think it best that we forget about the letters. We just act as if they never existed. No one will ever be the wiser. Agreed?"

"How much?"

"I wish you hadn't said that. I really do. Because it suggests to me that you don't give a damn about your family roots and your granddaddy's reputation. In my book, that's a cardinal sin."

A raucous display of laughter erupted from Vincent's shaking body. "Montgomery, you old scoundrel, you of all people—"

Montgomery leaned across the table and whispered, "Not so loud, man. Others are watching you."

Vincent breathed his alcoholic breath into Montgomery's face. "Everyone knows you like black meat and drumming your stick into that handsome Miss—"

"No names," hissed Montgomery, "unless you want a bullet also."

By the time they had finished dinner and reached Hungamon, Vincent had agreed that a family's standing mattered more than money. Besides, Vincent confessed, his pappy had told him whom to approach if he ever needed money.

A few days later, a janitor found Vincent's body in the parking lot of his workplace. According to his employer, he had stayed late to check some receipts and had agreed to lock up afterward. The police report said that he had been shot as he approached his car. One bullet had entered his right temple, and he had died immediately. Most surprising of all: According to the crime lab in New Orleans, the bullet that killed Vincent had come from the same gun that killed his father.

Judge Emory Waters and Samuel Hildreth met at the east end of City Hall in a room that during heavy rains attracted rat snakes, which slithered under the door. The judge believed, like many white people, that reptiles unduly scared blacks. Among the regular churchgoers of Hungamon, a Christian source for this belief could be found in Scripture. On this drizzly day only one rat snake thought to interrupt the colloquy between Samuel and the judge, but the former immediately forced it to retreat by efficiently applying the heel of his boot.

"I thought this place safer than mine," said the judge. "Miss Samantha has been staying close to the house lately."

"Lotta water passed under the dam since we last spoke real serious like."

"If the Crenshaw boy had received the death penalty, I suppose we wouldn't be sitting here."

"We had a choice, and you told me which way to go."

The judge ran his teeth over his upper lip. His stained dentals exhibited the effects of a lifetime of smoking cigars and other inhalants. Samuel avoided his gaze. Emory had mixed feelings about Samuel: pity and anger. He thought Samuel looked thin and alone. To repay the judge for his having gone easy on him several years before, Samuel had sworn to vote against the majority, which the judge knew would want to recommend capital punishment. In light of the vilification subsequently visited upon Samuel, the judge now wished he had advised the district attorney and jury to consider only one charge, manslaughter. He paused and looked out the window. Overcast and dreary. In the distance the Spanish moss hung like funereal crepe. "I understand that you and Vincent Dozier, poor fellow, have become chummy."

Well aware that the most informed man in Hungamon, Judge Waters, faced him, Samuel made no attempt to hide his congress with

Vincent. "We agreed to look into some lynchings back in the thirties, which involved Vincent's granddad and someone else from here."

"Montgomery Xavier French, you mean."

"Yes."

"Save your time. The law exonerated both men."

"Some letters suggest otherwise."

"I know all about them."

"They imply—"

The judge cut him off. "All circumstantial."

"I think both Doziers got killed 'cause of those letters."

The judge narrowed his eyes and said curtly, "In which case, Manny Crenshaw is probably innocent. Isn't that the conclusion you want me to draw?"

"At first I thought it happened 'cause of drugs. Now I'm not so sure."

Judge Waters pulled his chair so close to Samuel's that their knees touched.

"You want some advice from an old friend? Let the Crenshaw case go. Take the bit out of your mouth. I can assure you that neither drugs nor letters caused the Dozier deaths. Trust me."

"If what you say is true—"

"Of course it's true," the judge thundered.

Samuel ruminated for several seconds. "Then why am I here?"

The judge placed a hand on Samuel's shoulder. "Having done a few favors for you in the past, I want you to do one for me. Forget this whole business. You're barking up the wrong tree. Moreover, I don't want to see you get shot. Poor Vincent."

# A Home Away from Home

Even before Zoe approached the Shaws about housing Wayne and Lidia, she had begun to carpool with Adam each morning. Although she normally started work at Moss Hospital earlier than his usual arrival time, nine o'clock, Adam, still inspirited by Zoe, announced that in the interests of economy, he would leave earlier. Zoe had told Adam of her decision to house Ori and the child's parents. Today, as they approached the causeway, only the hardiest birds hovered over the lobster traps and the lines trolling for Spanish mackerel. The weather had turned unseasonably cold, driving the avian fishers back to their nests. Zoe took the dearth of birds as the occasion for introducing the subject of Wayne and Lidia.

"Since I'm taking the Panamanians in, I'll need a nest for my two kids. The house is too small for us all. I spoke to Miss Libby, but she doesn't have the room either."

Adam did not take the bait. "Perhaps it's time to look for a larger house."

"That or find a family willing to look after them."

She let the silence soak in before she continued. "You like Wayne, and he adores you. And Lidia's just as sweet as maple syrup."

From Adam's unresponsiveness, Zoe inferred that he understood her request, and interpreted his wordlessness as a no. Then he seemed to open the door a crack. "What you're doing for Ori and her family deserves my support. Maybe I can find a family for Wayne and Lidia to board with."

"Room and board," she corrected, annoyed that he seemed unable to swallow the hook.

"You may have those Naso Indians on your hands for years."

If Adam intended this observation as a way of saying that he or anyone else would find it disruptive to have children underfoot for a long time, he of all people would know. He had been adopted and then removed to a foster home. Zoe wondered whether his own experience prevented him from volunteering or whether he hadn't yet realized that she had the Shaws in mind. She said nothing further until that evening, when they drove back to Hungamon in a light rain. He stopped the wipers and idled the motor, usually the moment Adam took to say something personal and supportive, like "You're doing a great job," or "You're the best nurse I ever hired." Before he could speak, Zoe said, as if the idea had come to her only suddenly, "Why don't you and Miss Rachel take the children?"

Adam looked like a man who suddenly realizes that the shot he heard has struck him. He slumped forward and turned off the motor. Staring straight ahead through the rain-spattered glass, he said, "I see." But Zoe wondered if he did. "Rachel and I might be able to help from time to time or for a short period, but—"

A man convinced against his will, thought Zoe, is of the same opinion still. Rather than force the request, she suggested a trial period. If the kids behaved—and she or Libby would make sure they did—the Shaws might like having them on the premises. They would certainly liven up the place. "What if they come to you for just a week? Then if you don't want to continue, we'll make some other arrangement." She silently completed her thought: *But if you do want to continue, everyone will come out ahead.*

His reply left Zoe parsing his words not just for the moment, but for nearly a week.

"If I convince Rachel and we do this for you, what will you do for me?"

The next day Samuel took Wayne and Lidia to dinner at a small restaurant. The children wanted to share an idea. "From what you say about that painting hiding a story under its paint," said Wayne, "we think you ought to peel it off and take a peek."

Samuel's sardonic laughter, learned in war, provided a defense against unpleasantness. But the more he thought about the idea, the more he thought it had merit. "Now just for the sake of chewin' things over, how would you go about stealin' that paintin' or gettin' someone to do what you've just suggested?"

"Easy," said Lidia. "You and Miss Rachel is thick as molasses. Why not ask her?!"

Enjoying steak sandwiches and cranberry juice, the three of them kicked the idea around for a while, until he thought, *Why not*? Now that he and Rachel had shook hands and agreed to cooperate, he could fairly argue that his request covered the territory they both wished to explore.

Wayne excused himself to use the restroom.

Samuel asked Lidia, "How do you like Mr. Lumpkin and your tutoring?"

"All right."

"Just all right? I'm paying. I want you to learn something."

Lidia's mind traveled to her lessons. "Did you know that George Washington could've been president his whole life but said that he was no king? So he quit. And did you know slavery would probably have died out 'cause of the hardness of cotton picking and plucking, and that slave owners started losing money? The invention of the cotton gin made slavery profitable. In a way, then, you can blame Eli Whitney for the Civil War."

A confused Samuel scratched his head. "Is that what Mr. Lumpkin taught you?"

"Yeah, and some other things, too."

After Samuel took Lidia home, he stopped to talk to Zoe. Did she think Mr. Lumpkin a good teacher?

"With music or otherwise?"

"Otherwise."

"Well, that depends. All in all, I'd say it's what you'd expect in Louisiana."

Samuel wrote out a check for Lidia's next month's tutoring, returned to his trailer, and called Rachel. Adam answered, a circumstance that always flustered Samuel. One of these days, he thought, Mr. Shaw is gonna ask me why a black man is callin' his wife. But Adam merely said that his wife had gone off to her bridge club, and that he would have her return Samuel's call. How late could she call? "Hardly matters," he said. Shortly before eleven, Rachel buzzed him. When Samuel broached the subject of whether her father's painting had something underneath, she agreed to help him find out. She then used an unfamiliar word, *pentimento*, which she explained.

"Yeah, that's it. Maybe what we got here is some pentimento. But how do we get the painting to x-ray it?"

"Let me think."

"Call anytime."

"Even in the middle of the night?"

"I don't sleep very good. The war, you know. Bad dreams. So I'm often up . . . just thinkin' and rememberin', which the doctors say is the worst thing to do. But at least I'm not a druggie."

That same night, Rachel restlessly tossed herself into wakefulness. She had been dreaming about the car accident that killed her mother and injured her. All her senses had been engaged, from the splintered glass to the skid and the crash, from the burst gasoline line to the fire. She had been thrown from the car, but her mother, pinned by the crushed door, had burned inside. Rachel had seen the firemen remove the charred body, which bore no resemblance to anyone Rachel knew. In her dream her mother emerged from the backseat after the rescue squad had extricated the stranger from behind the wheel. Then she awoke, strangely finding herself sitting up in bed with her arms extended, as if expecting someone to enter them and embrace her.

She slipped into her wooly robe and fleece-lined slippers, went downstairs, heated some milk, and telephoned Samuel. The clock read 3:23 a.m.

He answered immediately, suggesting that Samuel, too, had yet to fall asleep. She told him she had the perfect excuse.

"What's that?"

"The painting needs cleaning and evaluating—by an expert."

"Who's the expert?"

"Leave that to me."

Samuel paced his trailer, thinking. By morning he had decided that his first stop that day would be the library, to learn as much as he could about art restoration. He knew virtually nothing, but he did know that if the painting had to leave the state, he would accompany it, and that when they stood at the expert's shoulder, he would know what to ask.

Once Adam decided to approach his wife about the possibility of housing Wayne and Lidia, he had to figure out the best time, the right occasion, and the ideal setting to introduce the subject. He chose to take Rachel to New Orleans for a splendid dinner at 209 Bourbon Street, Galatoire's, the famous restaurant built in 1905 that specialized in French creole cuisine. As they opened the front door, with its distinctive single letter, G, Adam gave the young woman at the reservation desk his name. He and Rachel had dressed in their finest evening clothes, befitting the stature of a restaurant that did not admit men without jackets and ties. They sat, as requested, at a quiet table. The wallpaper, Rachel noted, had begun to age, much like an old painting. The pattern of fleurs-de-lis, which ran from the ceiling to waist height, terminated at a long strip of molding that begged for a new coat of paint. The tables, covered with white linen, and the waiters in white, balancing plates on their arms, led Rachel to observe that Paris restaurants must be much in this mode, and how lucky of Libby to have visited the City of Lights. She requested a glass of white wine, and Adam a Tanqueray on the rocks. Both ordered the "Trout Maugarote."

"I can't understand," said Rachel, "why Libby never told us that she had visited Paris. If I had been there, all my friends would have known."

"Perhaps she had a bad time."

"Paris? Impossible, at least from what I hear."

"Would you like to go?"

"I'm packed and ready."

"Then do me a favor. Let Wayne and Lidia stay with us for a month or two."

Rachel, who had just sipped her wine, spluttered and sprayed her Pessac-Léognan across the table. "Are you mad? Absolutely not!"

As if explaining to a child, Adam slowly and sensitively described the situation in which Zoe found herself. Having offered to help others, she needed help. Could the Shaws lend a hand? In return, Adam offered Rachel a trip to Paris. He felt that she would readily accept. But to his surprise and chagrin she refused. Well, then, she could just forget Paris.

"We'd be the laughingstock of Hungamon. What in the world has got into you, Adam?"

"Not even for a trip to Paris?"

"Not even for the Hope Diamond."

He sipped his gin and said simply, "I've given some thought to your request that I write a check for the community center you want to build."

"I see, a bribe."

The Rachel he sat facing confused him. Although willing to dive into a lake to save a drowning black man, she had no desire to house one. And although willing to fight to see Manny buried in the Hungamon Cemetery, she had no wish to house two black children. "I won't mention it again," said Adam, seething with an anger that seemed incommensurate with its source.

They ate their dinner in silence and returned to Hungamon, neither digesting what the other had said.

Samantha Larkin had long known and worried about Emory Waters's cocaine addiction, which had begun shortly after Miss Julie died and an ex-con introduced him to the drug. A petty crook, Jackie Pyle, had come before the judge for a parole violation. In his chambers the judge, as per his custom, asked the young man about the reasons for the crime.

"I couldn't stand feeling down all the time," said the ex-con, "so I took to snorting Aunt Nora."

"You'll have to translate."

"Lady Snow. The Big C. Cocaine."

"Did it help?"

"Did it ever! It gave me a high and the feeling of being on top of the world. I no longer felt low—until it wore off. Then I needed another blow." The judge looked at Jackie sympathetically, and Jackie noticed. "To tell ya the truth, judge, you seem sorta in the dumps yourself."

Emory softly said that someone close to him had recently died.

"For some people it's addictive; for some it ain't. Try a snort."

Before Jackie Pyle left Emory's chambers, the ex-con had earned a second chance in return for supplying the judge with a small dose of Snow White. Emory justified his trying the drug on two accounts. First, antidepressants hadn't helped him, and perhaps a small dose of cocaine would; and second, Dr. Sigmund Freud had used cocaine. The first time Emory tried it, with Jackie's assistance, he felt euphoric. His demons disappeared, his sense of control grew, his vitality improved, and his capacity for work increased. He had always been loquacious, but now he perceived himself as eloquent and courageous—courageous enough, in fact, to invite Samantha Larkin and her daughter to move in with him. Unfortunately the effect of the drug faded, at which time he needed another snort. Result? He became addicted and required a regular supply. For more than a year, Jackie Pyle served him well, until arrested in Baton Rouge for dealing to students. A crime that serious meant Emory could do nothing to get Jackie off, though he did prevail upon the sentencing judge not to give Jackie life. The sentence: twenty years, with the possibility of parole after ten.

From the beginning of their cohabitation, Samantha had said nothing and kept Libby ignorant of the judge's drug habit. To protect her, she sent Libby to boarding school. With her away, the judge felt free in his own house to mitigate the sad memories that still periodically brought on a sullen depression. At least that's what he told himself. But since the imprisonment and death of Manny Crenshaw, the cocaine-distribution system in Hungamon had been haphazard at best. Now the unthinkable had happened. He had nearly exhausted his cocaine supply and needed to restock it. With Manny gone, the judge required a new courier, one who had ready access to the drug. Samantha immediately came to mind, the only person he could absolutely trust. As she rested on an ottoman next to his chair, he gently stroked her hand.

"My 'medicine' is running low and I suspect that Mr. Samuel Hildreth might be able to help. If not, maybe he can suggest someone."

"I wouldn't have the slightest idea what to say."

"Of course you can't come right out and ask him. But you could say something like, 'Among Manny's friends is there an Angie?' Sounds goofy to me."

"He'll understand. Angie, on the street, means cocaine."

Without knowing that Samuel had been Manny's source for the drug, Samantha approached "Mr. Hildreth." The moment she made her request, she confirmed, to Samuel's satisfaction, the judge had been buying from Manny.

"I'll take care of the matter," said Samuel.

He called LeShaun Jackson, a scrofulous young black man in his early twenties whom Samuel had originally recruited to service Slidell and points south. He told LeShaun to cut his dreadlocks and apply to Samantha Larkin for a job as a gardener. She would then tell him when to come and where in the woods behind the house to stash the stuff. He would follow the same routine that Manny had followed.

Less than a month after the Budapest trip, Larry Weiss received a parcel marked "Special Delivery." The return address bore the name Bela Baranyi, Budapest. He had enclosed photocopies of birth certificates, arrest warrants, deportation orders, adoption papers, and exit visas. Buried in the words of those gray, formal documents lay a vibrant family, one that Larry wished Adam had known. He took the parcel to the university, made copies for himself, translated all the documents, and posted the contents to Adam. He knew that he would soon receive a telephone call from Louisiana.

The package rested on the inlaid antique table in the Shaws' entry hall. Adam, exhausted from a day at the hospital, initially gave it only a cursory glance. Rachel's mail, no doubt, he thought. But seeing Larry's return address, he gathered it up, as if cradling a child, and retreated to the den, where he carefully peeled back the wrapping. At first stunned, he then cried. Rachel had heard him enter the house and thought it strange he'd failed to greet her. She found him teary eyed, bent over sheets of paper that he gingerly fingered with the same care as if they had been the Dead Sea Scrolls.

"My parents," he said mechanically, unable to deny the authenticated report, "were József and Abagail Rashi. My grandfather had been a prominent art dealer, Mordekhai Rashi. He and my grandmother, Sára, died at Auschwitz."

By this time, Rachel had seated herself beside him, with her arm resting consolingly around his shoulder. Before Adam could remove his handkerchief, she eased it out of his back pocket and dabbed his face.

"Tell me," she said, and embraced him all the tighter.

"They died in early 1945. If only they could have held out until the Russians liberated the camp a few months later. Mordekhai and Sára . . . observant Jews."

Adam could feel an involuntary shiver run through Rachel's body, but she said nothing. "Their son, József, married Abagail Baum. Look," he pointed to the papers. "Larry has translated everything. You can read if for yourself."

Rachel gently lifted the papers and rested them on her lap. She too regarded them as a kind of holy writ. The sacred silence between them lasted for several minutes, until Rachel softly read:

"Report of the Hungarian Border Patrol, August 1954. A couple identified as József and Abagail Rashi apprehended trying to cross into Austria. The man, a lawyer, sent to a prison factory, and the woman, pregnant, to a nursery."

She read from another report, "Annual Proceedings: Collective Farm SP4, 1955." On the second page, Larry had put an asterisk next to the following, which Rachel read.

> *Felons József and Abagail Rashi and their infant son . . . resettled in July. The parents immediately incurred resentment for declaring their wish to worship as Jews. Their farm work is poor and they have frequently been reprimanded. Their laxity led to their losing their infant, given up for adoption to Berta and Fulop Vadas, recommended to the government by Vilmos Kovács, their former employer. Mr. Kovács has arranged for the transport of the child and the adoptive parents to Budapest.*

Another document that Larry had starred came from the Immigration and Visa Office:

*Exit permits for the United States granted to Berta and Fulop Vadas and adopted son, Adam. Family sponsored by Vilmos Kovács, former Budapest gallery owner and former employer, who is paying for their transportation. Valuable possessions: cash (the equivalent of $5,000); a gold wedding band; a small diamond; a painting, donated by Mr. Kovács, deemed the work of an amateur and therefore allowed to leave the country.*

Another page included a brief description of Mr. Kovács.

*A patriot. Fought in the underground. Part owner with M. Rashi of an art gallery, now a youth center. Owned a large house in Buda, now apartments for workers. Previously employed the Vadas couple, Berta as a cook and Fulop as a groundskeeper. The couple have a brother in America. Recommendation: the family be granted an exit visa.*

Without speaking, Adam and Rachel had similar thoughts, which they shared later. At the time of Mordekhai and Sára Rashi's arrest and deportation by the Germans, Vilmos Kovács had hidden their son and his wife. Later, with well-placed bribes, he had arranged for the release of József and Abagail from their penal camp. He had, as the documents made clear, arranged for Adam's adoption and the emigration to America. The painting, which Vilmos had almost certainly taken from the gallery before either the Germans or the communists could requisition it, constituted the Rashi patrimony. There could be no question: Vilmos Kovács deserved to earn the honorific title "Righteous Gentile."

The last thing Rachel said that night before Adam turned off the light and gently made love to her gave him slight consolation:

"Do you suppose your parents might still be living?"

Again, since Manny's death, Adam could not reach a climax.

---

With Zoe at a teachers' meeting with Wayne, Samuel and Lidia ate dinner together in the trailer. They talked about their search of David Dozier's house and the discovery of the letters. She urged Samuel to search the house one more time.

"Maybe we missed something."

"I don't think so. Besides, it's too risky."

They had been playing poker, and she kept winning. Lidia shuffled the cards. "You never know when an ace might turn up."

Samuel raised a window shade and thought: *Tonight, almost moonless, would be a good time.*

"Let's go," said Samuel, throwing down the cards he'd been dealt.

"Bad hand, huh?"

"Lidia, you oughta be workin' in Vegas, the way you shuffle and cut those cards. I'd swear you're palmin' a few."

"Just a trick I learned in Mexico."

They parked two blocks from David Dozier's house and put on gloves. The fading yellow tape, warning off trespassers, fluttered in the breeze. Samuel hoisted Lidia onto the low-hanging roof. She scampered to the top and, as before, swung down from the eve and opened the window with a push of her foot. Once inside, they crept to the second floor, which on their first break-in, they had treated cursorily. The beds stood made and the pillows fluffed. Nothing under the beds. The clothes closets yielded nothing, not as much as a stray penny, even though they went through all the pockets of every suit and jacket. The same proved true of the shirts that they carefully removed and refolded from the dresser. In the bathroom, towels hung neatly from racks and toothbrushes and toothpaste rested comfortably in a glass.

A well-stocked supply cabinet beneath the sink held toilet paper, soap, and toothpaste. Lidia peeked over Samuel's shoulder.

"Hey, grab one of those tubes for me. Zoe's running low."

"You're a born thief."

"Why waste things? You Americans . . . a person could live easily off the stuff you throw away. Behind every hotel in Mexico, the kids rake through the trash and find enough to keep their families alive."

"Not all the toothpaste tubes have the same brand name. Which kind do you want?" Samuel asked.

"You decide."

He counted five, which he thought an unduly large number. As he reached for one, he tipped over another that felt light as air. He then balanced each in his hands. Two of the five weighed virtually nothing. Opening one of them, he smelled. "Jesus!" he exclaimed. "Cocaine."

"Grab it!" hissed Lidia, spraying him with saliva.

"All of 'em?"

"You bet."

Samuel knew enough runners to easily distribute the drug, but if found with this much cocaine in his possession, he'd get life in prison. He had always made it a point to use a middleman for distribution, and to keep his own house and car and person clean. He ran enough risks just bringing the stuff in from Mexico. Caught red-handed in the United States owing to carelessness . . . not a chance. He stuffed the tubes inside his shirt and crept down the stairs to the den, while Lidia continued to search the upstairs rooms and the attic, reached by pulling a rope that lowered a folding staircase that led to a finished room under the roof.

An entire wall of the den held videos. The movies ranged from silent to epic, from mysteries to pornography. Mr. Dozier had alphabetized his collection by title. Under the Ws, Samuel saw a space. He went to the player, pressed the ON switch, and hit the eject button.

A drawer opened, and a video slid out. Samuel read the title: *Witness for the Prosecution*.

After a thorough search of the downstairs, Samuel pocketed the video, softly called for Lidia, who had found nothing suspicious, and took one last look around. They exited the rear door and hiked through the woods until they reached the connecting road that led them back to the car.

Once in the trailer, Samuel took a large knife, removed some sod from the weedy garden out back, and buried the tubes, which he had wrapped in a plastic bag. Lidia watched from the trailer, as he restored the sod.

The Panamanian family had already moved into Zoe's house when Libby summoned enough courage to have a talk with Rachel. Her fear that any day now, Rachel would unearth a compromising letter or document had become obsessive. They sat in the sunroom and watched a slanting rain ripple the lake in a vertical pattern. Rachel had made coffee, and Libby had brought homemade peach cobbler. China and silver rested on the table. Rachel had a feel for social events, even when they comprised only two people. She had learned tea manners at her private school in Virginia and how to get someone to pass an item she desired. Never, for example, would she ask for the jam. Rather, she would say, "Are you finished with the jam, Libby?" And Libby would know to say, assuming she had finished with it, "Let me pass it to you." The school transmitted the code from one generation to the next.

Libby took the cake knife and cut into the cobbler, putting a piece on each of their plates. She smiled at Rachel. "We have to talk, honey, talk like never before."

When Libby's eyes began to tear, Rachel knew that this talk would hurt, that it would amount to a kind of moral surgery. But she thought that Libby would be disclosing some secret about Adam and Zoe, given that sex between her and Adam had become infrequent. She could almost feel betrayal in the pit of her stomach.

"It's about Adam, right?"

"No, honey, you."

"Me! I'm just an old-fashioned housewife. No lovers. No drinking problem. No skeletons in the closet."

Libby breathed deeply. "I'm the skeleton in the closet."

Rachel stared, uncomprehending. Then a thought dawned on her. "Libby, I've known forever that you and my daddy . . ." Proper ladies didn't have to finish such sentences.

"It goes back, honey, even further than you imagine."

The rain had increased. On the roof it sounded a constant beat, like a snare drum.

"Perhaps I'm all wet," said Rachel, "but aren't we talking about the same thing? Once Mommy died, you and Daddy . . . Isn't that it? Or am I missing something?"

At this moment Libby debated whether to continue. But having come this far, she knew that to reverse direction would just prompt Rachel to pursue the subject. Libby had set loose the Devil, and now she had to pay his infernal price. Of course she knew that the tempter had snared her years before, but only now had he come to collect his portion. What did the Bible say about the wages of sin? Romans 6:23. Surely she did not deserve death when the worst she had done, she had done for love. "As a young woman, I loved your daddy, and he loved me. A baby—"

Before Libby could continue, Rachel blurted, "Yes, he and some other woman."

"No, honey, with me."

Normally Rachel's intelligence didn't mislead her. But owing to her staunch belief that her daddy had fathered a child with some shady woman, she could not bring her mind to focus on Libby's confession. Like so many others, Rachel held fast to what she wanted to believe;

but when facts contradicted her belief, she rejected the facts. "If my daddy had a baby with you, where is it?"

Libby pointed to Rachel. "Sitting in front of me."

The world exploded. Armageddon had arrived. The demons had been released from the deep. Rachel slumped in her chair, covered her eyes with an arm, and cried, "It can't be true."

"I went to Paris just before your birth. Miss Ellen treated me kindly. Your daddy, too."

"But why didn't they put me up for adoption?"

"Because Montgomery French is your father, and you have his blood running in your veins."

"And yours."

"True. But your mamma couldn't have children. So why not you?"

Rachel laughed stridently. "Then I'm an octoroon. No better or worse than all the women who slept with their massas and gave birth to—" She couldn't bring herself to say the words.

"Honey, no child ever had more love than you. What else can you ask? I even moved in to help care for you."

"Montgomery French's bastard child. His half-breed." There! Now she had said it. The foundation of her cherished status crumbled. Although she had felt safe fostering liberal attitudes and speaking out against racial discrimination, she now felt vulnerable. She sarcastically remarked, "Perhaps we ought to sell this house and move into the black section of town. Adam would be in no position to complain. After all, he's Jewish!"

Libby, as she had a thousand times before, hugged her daughter consolingly. "What's this about Adam?"

Rachel told her the story of Adam's real family. "I think that at this very moment, he's making plans to fly to Budapest, to try to locate his parents."

Libby held her tightly and said, "I hope he does, and I hope you go with him." She took one of the linen napkins and dabbed Rachel's face. "Knowing Adam, as I do, I can't imagine him giving a hoot about who your mother is. But there's no reason for him to know."

"Why, then, did you have to tell me?" Rachel cried. "I could have lived happily without knowing."

"Yes, but I couldn't. I lived in fear you would one day find out. I knew I had to tell you myself. In truth, at this very moment, I feel freer than I've ever felt."

Rachel reflexively murmured, "The truth will set you free."

"John 8:32," said Libby. "I know the passage by heart. 'And you will know the truth, and the truth will make you free.' Those words have been smoldering in my heart since the day you came into the world. All these years I have suffered the pain. But now things have changed. Your daddy said you've been reading his papers. So I decided to speak. At last, I can say the fire in me has been extinguished."

Making no attempt to find in Libby's happiness a vicarious joy, Rachel said, "And my hellfire's just beginning."

"I don't see why, Rachel. You're not to blame."

That Libby had used the name Rachel instead of honey signaled Libby's displeasure. It always did, and Rachel noticed, causing her to backtrack.

"Pastor Rominy says a person's no better or worse than his acts. I suppose," said Rachel, "that goes for me, too. If I didn't tell anyone, I couldn't live with that secret. I'd prefer that others knew. An open book, no matter what it says, is better than a burned one. If nothing else we should have learned that lesson from the Nazis. Not that I plan to send out announcements to all my friends and acquaintances. But if the subject should ever arise, I'll be the first to bear witness to my roots."

"There's one problem, honey, and it's the same one I've had to bear for years. Your daddy won't let you say anything, just as he wouldn't let me or Miss Ellen talk about what happened. If he knew that I told you, I can't even imagine the consequences. He's already moving his papers to a safer place."

"Libby, do you hear what you're saying? You're free now, but I'm not."

Both women fell into a ruminative state. Their heavy breathing and the beat of the rain invited lugubrious thoughts. And here they sat: Libby fearing she would have to leave Hungamon and live elsewhere; and Rachel, wrestling with whether she could live with her secret. She thought of her father's papers and collections willed to the library with the understanding that they would not be made public until after his death. She therefore decided that she would say nothing, unless something untoward arose.

The request to house Wayne and Lidia came from Zoe. A month had elapsed with her caring for five people in her small house.

"Adam has already spoken to me, and I said no."

Undeterred, Zoe explained her situation and asked that Rachel merely keep the children for a week, on a trial basis. If the situation proved unmanageable, she would bring them home. "You don't have to change anything for the kids. For my sake—and theirs—I beg you to help."

How could Rachel refuse Zoe, whose generosity toward the Panamanians made her look uncharitable? "I'm willing to have them stay for a week, but not until I've prepared the rooms. Can you wait?"

"If I have no choice, I suppose I'll just have to."

Adam agreed to her plan, and actually thought it might be great fun to have children to tease and embrace. Ten days later, the children moved in, and the Shaws' life changed markedly. For one thing, their innumerable friends became numerable; but Rachel soldiered on without so much as an apology. In fact she proudly announced that Adam had unearthed the history of his Hungarian family and his Jewish roots. For a second thing, the Shaws found themselves laughing in a house heretofore steeped in silence or fragmentary conversations.

The foibles of the children provided an endless treat. For a third thing, Wayne sang for them, with Lidia on clarinet accompaniment. This kind of evening made Rachel remember a time when people would spend Sunday afternoon around the piano singing songs. The old-fashioned and salubrious quality of such days appealed to her. And last, the children kept them from thinking of themselves. Having others to care for enriched their hours.

By the end of the week, Rachel and Adam would not hear of the children leaving. They insisted on their remaining with them. Although Rachel wondered if her changed feelings had anything to do with the discovery of her bloodlines, she genuinely felt that life had become fuller with the children in the house. She now had reason to cook from recipes she previously avoided; she liked having some control over lives that she felt would benefit from her experience. After several weeks, she wished she had a child of her own. Damn that horrible accident!

Did moments arise when she questioned her decision to keep the children? Of course. They exhibited numerous failings: sloppiness (she would school them in tidiness), poor speech habits (she would correct their grammar), ignorance of high culture (she would introduce them to literature and art), and occasional unruliness (she would impose discipline). Did she succeed? Only partially. Because children have a way of avoiding parental orders, Rachel settled for half a loaf, which she treated as a feast.

In bed one night, Rachel, out of the blue, apologized to Adam for her sterile condition.

"Don't be silly," he said. "We agreed from the start . . ."

"But you see now how much fun we have missed in our lives. With children . . ." She saw no need to complete the sentence.

"Please, Rachel, no need to regret your condition. We have two now."

She failed to respond.

Libby's revelation seemed to effect a chemical change in Rachel, who became less formal and more forward. She no longer felt the need to maintain some abstract standard of right behavior. In a word, she could act on her feelings. And soon she discovered that she liked herself more than before. Adam noticed the change as well. She let her hair grow, she stopped using nail polish and perfume, and she wrestled with the children on the living room rug, took them on nature hikes, and drove them to New Orleans to visit her favorite bookstore. Although Adam never felt in competition with Rachel for the children's affection, he had his own ideas of where to take the kids: the public golf and tennis courts, New Orleans Saints football games, fishing, the art museum, and a four-day family trip to Mexico, where Lidia handled the Spanish—and the Kaopectate—for them all.

Zoe and Samuel saw the children often, so homesickness never arose. Mr. Lumpkin's private tutoring soon ended, and the Shaws, with the parents' permission, enrolled both children in a small private school, the Fry Academy, run by descendants of English Quakers. Adam insisted on paying. No one questioned Lidia's lack of a birth certificate or papers, and the Shaws offered no explanations. The children quickly blended into the school and excelled. Wayne's voice earned him a leading role in the choir, and Lidia's prowess at soccer elevated her to the varsity team.

Zoe, pleased with the current arrangement, could not help observing for Adam's benefit that money had magical powers. "I'm sure a great many other children are equally talented, but without the opportunity, they will never or rarely succeed. If all the schools in America cared as much as this one, we'd have a much different country."

"Money and the right parents," said Adam, prepared to pay tuition for as long as necessary.

"Yes, both matter," said Zoe. She and Adam were driving to Moss Hospital on an early spring day in 1989, and a mist hovered over the trees and grass. Buds had begun to issue from the profusion of plant life. "When this whole matter first came up," said Zoe, "you asked me: 'If I convince Rachel and do this for you, what will you do for me?' I decided that you meant only one thing: sex. Right?"

Adam took a while before replying, "Yes, but now I'm thinking in different terms."

"Because of the children?"

"And because of Rachel. She's changed. Less stiff, more relaxed."

Zoe chuckled with a knowing twinkle in her eyes. "More affectionate?"

"Partly."

"And the other part?"

"Me. I've begun to understand her struggle to free herself from her parents and schooling and place in society. In college her wealth and social standing made her different from me. I grew up a poor kid from the streets of Newark. When I got close to her perfume and perfectly coiffed hair, when I got to escort her to sorority dances, to embrace and kiss her . . . I felt as if I had accidentally entered the crystal palace where others mistakenly treated me as one of the rich."

"Well, I certainly hope the children have something to do with her change. That would be nice."

Adam failed to answer because he couldn't. He had these last few months tried to understand the transformation in Rachel, but whichever explanation he entertained, he saw that it lacked the essence of truth. He had realized only recently that when you love another, you see yourself reflected in that person. And of late he found Rachel's presence truly nourishing.

Recovering his voice, he said, "I might yet ask a favor of you, but I can't say at the moment."

"Fair enough."

Adam drove home and greeted the children with a challenge. "Hoops after dinner?" He meant shooting baskets.

"Not until they have finished their homework," said Rachel.

The children greeted her comment with moans, but they followed her orders. When they finished, they charged outside to the spot where Adam had sunk a post with a backboard and rim.

"Mr. Cotton, the headmaster, agreed to let us keep turkeys on the school grounds," said Wayne. "He's building a pen, and all the children get to look after them."

Adam approved and observed that Wayne would be way ahead of the other children because he had once kept a turkey as a pet.

Lidia said, "At Thanksgiving you never said what happened to Hector, your pet turkey. Do you still have him?"

Wayne shook his head no and looked away. "Some guys from school broke into our backyard and strung the bird up on our tulip tree."

"Well," said Lidia, "if anyone at school tries that, and I know about it, I'll punch them right in the nose."

And she would. Wayne had a pacific personality, Lidia a feisty one. Her free spirit, in fact, had led Adam and Rachel to worry about her association with Samuel Hildreth, whom she would meet at night, at his trailer. Both the Shaws had the same troubling thought. Did these meetings have a sexual component? Should the surrogate parents worry? Neither Rachel nor Adam dared to ask Lidia about her evening rendezvous. They feared they would destroy the trust that had grown between them and the children.

Samuel drove to New Orleans to meet with the director of the art museum to ask about restorations. He described the painting: an oil on canvas, which over time had lost its luster. Where could he find the best restorers? The director mentioned museums in New York, Chicago, and Los Angeles.

"I even know a superb restorer in Kansas City, at the Nelson-Atkins Museum of Art, a woman, Katie Garland."

Now Rachel had to persuade her father to relinquish the painting for cleaning. Although he could see how the varnish had browned, he resisted, dismissing her concerns about the state of the canvas. Rachel could restore it after his death, but for now it remained with him. She suspected that his fears regarding the painting mirrored her own. The painting might open a chapter in Hungamon history that Montgomery had spent a good deal of his life initially denying and then editing. Neither the father nor the daughter, if asked, could have explained how or why the painting could implicate the first Montgomery French, but they both felt that behind the painting lay damaging evidence.

Rachel told herself that the painting might easily be removed in her father's absence, but he would know in an instant that she engineered it; and his sense of betrayal would come between them. She would just have to persuade him to agree to the restoration. But what excuse could she fabricate that he would buy? She decided to ask Adam, without telling him about her suspicions regarding her father's and grandfather's history.

Adam responded by explaining, "Few people realize that canvas moves, and paint and varnish shrink, creating a condition we call *craquelure*, which means that a network of fine cracks or crackles appears on the surface of the painting. To repair the damage, restorers normally glue another piece of canvas to the back of the original, to stabilize it. Craquelure also explains why museums carefully maintain a certain temperature and humidity in their galleries."

The floor creaked. Rachel looked up and saw Wayne standing in the doorway. He had obviously overheard what Adam had said, because he added: "That gloomy painting could sure use some cheering up."

Adam laughed, remembering the canvas. "It's probably covered with linseed oil."

"Linseed oil!" Rachel exclaimed.

"Sellers sometimes rub the oil on the varnish to make the painting appear older. To remove the stuff takes some doing. If you want me to investigate, we can drive over later."

When Rachel called him, Montgomery replied that he'd be out for the evening but that Adam could inspect the canvas. He mulishly observed, "I thought we agreed that you'd clean the canvas after I'm dead."

"As you know, Daddy, Adam recently discovered that his painting is worth a lot of money. He says maybe yours is as well."

"Already the Jew in him is coming out," Montgomery quipped. But Rachel didn't laugh.

"Your son-in-law wants to do you a favor, and you come up with a remark like that? I'm disappointed in you, Daddy. What would Libby say, if she heard?" Rachel, playing on the fact that blacks and Jews still shared pariah status in provincial America, wanted her daddy to see that if he slept with the one, he could at least respect the other.

"Just a bad joke, honey. You know how much I like Adam. Feel free to come over tonight, and tell me Adam's verdict."

Adam drove. Rachel unlocked her father's door and turned on the lights. Adam went straight for the painting. Well aware of the house's poor lighting, he had brought along a special desk lamp with a high-powered bulb, and his magnifying glass. Focusing the light on the canvas, he studied the condition of the paint under the glass. With Adam preoccupied, Rachel walked around the room and shuffled some papers resting on her daddy's worktable. She noticed a volume about the history of American gangsters. Her father had bookmarked the chapter on Bonnie and Clyde. Next to the sentence about their death caused by a traitorous friend, Montgomery had written "Untrue." Rachel could not keep from smiling. Her daddy remained indefatigable in his belief that Ivy Methvin had not conspired with the police to capture Bonnie and Clyde. She supposed that if he had had the means, he would have prevailed upon the movie producers to rewrite the film's ending, putting the blame where he thought it belonged: on the trigger-happy police. Adam had been talking to her, but in her absorption, she failed to hear what he said.

"The stretcher bars have creased the canvas, and I see considerable craquelure. If your father wants this painting to last, he'll need to get it restored. The materials available to artists in the 1930s lacked the quality available today."

"Would you be willing to tell him the painting is valuable?"

"But it's not."

"Just tell him it is. Maybe mention half a million dollars."

"Based on what?"

"You're the expert. Think of some reason."

"You're scheming, Rachel. What's up?"

Rachel raked her hands through her hair and rubbed her neck, her tension palpable. "I can't say now, but I will later. You'll just have to trust me." She bit off a cuticle. "It's important. Please help me."

Adam, struck by the force of her request, replied, "If it matters so much, then of course I'll say what you want." His thoughts raced through his catalog of art memories.

"Okay, what I plan to tell him is this: The painting is from a particular school of 1930s artists now being collected, and now commanding top prices. Will that do?"

She hugged him and whispered, "Perfect. Thank you, thank you."

On their way home, Adam deliberately asked in a colloquial manner, "What happens if your old man refuses to give up the canvas?"

He hoped his diction would emphasize Montgomery's stubbornness.

# Art for Truth's Sake

"How much did you say?" exclaimed an incredulous Judge Waters.

"Half a million."

"And you're telling me, Montgomery, you're prepared to turn down that much money all because you're afraid someone will look into the background of the canvas and who painted it?"

"I've done some reading of my own. No one pays prices like that unless they're sure of the provenance."

"The what?"

"The history of the painting."

Both men, nearly horizontal from Samantha's home brew, sprawled on the judge's leather chairs and ottomans in the paneled den. Samantha, not for the first time, had entered the adjoining room to eavesdrop. As the liquor loosened their tongues, their talk became increasingly frank and unfocused, swerving from one subject to another, merely on the basis of a word or a phrase.

"My daddy—"

"A good man," said Emory, "but too quick to judge. And that observation comes from a judge." He laughed robustly, thinking his play on words had been immensely amusing.

"What choice did he have, what with him and his friends caught on film? You can't have some darkie blackmailing you."

"Blackmailing," repeated the judge. "What's more suitable for a darkie?" And again he laughed at his perceived wit.

Samantha could feel her anger surface and her temper rise. But she bit her tongue, as she had often done. Oh, how she wished she could have upbraided both men for talking drunken nonsense. She tried to remember some Latin phrase the judge often used. Oh yes, in vino veritas.

"When I heard about Rachel nosing around the old library, that's when I decided better safe than sorry."

"You did the right thing, Montgomery, pulling your collection out of that shack and bringing it home."

Mr. French took a long sip of the booze. "Damn good stuff. Whew!" It took a moment for him to catch his breath. "In fact, I put the most sensitive papers in the basement, in green accordion folders. I ordered a Chubb floor safe. When it comes, in they go."

Samantha's growing suspicions made her want to ask her own questions. She entered the den and announced her presence by volunteering to provide the men with another bottle of her moonshine.

"I think we're fine for the present," said the judge.

Before exiting, she planted a seed. "I heard you mention the old library. Since they got the new one," she lied, "I understand they're gonna be movin' their photo collection from one to the other." On that note she left—and listened from the next room.

"Photo collection," said Montgomery. "What do you know about that, Emory?"

"Nothing."

"Maybe that kid's picture's in there."

"God, we're talking about ages ago. Fifty years."

"Mary Judd."

"I thought your daddy took the original and destroyed the negative."

"I know of at least three copies. Several of the men wanted one, including old man Dozier. But his seems to have disappeared."

The judge belched. "The painter. His name again?"

"Godwin Rush. Three men who knew him are still alive; and one, I understand, still has his wits. Jeremiah Lincoln."

"Well, at least you got the painting. The photo and witnesses don't mean anything unless you can put them together with the painting and all that other stuff."

"That's why I don't want to let the painting and 'all that other stuff,' as you call it, out of my hands."

The judge pondered the force of his friend's argument and then concluded, "A half million is a lot of money."

Montgomery held up his glass. "Here's to Chubb safes!"

Samantha had heard enough to script a plan. In the next day or two, when Montgomery called on Libby and parked his car, as always, down the street in front of a vacant lot, Samantha would have someone let the air out of a tire or jack up the car and remove one, a prank that would give Rachel time to go through his papers in the basement. But if the Chubb safe came immediately . . .

Resuming her perch at the half-open door next to the den, Samantha tried to fit together fragments of conversation she couldn't quite fathom. She felt as if the pattern of talk resembled a jigsaw puzzle, and she lacked a picture or context to guide her. Montgomery said that "in those days," although the police sided with them, one still had to have an alibi, deal with witnesses, and destroy evidence or bury it beyond the reach of the law.

Judge Emory pontificated. "Fatal mistake that girl made. Foolhardy."

"Godwin Rush should have known better."

"An act of defiance or stupidity, if you ask me," said the judge.

"Did he think he could blackmail my daddy?"

"What irony! The painting now hangs on your wall and nobody has any idea about its history. Thank goodness our local people, like most Americans, have no familiarity with their own past."

"I'm pained to think that that poor child just wanted to brag up her photo, when she showed it to Godwin."

The judge sighed. "A cruel turn of events. I wonder if she knew how he intended to use it."

"No way of proving that now," said Montgomery.

"Strange." The judge took a healthy draft of Samantha's brew and leaned back in his chair with his eyes closed. "So much of what you and I once took for granted has changed, Montgomery. We live in a world governed by self-interest and money changers. Just look at Dozier and his son. And yet for all my misgivings, I have to admit that the pleasures I've known with Samantha would not have been easily available to my father, at least not in the public way that I've lived. And the same goes for you and Libby. What's my conclusion? That even with our former, and maybe current, prejudices, we have it better now than our fathers did." He sighed. "Of course, you might say, the slaveholders had the best of all possible worlds. They had their wives and their families and their slaves and their every wish satisfied, from material luxury to nannies to sex."

Montgomery didn't answer. He had fallen asleep.

The judge murmured audibly, "The French family never did have the staying power of the Waters'." He relaxed and a moment later snored softly.

Samantha jotted down Jeremiah Lincoln, Mary Judd, Godwin Rush, and green accordion folders, and hurriedly left the house.

In April 1989, on a Tuesday, Mars day, the day of war, the day that hosted medieval tournaments, Rachel joined the struggle to demystify past and current events. Her father, having learned from Adam that his painting might fetch up to half a million dollars, spent the afternoon with Miss Libby; Adam and Samuel, becoming fast friends, traveled to Kansas City with the carefully wrapped and padded painting in the back of the car; and Rachel sat in the basement of her father's house reading papers in green accordion folders and in files labeled "Bank Statements."

The number of papers, too great for her to read in a day, led her to read selectively. She removed the contents of the green folders and replaced them with files from other boxes stacked in the basement. It took two trips to her car to transport all the material, but she completed the task before her daddy returned. In fact, just as she prepared to leave the house, a delivery truck arrived with a floor safe. She unlocked the door, watched the two young men, sweating profusely, put the safe in the basement, tipped them, and drove off.

At home, she unloaded the papers, stuffing them into empty hatboxes stored at the top of her closet. She had saved them because each one came with a memory: her honeymoon; a trip to New York; an Easter bonnet; a Mediterranean cruise. The helter-skelter manner in which she had scooped up the papers and thrown them into her car merely compounded her work. She would now have to sort and file and date and categorize them by subject. For the moment, fearing discovery, she didn't want the papers in plain sight; hence her resorting to the hatboxes and their place of storage in her large clothes closet. She paused. What had happened to all those hats?

Although Adam had gone for a few days, Wayne and Lidia would still have the run of the house, so she could not, until they slept or went off to school, read her father's files. The job would therefore take longer than she'd hoped. But Rachel, a patient and fastidious woman, prided herself on being organized and skilled in taxonomy. Alphabetizing would prove helpful, and dating would provide context, but real meaning would issue from typology, phylum, and precise classification—virtues she would bring to her reading.

By the time Adam and Samuel returned, she understood why the papers had been put under lock and key. She also knew the impossibility of separating the different issues: race, culture, manhood, fear, governance, integration, miscegenation, religion, and, not least, jobs. With the picture almost complete, she needed only to read the letters in Samuel's possession. He had promised to show them to her "at a later date." That date arrived when he and Adam returned.

A warm spring rain had streaked the windows of the Shaw house, and the dappled lake had attracted a few anglers, those who claimed that the rain improved the fishing. Adam spied the lake longingly, and wished that instead of huddling with Rachel and Samuel in the sunroom, he could be out on the water with his neighbors.

"We told you everything we learned," said Adam, "and now after having had the painting cleaned and getting your dad's hopes up, we have to explain to him that it isn't worth more than a thousand or two."

"You saw them x-ray the canvas?"

Samuel came to Adam's aid. "We're as frustrated as you, Miss Rachel. We thought we'd find more. Like Adam said, the belt buckle read 1933, so the only real difference was that the original painting used the word *Klansmen*, not *Kinsman*."

Adam sighed, visibly annoyed at the trouble they'd gone to and the little they'd found. "We couldn't make head nor tail of the damn words. I mean, sure, we thought of the KKK, but did Godwin intend to paint a visual joke? And if so, what's the joke?"

Putting her folded hands behind her head, Rachel leaned back and stared into space, thinking. She remembered a word from one of her English classes, *ratiocination*, meaning "to think or argue logically or rationally." She told herself to ratiocinate, to go beneath the surface. What symbols lay hidden there? Adam had put his finger on it: a visual joke. But Adam's grasp of the historical background could not compete with Rachel's or Samuel's, both of whom had, so to speak, done their homework. Hence Rachel knew that Samuel would have to provide the final clue. They sat in silence and watched the fishers. Rachel went to a sideboard and collected some brandy and snifters.

Samuel held his glass up to the light to admire the fine glasswork. Rachel poured, the men drank, and still no one ventured to speak.

The silence felt like a suffocating blanket. Finally Samuel murmured in a manner that suggested he wished to test an idea. "If those letters I got can be trusted, and I can't see why they couldn't, after all they led me to the newspaper reports, and those reports never contradicted the letters, then I'm guessing that 1933 refers to the first of the two lynchings, Ned McLaren's murder. Mr. Rush hoped to say what?"

Rachel smiled. Samuel had just solved the mystery. In light of her father's letters, she could now say with some certainty, "My grandfather had initially been reluctant to go along with lynchings and cross burnings and shootings, although he had nothing against a good whipping with a wide leather strap. He said so himself in a page from his diary that my daddy preserved. Too bad Daddy didn't preserve all of it. But for some reason, in 1933 my grandfather lent himself to a lynching. When Godwin Rush painted him and his accomplices, Godwin depicted in a visual joke 'The Fall of Man.' That's what the date on the buckle means: Montgomery X. French fell from grace in 1933. The reins painted like snakes and the garden lushness . . . it all fits. Once my granddaddy came into possession of the painting, he had Godwin change the word but left the date. Why? To mock Rush, who needed the money and therefore did as Grandfather asked."

Rachel's explication of the canvas rendered Adam speechless. As the one skilled in the "reading" of paintings, not she, he marveled: "How did you figure it out?"

Rachel felt that an explanation would have to wait until later. For now, her father had not yet discovered the theft and the exchange of papers, and she had no desire to reveal any clues that might point to her. After all, her daddy had always treated her lovingly and generously, and she felt enormous affection for him. Besides, he had not been party to a lynching; her grandfather had. At the right time, she would confront her daddy, but not now.

The two men sat with fixed gazes, staring at Rachel, and obviously waiting for her to continue her narrative. She had to admit to herself that she loved the role of cynosure, and at this moment she held not only center stage but also the rapt attention of her audience, albeit composed of only two men. For some reason her mind flashed to a time, not long ago, in church, when she had been sitting next to a man she had never seen before, and she knew that his eyes focused not on Pastor Manders but on her.

"Godwin's painting," she continued, "was selected for exhibition in New Orleans as part of a Federal Art Project show. Presumably he started the painting in 1933, but he didn't complete it and qualify for a government grant until 1935. The certificate of purchase lists the title as 'Klansmen' and the sale price as one hundred dollars."

Still stunned by her grasp of provenance and her having unearthed information that, in most cases, proved virtually unattainable, Adam sputtered, "Where in the hell did you find all that out?"

"Records," she replied coyly.

"Whose records?" Adam pursued. "Samuel and I drove all the way to Kansas City, and we couldn't discover anything more important than the original inscription on the frame. And here you turn up a certificate of purchase." He paused, and then hit the table. "Geez, what an idiot I am! The damn painting is hanging in your father's house. His father must have given him the papers. But how did you get them?"

"By looking."

"Where?"

"Ah!" she said, but refused to say more, reasoning that in silence is safety.

Samuel audibly murmured to Adam that he wanted "to hear Rachel out," and that Adam and his "providence" questions could just wait. "Miss Rachel, you said something about changes to the painting. What's that about?"

She couldn't reply that the certificate of purchase contained that information, because clearly it didn't. She also didn't want to show her hand with respect to the papers now resting in hatboxes at the top of her closet. One could never be too careful. Her explanation would require invention.

"Judge Emory Waters," she said, "told me the whole story."

"Whew!" exclaimed Samuel. "That man's got his fingers in every pie in the parish. Others, too."

Now composed and slightly skeptical, Adam observed that the original story would have had to issue from the judge's father. So how did he become involved?

Rachel had hoped that the mention of Judge Emory Waters would end the interrogation. Now in a pickle, she'd have to come up with yet another lie. Of course lying requires a good memory, and Rachel just hoped she could keep all of her inventions in mind. "Adam guessed it. The source of this story is Emory's father—"

"His name?" Adam asked.

"I don't remember. But he had run into the first Montgomery French at a convention, where Montgomery shared it."

For strategic reasons, she decided to leave the "it" indefinite.

"Probably some KKK meeting," Samuel muttered.

"You might be right," said Rachel. "Godwin Rush attended the show in New Orleans. He also had other work on exhibit. My grandfather offered him a price with the understanding that Godwin would call the painting 'Kinsman' not 'Klansmen.' Godwin, living on next to nothing, accepted the deal." She grinned with self-satisfaction. "That's the long and the short of it."

"I'm wondering," added Adam, "whether the meaning of the canvas—the snake and the garden and the fall of man—led to Godwin Rush's death?"

She paused. "It all begins with a photograph, which the painting drew on. A young woman—"

Samuel nodded his head in agreement.

"Mary Judd," said Rachel. "She secretly took a picture of some men in a meadow, the Sons of Dixie. Mary had briefly worked for my grandfather as a housemaid. She immediately recognized him sitting on his horse and, I suppose, that led her to snap his picture, with his friends in the background. When the painting surfaced, the Klansmen exploded. As I told you, my granddaddy bought the painting, thinking that once he owned it, he owned the evidence, and the furor about people being discovered and compromised would die out. But Godwin Rush had apparently been working on a second canvas, based on the same photograph. The Sons of Dixie decided to put an end to both their lives—Godwin's and Mary's." Rachel's voice trailed off, and she found herself sniffling.

The three of them sat silently thinking their own private thoughts. Adam couldn't get over Rachel's detective work. Samuel now had answers to many of the questions that had been bothering him since talking to Jeremiah Lincoln. But he felt intuitively that Rachel's findings pointed to David Dozier's murder, and that if he could unriddle the rebus, Manny Crenshaw's name would be cleared. Rachel worried that even worse revelations lay ahead. In the coming weeks she would read all the papers she'd stolen; and she feared that they might contain land mines and time bombs of unimaginable harm.

LeShaun Jackson, the twenty-two-year-old black man whom Samuel had recruited to sell Judge Waters cocaine, had been leaving the plastic-wrapped powder, as directed, behind the house, for Samantha to collect. But LeShaun saw himself as an entrepreneur, not a runner, an ambitious fellow who could rise to the top and to riches if only he played his cards right. He had watched in the woods as Samantha retrieved his packages and carried them back to the house. In its place she always left a brown bag of cash. LeShaun reasoned if the judge had that much cash on hand, he probably had more. But he didn't think of himself as a common house thief. He would approach the judge and suggest that the two men go into business together. With the judge fronting the money, and LeShaun not only distributing but also buying, the two men could turn a handsome profit. And if the judge refused his offer, LeShaun could always threaten to expose the judge's addiction.

One evening LeShaun rapped on the judge's front door, and Samantha led him into the study. The young man had never seen such tasteful splendor. Suddenly he wanted to remove the gold chain around his neck and the large pinky ring and his diamond-studded watch. He cleared his throat and shuffled his feet. When he finally wended his way into the subject, Judge Emory Waters peered at him with venomous eyes. A second later he frothed at the mouth: "Do you really think, you jackass, that anyone would believe a black drug dealer? I ought to kill you. Rile me again and I'll issue a warrant for your arrest. So, just pull up your pants and go back to what you know best, cocaine distribution. Maybe you never heard about my temper. Don't ever test it again. Or—" He backed LeShaun toward the door and held a letter opener to his throat. "Understand?"

The judge opened the door and shoved LeShaun across the threshold. "You're lucky to be alive, boy. Just remember that." LeShaun left the house and drove directly to Samuel Hildreth's trailer, where he cooled his heels for a couple of hours until Samuel returned. As Samuel unlocked his door, LeShaun slipped out of the shadows and came up behind him. Samuel instinctively swung around and, with a hand chop, dropped LeShaun to the ground. The young man's nose bled.

"You dumb shit," said Samuel, "don't you know better than to sneak up on a man? I coulda broken your nose."

Samuel helped LeShaun into the trailer and attended to his injury. Once LeShaun could compose himself, he told Samuel what he had done.

"You're even dumber than I thought," said Samuel. "You got rocks in your head?" But after a moment's reflection, Samuel said, "Maybe you're a lot smarter than I'm givin' you credit for." He screwed up his mouth and mused aloud, "Twice now that old bird has threatened, first me, now you. That man has death on his mind. What's he protectin'? Reputations? He says so, but I don't believe it. For example, he don't care what others say about his livin' with a black woman. And then there's—"

Staring at LeShaun, Samuel realized that the lad couldn't be relied on to maintain a confidence. When the time came, he would give LeShaun his marching orders and stage props. With LeShaun hardly out the door, Samuel telephoned Adam. Ten minutes later, Samuel heard a car roll to a stop on the gravel parking space next to his trailer. As good as his word, Adam had come at once.

"I heard a crackling under my tires. Do you keep an armadillo?"

"There's one that lives back of the trailer."

"Not anymore."

Samuel left the trailer and returned holding the dead animal. "I just hope this ain't an omen. Excuse me." He retreated to the woods, put the remains under some leaves, returned, and washed his hands. "They got a musky smell."

"I should have noticed," said Adam. "How could I have been so blind?"

Samuel offered him a beer; Adam declined, saying he never drank after dinner. Apologizing for the lateness of the hour, Samuel outlined his suspicions. The judge had a cocaine habit; David Dozier had dealt in drugs; Samuel (and this confession pained him) had once ferried drugs from Mexico to the United States and sold them to David Dozier; Mr. Dozier, a middling lawyer, always paid for the drugs with large sums of cash; Manny Crenshaw worked as one of his runners; and by all accounts, Mr. Dozier frequently shorted his runners.

"That's the true facts," said Samuel. "I would guess that Dozier had a bankroller, and he crossed that person for some reason, which cost DVD his life. Somethin' tells me the judge knows the person."

"And how do you propose to prove that guess of yours?" asked Adam, now frankly shaken by Samuel's admission that he had been carrying drugs from Mexico and selling them to David Dozier. Adam even wondered about Samuel's own motives. He had had a good reason to silence Dozier. But he chose to turn a blind eye to facts that would cast Samuel in a bad light and might even lead to his imprisonment, to say nothing of Adam's culpability for aiding and abetting. So any plan demanded craft.

"I know what you're thinkin'," said Samuel. "You think I'm involved. Well, before I map out the terrain, I want you to meet someone, a kid who took Manny's place supplyin' drugs to the judge. LeShaun Jackson. Not the quickest man on the track, I admit, but he can finish a race. I can have him here tomorrow night. You free then?" Adam shook his head no, but before he could explain, Samuel continued, "I want you to meet him and give me your impression. If he passes muster, then I'll put you both in the know. That's simpler than havin' to explain twice."

Adam had been planning a coming-out party at the New Orleans art museum for his Mihály Munkácsy painting. Persuaded of its authenticity, he wanted to share with fellow collectors his Hungarian treasure. All the aficionados and connoisseurs of the local art world would be on hand, as well as Scot Marco, who volunteered to fly into the city for the event.

"Let's make it for the day after next. I'm planning a big splash tomorrow night."

"That's what I'm plannin', too," said Samuel cryptically, "in a rich man's backyard."

The New Orleans art crowd, gathered in the marbled entry hall of the museum, appeared stunned by Adam's painting and the proof of provenance. Numerous people offered to buy it, and Scot Marco proposed auctioning it in Los Angeles. To all of them, Adam said, "I plan to keep it." But he knew full well that no insurance company would cover the painting unless he safely secured it, and Adam did not plan to turn his house into Fort Knox. So he reasoned that he would lend the painting to the museum, where he could see it virtually whenever he wished; and if he should ever decide to reclaim or sell the painting, he could do so freely.

"You're sitting on a lot of money," Scot whispered, "and maybe even a hornet's nest. Remember what I told you. If the Hungarian government has a change of heart about the worth of the painting and its leaving the country, they might try to repossess it."

Unlike before, Scot's words lingered. Adam pondered what he would do if sued for the painting. Perhaps this showing had been a bad idea, and keeping the painting under wraps, so to speak, might have been the wiser course. His thinking led him to wonder about the wisdom of Rachael's hope to raise money for a Black Arts Festival, which she had dreamed up. To the dismay of many of her friends, she wanted to feature paintings, sculpture, photography, pottery, and jewelry. Her father's canvas would be on display and so, too, would the photographs of Mary Judd. Wayne would sing at the event, and Lidia would play a clarinet solo. Rachel had already rented a space on Magazine Street in New Orleans and had the approval of the local merchants, who knew that the spillover would mean ringing cash registers.

Watching her hit up the wealthy city patrons, Adam could only admire her gentle but firm touch. She behaved like a seasoned political campaigner. He had no idea what had decided her on this event, but several weeks earlier she had run an advertisement in the *Times-Picayune* requesting owners of Godwin Rush works to contribute to the show. To date, she had heard nothing, and Adam doubted that any paintings beyond her father's would surface. By the end of the evening, she beamed with pride over her husband's painting and the amount of money she had raised. She sidled up to Adam and whispered, "You'll never guess."

"I'm listening," he said, bending an ear toward her lips.

"Stephen Epstein, the historian and collector, told me that he has a Godwin Rush painting. It depicts a poor farmer standing alone in a field. He's willing to lend it to the show."

How could Adam not admire this enterprising wife of his? She and Zoe shared a penchant for getting things done. If they joined forces, they could probably effect a miracle.

With the Shaws in New Orleans, Libby remained in Hungamon looking after Wayne and Lidia. The children often explored in closets and dark places. In Rachel's closet, Lidia saw the hatboxes and thought how much fun it would be to model some of the hats. To her surprise, she found not hats but papers and letters. Although the children had no idea of their importance, they told themselves they had unearthed a secret and hoped to extort some special favor from her by promising to keep silent about their discovery.

The next day the children had enough sense not to include Adam in their plans. Besides, he left for work early, well before they departed for school. Over breakfast Lidia and Wayne began giggling. When Rachel asked what they found so funny, Lidia sputtered, "Hats," a reply that sent both children into hysterics.

"I confess," said Rachel, "you're way ahead of me."

Wayne boldly suggested that for a boat ride on the Mississippi, he would share the joke. Lidia immediately added that the trip would have to take place on a school day, making it a *real* vacation.

"What are you up to?" she asked.

"Hats," repeated Lidia. She waited a moment and then added, "Hatboxes in someone's closet."

The children could virtually feel the flush that reddened Rachel's face. Without realizing it, Rachel then made two mistakes. One, she refused the children's request. Two, she said that her father had left the papers with her for safekeeping. Unfamiliar with the experience of raising children, she failed to take into account that they would, when the opportunity presented itself, brag to their "grandfather" Montgomery that they knew the hiding place of his papers. Two days later, Mr. French called on his daughter. The children greeted him with a nonsense rhyme.

We have a wonderful secret,
Which we will share for an egret;
If you want out of the pickle,
Give each one of us a nickel.

Rachel immediately suggested that she and her father go off for a talk, one, she whispered, rare in its candor and raw in its truth.

In fact Rachel had been looking for an occasion to speak to her daddy. Her two mistakes therefore proved serendipitous. Their talk took place on a warm spring afternoon, with the irises in full bloom.

The second time LeShaun Jackson knocked on the judge's front door, he sported a new suit and had been tutored by Samuel Hildreth. He told Samantha he had come to make amends and had brought along a gift. Moments after Samantha left him in the hallway, he could hear the judge's booming voice in the study, "One minute. Not a second more." LeShaun waited for Samantha to leave, entered the study, and handed the judge a package with two airy light toothpaste tubes.

"Is this some kind of tasteless joke—," the judge began.

"Just unscrew the cap and take a sniff."

A second later, Judge Waters calmly asked, "Where?"

"The Dozier house."

"Police searched it."

"Not closely enough."

"How did you?"

"I'm guessin', judge, my minute is up. Good day to you, sir."

Never again did LeShaun Jackson feel so much satisfaction in leaving a man's presence. Making directly for Samuel's trailer, he related the moment.

"You guessed right on every account. He shouted, warned that he had only a minute for me, and wanted to know where the stuff came from. When I told him, he looked as if he had pissed his pants. Then I left the great man's house. God that felt good!"

"Hang around. Adam Shaw's on his way here. We need a white witness for the second part of the plan. If this thing works, Manny Crenshaw will be smiling in heaven. Whatever happens, I'm proud of what you done."

LeShaun beamed.

With Adam's arrival, Samuel opened three beers and shared his conclusions. "Letters, drugs, or double-dealing . . . it's gotta be one of the three that led to Mr. Dozier's death. Maybe all three. His son's death . . . I ain't figured that one out yet." Turning to LeShaun he said, "Like I told you, the next step is to fit you with a body wire and a miniature transmitter. Adam and me will be nearby in a car with a receiver." The courage drained from LeShaun's face. Samuel removed a C-note from his wallet and slid it across to LeShaun. "You do what I tell you and there's more where that came from. Now listen closely, man. You stop the judge the next time he's leavin' the courthouse." LeShaun's yellowed eyes looked like fog lights. "Before you guys meet, go over and over what I told you. After that, I'll do the rest." LeShaun sat strangely mute. "One last thing, man. Don't you be showin' up for that meetin' high on booze or weed."

LeShaun put his hands in his pockets to stop them from shaking. Working as a runner ran its own risks, but Samuel's plan . . . that entailed real danger. "I need to go now," he said, slapping hands with Samuel and Adam, and stumbling out of the trailer.

"You know where he's goin'?" Samuel said, anxiously biting his lower lip. "For a stiff drink."

"I would too," said Adam.

Samuel laughed. "Now, my friend, this is where you come in. I need a white witness. When LeShaun arrives at the judge's house, he'll be wired for sound. You are my honest broker. I'll set you up with earphones so you can listen to what LeShaun and the judge have to say. Unless I'm mistakin', the judge knows who bankrolled Dozier. When LeShaun leaves, you put the tape in a safe place."

Samuel felt he owed Manny Crenshaw his best efforts, to make amends. Adam asked whether Samuel felt any guilt for compromising Judge Waters, a man who had kept him from doing serious jail time.

That question, in fact, had been haunting Samuel. He owed the judge a favor, but he also thought Manny had been railroaded. Like many people, he believed it better to see a dozen guilty men go free than to imprison one innocent man. Although the judge had overlooked Samuel's involvement with drugs, he had put Manny in jail. So which mattered more: the judge's drug habit or Manny's reputation? From Samuel's standpoint, Vincent's murder didn't even weigh in the balance. He felt certain that when the judge let him go, he didn't expect Samuel to forfeit for life his moral compass.

A fearful LeShaun remained sober throughout the whole operation and then some, the longest period in his adult life that he had gone without a fix. As directed, at his first opportunity, a Thursday, he approached the judge outside the courthouse and repeated what Samuel had told him.

"I think we need to talk, judge, about DVD's banker. I got a few names in mind. Let's say we meet at your place. I'm free, except for today."

As Samuel anticipated, Judge Waters pleaded incomprehension. LeShaun, following his script, said, "I think the list might interest the feds," and strolled off. Before LeShaun reached his car, the judge called to him.

"How about Sunday afternoon next week, in my office behind the house. You know, the garden cottage. Say two o'clock."

Instead of a walk, Rachel and her father drove to his house. She had declined his offer to take her to lunch. On the way there, she hinted at her concerns. Montgomery grimly clutched the steering wheel but said nothing. Inside the bungalow he immediately seated himself at the old, familiar table that held his current notes regarding Bonnie and Clyde. Eyeing his daughter, who paced the length of the room, he had no inclination to assuage her unease.

"At first," he said, "I saw nothing amiss. But when I started putting files in the safe . . . then I knew."

"Daddy," she finally said, "you've been falsifying the historical record, and I think I know why: to preserve the family reputation."

But Montgomery wanted to shift the focus from his crimes to hers. "You stole from your own father. I never thought that a daughter of mine—"

Rachel stopped him dead. "Perhaps it's because I'm part black," she said. "We mixed bloods can't be trusted."

"An ugly slander!" her father thundered.

"Not good enough," she replied.

Her father sat crestfallen. He tried unsuccessfully to explain, to gesture, to rise. Nothing worked. After a long silence, during which he inhaled deeply several times, he finally managed a few fragmentary words. "Then you know. I had hoped—but—if you." He quit the sentence in defeat.

"Yes, I know."

"The papers . . ." Again he fled the field.

"I wanted to learn about our family."

"What did Libby tell you?"

"Nothing."

"In my generation—"

"Don't try to pass off crimes and unseemly behavior as a generational trait. I care as much about our family as you do. But I'm not about to rewrite history."

A great silence can make a large noise. Montgomery's failure to respond echoed through the house. He had feared this day would come, and it had. But like all who know that the angel of death is perched on the garden gate, Montgomery thought that in his case he would receive a special dispensation. No believer in miracles or in an afterlife, with harps and a choir singing Handel, he did hope that he would escape judgment, particularly from his daughter. At this moment the worst of all possible fates had befallen him. His daughter expected him to answer for his father's crimes and his falsehoods.

On the Saturday, Adam and Zoe took the children to a school soccer match. Unlike Lidia, Wayne had no special talent for the game, but they both ran hard, blocked kicks, passed the ball, skidded on the grass, laughed, and, all in all, had a wonderful time. Sitting in the stands watching, Adam and Zoe chatted about work, the game, Ori's parents. In a month's time, the Naso Indians had completely redesigned Zoe's garden, turning it into a pleasure parade. Once her neighbors saw the brilliant transformation of her grounds, they wished to hire the Panamanians. Before long the Nasos were much in demand, though still pining for Panama.

With sadness Adam said, "Watching the kids makes me wish to keep them."

"They are yours—for now."

"I'm just a substitute."

"From what Wayne tells me, a darn good one."

He smiled generously and dropped the subject, appreciative of the life that he had. His wish for an affair had ebbed in parallel with the transformation of his wife. Moreover, he had become fond of Samuel; and the Hildreths, though separated, remained married. Still, he treasured his fantasies about the beautiful and electric Zoe. In college he had read a novel about a man pursuing the perfume of infidelity; but the man knew that the intoxicating scent would be so addictive that he could never escape. He would become a slave to trysts, a condition that only a madman could fancy.

Adam's thoughts left him feeling uneasy. He could not imagine Rachel telling him that she no longer found him attractive or supportive or compatible, but he could see himself saying that if he could not make her happy, she should have the independence to find love elsewhere. Did he entertain these thoughts because he wanted her to feel the same way, or for some other reason? How terrible and magnificent is passion, he thought, but what if desire ultimately concerns not loving another, but desire itself? His meandering thoughts finally led him to conclude, rather prosaically, that once betrayal supplants fidelity, then anything is permissible. His course in Russian history at Vanderbilt had taught him that much.

The game over, the four of them drove to the supermarket to buy ice-cream sandwiches and pretzels. The combination made Zoe roll her eyes, but Lidia, learning American idioms, thought there's nothing finer in the state of Carolina, even though they lived in Louisiana. Adam drove to Zoe's house, where they relaxed in the splendid garden. While the children ran after frogs, Adam and Zoe contentedly watched. A sudden cry from the children brought them running. A snake slithered through the thick grass.

"It's harmless," Zoe announced, having spent a childhood roaming through a jungle full of poisonous reptiles. She reached down and picked up the garter snake, which coiled around her warm arm. The children jumped for joy at the sight and wanted to have their chance to hold it. She told them that they could keep the garter snake as a pet—at her house—given its low maintenance and calm temperament. Would they like that? You bet!

The church elders occupied the first two rows of the sanctuary to discuss Rachel's proposal. She felt on edge, having only the day before confronted her father. She sat in the third row. Fearful of speaking in public, she worried about the wisdom of quoting Shakespeare. Pastor Rominy, dressed in street clothes, faced the group. In the background stood the altar, bathed in sunlight from the stained glass window depicting a crucified Jesus. In attendance sat nine white men, two of whom also served on the city council and had supported her proposal. If they remained steadfast, she would have to persuade only three others. Three out of seven. She liked her chances—until Mr. Blunt immediately announced his opposition.

"A murderer, drug runner, and suicide! What are we thinking?"

As an insurance agent, Mr. Blunt always calculated the odds, whether of longevity or illness, fire or flood. He prided himself on knowing the safe drivers from the careless. But what did he have to lose in the current situation? A moment's reflection and she guessed. Word would get out. He might jeopardize his business interests. As she calculated the leanings and prejudices of the remaining six, she figured that at least two of them would object. Mr. Slagman, a no-nonsense retired serviceman, had a son in the Marines. Rachel mentally put him in the no category. Then she studied Dr. Frumer, a gynecologist, who generously served the black community, but railed against the black crime rate in town and the cost of food stamps. If she counted him as a no, the remaining number stood at four. She mentally reviewed their backgrounds.

Dr. Drillman, a dentist, had a recently divorced daughter owing to domestic abuse. His son worked as a counselor at LSU in Baton Rouge. She figured Dr. Drillman for a no. Staring at the balding head of Marcel Lucas, a restaurant owner, Rachel hoped he appreciated how many times she and Adam had eaten at his establishment. Something of a peacock, Mr. Lucas fashioned himself a cook in the Parisian style. Unmarried, he had "a lady friend" in New Orleans. A possible yes for him. Mr. Ellis, sitting as straight and stiff as a broom handle, had retired from teaching math, fascinated by the historical origins of zero. How did that number come into being and why? The absence of zero, as he often explained, made a mathematical system impossible. His wife, a retired librarian, belonged to some committee that fought the banning of books. They had four children, all of them professionally successful. Put him down as a yes. Messrs. Knight and Gautier, the first an undertaker and the second a tech writer, she regarded as unknown quantities. She couldn't even guess how they might vote. The last person, Mr. Gaylord, the youngest of the elders, remained a mystery. He and the pastor seemed especially companionable, perhaps because Mr. Gaylord wrote articles for some religious journal. Like the pastor, he had never married, but unlike the pastor, shyness had virtually rendered him mute.

After an exchange of opinions, in which the elders bandied about the word *justice*, leaving her unsure of the vote, she asked to speak. Pastor Rominy, hearing no objections, invited her to join him in front. She had made it a point to dress conservatively, in a simply tailored navy blue taffeta tunic dress, accented by a white silk scarf. She wore black patent leather shoes and sheer stockings of sunburn tan. None of the elders could fail to notice the attractive woman, handsomely garbed and softly well-spoken.

"Gentlemen, you know why I've come and the nature of my proposal. What you don't know are my reasons." She folded her hands at her waist. "I begin with an apology. Though we all meet here as Christians, instead of invoking the Bible, I wish to call your attention to Shakespeare's *The Merchant of Venice.* In particular, I wish to speak of mercy, as does Portia. In college I majored in English. We memorized her speech, the one that begins, 'The quality of mercy is not strain'd.' Unlike justice, which may not include mercy, mercy is compassion's other name. Portia says that the 'quality of mercy is not strained,' by which she means it is not rationed; it is not unnatural or forced. Rather it is a quality that we all possess. Like the gentle rain from heaven, it touches us all naturally. And when we express it, we are twice blessed. We bless ourselves and the person who receives our mercy. It is a god-like quality, greater than kings and majesty. We come closest to Our Lord when we show mercy. Is it not mercy that we ask of God, because if He held each of us to a strict standard of justice, none of us should see salvation? Justice resides in courtrooms and laws; mercy is heaven sent. Justice condemns; mercy forgives. Justice is harsh; mercy is gentle. And although justice is at the heart of a well-ordered society, 'mercy seasons justice.' So when you vote to decide the eternal resting place of Immanuel Crenshaw, I urge you to exercise mercy, a gift of the human heart."

As if ready to take flight, she spread her arms in appeal.

"Now it is time for me to fall silent and for you to vote, not on the basis of a children's center, though we can surely use one, but on the basis of a shared humanity."

The elders and pastor left the room for the vestry. Rachel remained seated in the sanctuary. Looking up at the stained glass window, she wondered about His last thoughts.

# Death Comes to Hungamon

WITH SAMUEL AND ADAM PARKED ACROSS THE STREET AND equipped with earphones, LeShaun crossed the back lawn toward the garden cottage, the inviolate space where the judge sat perusing old photo albums and composing his memoirs. It held a small desk, a bookshelf, and a safe, with a concrete casing, embedded in the ground and reached by lifting one of the floorboards. The safe, the soul of his hidden harmony, he knew to protect at all costs and from all intruders. This conviction the judge had often impressed on Samantha, who at the moment saw LeShaun approaching, with a small backpack that she feared might conceal a weapon. She knew that the judge had brusquely dismissed him from the house regarding some deal. She therefore intercepted him.

"Can I help you?"

"The judge told me to meet him at two."

"I'll just see."

"He told me to come alone."

She chuckled. "I don't count as anybody."

At the cottage door, she rapped. No reply. "He's hard of hearin'," she said and knocked harder.

A muffled voice from inside responded, "Yes?"

Many years before, the judge had decided that he and his family composed so much of Hungamon's history that to understand the one, you had to understand the other. Because some of that history qualified as unsavory, he kept his compromising documents in his floor safe, with a .45-caliber pistol. When Samantha knocked, he sat studying a photograph of a second cousin, Erma Rae Sutton, and her two daughters, Myrna and Raylene. Taken in 1965 at a Hungamon civil liberties rally by black demonstrators, the photograph cast an unfavorable light on the family. Erma Rae, an implacable opponent of integration, stood between her two young teenage girls. With arms aloft, she held a protest sign. Her handbag hung from her right arm, and the left, while anchoring the sign, also held two small Confederate flags. The placard read: "Nigger don't you wish you were WHITE."

Judge Waters pondered Erma Rae's thin, tight lips and facial plainness, her unattractive slacks and short-sleeved shirt. He remembered her no-account husband drinking himself to death, an undisguised blessing. At the moment of the picture, what did Erma Rae's two attractive daughters think? Now grown, with kids of their own, they had joined the ranks of the poorly educated fundamentalists. All their menfolk worked in the mill. The daughters and their children had grown up in abysmally ignorant families. Just look at the sign, which exhibited not only a KKK mentality, but also a rudimentary lack of education. Hell, he thought, where's the question mark?

His life with Samantha and his love of his community had led him to accept some change—albeit grudgingly—and to see that town and country had no future unless white folks acknowledged past injustices and set a table at which all could dine. The photograph, taken over twenty years earlier, led him to think: *We can't wait another generation to right the wrongs of the past.*

Someone called his name again. It wouldn't be Samantha, who knew better than to disturb him in his garden retreat. Then the judge remembered his two o'clock appointment. He began to fume, as his irascibility eclipsed his generosity. That LeShaun kid wanted to blackmail him.

Samantha leaned her face against the door and cupped her mouth, speaking into the peephole. Since the judge had not responded to her calling his name—she intended to say, "LeShaun is here"—she tried again, but managed to utter only "LeShaun," and then a shot rang out. The bullet came through the peephole and hit her in the side of the head. She staggered and fell. LeShaun, terrified, bolted into the woods. Adam used his cell phone to call 911, while Samuel ran to the body. Opening the door, the judge found Samantha lying on the ground, bleeding. Howling like a wolf caught in a leg trap, he cried: "Samantha, my beloved Samantha! What have I done? I saw the brown skin and was blinded . . ."

The police found Emory sprawled across Samantha's body. He had lacked the presence of mind to dispose of the gun. A few minutes later an ambulance arrived and removed the dead woman. The judge received the courtesy of not being shackled, though he left the scene of the crime in the backseat of a police car.

Shock swept Hungamon. The eminent Judge Emory Waters, alleged to have killed Samantha Larkin, a woman whom most people regarded as his mistress, had acted owing to passion, race, theft, infidelity . . . which? A check of the gun provided the greatest shock of all: The same weapon had been used in the shooting deaths of David and Vincent Dozier, but the gun had been bought by and registered in the name of Montgomery French. Other than not guilty by reason of insanity, what could the judge plead? The papers in Washington Parish relished every moment of the scandal. While the parlors of the parlous buzzed, a silent cortege walked behind a black hearse that brought Samantha to her final resting place. Libby had asked Pastor Williams to conduct the service, which he did at the grave, with Emory's friends in attendance. After reading passages from the Bible, he spoke softly to the modest crowd of mourners, among them Judge Waters, allowed to attend in the company of a policeman. The judge never said a word, but throughout the service silver streaks ran down his cheeks.

"A child of this land, Samantha loved Louisiana." The pastor laid a hand on Libby Larkin's shoulder. "She often told her daughter that Louisiana, for all its racial difficulties, provided a home for musicians and gourmets, for football fans and happy feet. She told her that the lakes and waterways gave her a peace so great that she could not imagine anything more lovely than spending her days in this part of the world. It is no doubt fitting, then, that she will be laid to rest in a land, for all its travails, she loved best."

The judge threw some dirt on the coffin as workmen lowered it into the earth.

With Judge William Bowie of Shreveport presiding, a jurist known for his sharpness and steely resolve, jury selection and the start of the trial took place in July. At the time of arraignment, the local prosecutor recused himself on the grounds of his friendship with Judge Waters, who declared his intention of defending himself and pleading not guilty. He intended to argue accidental homicide, namely, that he had mistaken Samantha for LeShaun Jackson, who had threatened his life. Although accidental homicide failed to meet any legal categories in Louisiana, Judge Waters hoped to use it to gain the jury's leniency. The townspeople groused about the choice of a New Orleans prosecutor, Carl Mantye. A balding fellow, he looked as if he had been tonsured, walked with a slight limp, and enjoyed a reputation for having a first-rate analytical mind. Unable to prevent Mr. Mantye's appointment or question his qualifications, Judge Waters's supporters complained that Mr. Mantye knew nothing of the local culture. Big-city lawyers were slick, untrustworthy. The citizens of Hungamon had undoubtedly hoped for a good ole country boy, like Judge Augustus Bowie. Mr. Mantye ignored family ties and went right to work, poring over the documents removed by the Hungamon police from Judge Waters's cottage safe. Chief Detective Peter Hansen had sorted them neatly.

The safe's contents revealed a great many family mementos; numerous newspaper clippings treating the local 1960s integration struggles and the recent suicide of Immanuel Crenshaw; a large supply of cash; a box of bullets that matched the murder weapon; several unsigned cryptic notes reading "DTA," followed by a date; and a thank-you card from a Samuel Hildreth that read, "You did me a favor. I hope I can do one for you." Looking over Detective Hansen's notes, Carl concluded that for the sake of context he needed to talk to LeShaun Jackson, Samuel Hildreth, and Rhoda Dozier. If necessary, he would promise them all immunity. For the interviews, he would use neither a recorder nor a stenographer. He simply wanted to understand the background of the crime. They did have to understand, though, that Judge Waters could call them as witnesses if he chose; but Mr. Mantye opined that he thought it unlikely, given the open-and-shut nature of the case. He met with them individually at the local courthouse, in a small room provided by Detective Hansen. Besides a table and two chairs, the room had one amenity, a framed photograph of Hungamon, dated 1935, prominently featuring the saw mill. *A company town*, thought Carl.

LeShaun Jackson arrived in his usual slouch, with his jeans low enough to reveal his plumber's crack, and wearing a hoodie, inscribed "New Orleans Saints." The men sat at the table, facing each other. LeShaun shook with fear, knowing full well the violence drug lords might visit on him if he named names.

"I got immunity, right?"

"Right." Mr. Mantye shoved a paper across the table to LeShaun with the promise of immunity in writing.

"You realize some things I can't talk about."

"Of course." Although Mr. Mantye worried that LeShaun would be less than forthcoming, he gently proceeded. "The police tell me," said Mr. Mantye, "that at the time of his arrest, Judge Waters admitted to drug addiction and claimed that numerous dealers, at various times, tried to blackmail him. Your name surfaced." Carl leaned across the table and asked, "Did you attempt to extort money from him?"

"No, sir."

"But I gather you had a falling out with him."

"Yes, sir."

"Can you explain?"

"I wanted to offer the judge a business deal—a fair and square one—but I never made it to the cottage. Miss Samantha rapped on the door and called to the judge. Then I heard a shot. She dropped to the ground, and I ran into the woods."

"What kind of a business deal?"

"I'd be bringin' in drugs from Mexico."

"Is it that easy?"

"Let's just say I know some people."

"And you wanted the judge to back you?"

"Yeah."

"I gather he refused."

"Played hard-ass with me."

"Can you be more specific?"

"He blew a fuse."

"Because you threatened to make public his drug use?"

Now staring at Mr. Mantye intently, he said, "If anyone done the threatenin', blame the judge, not me. He held a letter opener to my throat."

Two hours later Carl interviewed Samuel Hildreth, who showed up in fatigues and a cap with a Marine insignia. Mr. Mantye handed him a signed document promising immunity. "As promised," said the counselor. "The police tell me that rumors abound in Hungamon about drug deals and illicit money. In fact, FBI agents are currently scanning bank records and inquiring about large sums channeled to some unnamed person, who in turn deposited them in foreign banks. Do you know anything about this matter?"

"A lot, but not everything."

"I gather that at one time you got mixed up in some nasty business."

"Yeah, but the judge set me straight. He befriended me."

"Why would LeShaun Jackson have approached the judge?"

"LeShaun needed seed money. He offered the judge a cut."

"And the nature of this business?"

"Buying and selling."

"That description, Mr. Hildreth, could fit almost any commercial enterprise in the world."

"Coke."

"I'm surprised at your implicating a man who kept you from jail."

"I owe him, but I also owe Manny Crenshaw, a good kid, railroaded for a murder he didn't commit."

"I heard about his case. His conviction and suicide caused quite a stir." He paused to study his hands, with their long elegant fingers. "Do you bear a grudge against the judge?"

"No, I've always liked the judge. Hell, he gave me a second chance."

"Did LeShaun Jackson work for you?"

"I wouldn't say work. He did me a favor 'cause someone else needed one."

"I'm confused."

"Supposin' you ask me to cut your lawn—as a favor. And supposin' I do. Am I workin' for you or doin' you a favor? I can't rightly tell. But as you're a college person, maybe you can."

"Did you pay him?"

"No."

"This *favor* . . . did it involve what you called the judge's habit?"

"Yes, sir."

"The 'coke' . . . where does it come from?"

"New Orleans by way of Tampico and South America."

"I mean, the kingpin."

"At one time, Mr. David Dozier."

"And who else?"

"Some silent partner who puts up the money."

"How do you know about a silent partner?"

"DVD said so."

"Do you know the person's name?"

"I can think of several people, but I'd rather not say."

"For safety's sake?"

"Hell, one of them works for the governor."

"Can we return for a minute to Judge Waters? He has confessed to using cocaine. Did any of his intimates know about his habit?"

"Samantha knew."

"Would you agree that when the judge pulled the trigger, terror had blinded him?"

"I would agree that Judge Waters accidentally killed Samantha Larkin, mistakin' her for someone else."

"The gun found in Judge Waters's possession killed Mr. Dozier and his son."

"Yeah, but registered to someone else."

"As far as you know, did the judge have any reason to resent either of the Doziers?"

Samuel rubbed his unshaven jaw before answering, "That's a tough one. In this part of the country, people hold grudges for all kinds of reasons. The truth is, I really can't say."

Mr. Mantye thanked Samuel and asked him for a ride to the local library, where he spent the rest of the day reading about Immanuel Crenshaw. The next morning, at the courthouse, he interviewed Rhoda Dozier, who received the same written assurance of immunity. A heavily rouged short woman, sporting a dress that conspicuously displayed her bountiful bosom, she ran a hand through her short, curly brown hair and waddled on high heels that threatened, at any moment, to upend her. She smiled at Mr. Mantye in such a way as to suggest that she expected applause for her appearance. Her little mouth, fashioned in a Clara Bow heart-shaped manner, seemed even smaller given the way she minced her words. Mr. Mantye asked her whether she knew Judge Waters. She wept a few tears. He waited. She then removed a lacy handkerchief from her bosom and dabbed her eyes.

"Only through my dear husband."

Carl condoled with her over his death and circled into a question. "Judge Waters claims that he shot and killed Samantha Larkin in a fleeting moment of temper, suggesting that normally he kept his temper under control. Does your experience comport with this image of the judge?"

"Comport?" she asked, uncomprehendingly.

"Do you remember any time that the judge seemed uncontrollably angry?"

"Oh, yes. One time in particular when me and my husband stopped at my father-in-law's house and Judge Waters dropped by, they—"

Carl interjected, "Judge Waters and Mr. Dozier?"

"Yeah, them. They got in a terrible row about some letters. To Vincent and me, in the other room, it sounded awful. So Vincent went in to see if he could quiet them down, and the judge called him vile names."

"For example?"

Rhoda blushed and cleared her throat. "Asshole, shithead, imbecile, cocksucker."

"Did Vincent provoke him?"

"Not that I could tell. Vincent just tried to make peace, and the judge called him names."

"Did the judge ever threaten your husband?"

"Not that I'm aware of, but Mr. French did."

"When?"

"He took Vincent to dinner in Varnado." She blew her nose and clutched the handkerchief. With puckered lips she replied, "He told Vincent his, Vincent's, life could be in danger for saying the wrong things."

"Can you give me an example, Mrs. Dozier, of what 'saying the wrong things' might mean?"

"Well, Vincent knew if he talked about those same old letters his daddy left him, he could be asking for trouble."

Skeptically, Carl repeated, "Asking for trouble . . . I wonder why."

"I think it may have something to do with a painting."

"Whose?"

"Montgomery French's."

Before the trial began, apologists and detractors took to the local newspaper to express their support or condemnation of the accused. Friends of the judge wrote that he had been a benefactor to both black and white communities, and that his many contributions—financial, journalistic, and humanitarian—ran into numbers too great to recount. But his detractors decried the "cold-blooded killing" of Samantha Larkin. From Miss Hattie Lee came a disdainful letter deploring "the illicit relationship between the judge and Mrs. Larkin," a charge she repeated to every newspaper in the state. In front of dozens of cameras, she recounted the experience of living next door to "a race mixer." During a television interview, she admitted that she took great pleasure in seeing her name in print for exposing "the sinful judge."

On the day of jury selection and the start of the trial, Monday, July 17, 1989, a boisterous crowd sat outside on the lawns, under trees, beneath umbrellas, and under tents powered by mobile generators. People picnicked, vendors sold snacks and soft drinks, and a pastor distributed pocket-size copies of the *New Testament.* The more vociferous harangued the crowd about good and evil, right and wrong, sanity and madness, mercy and justice. Some patriotic women had made skirts and dresses or blouses out of red, white, and blue flag material. Most everyone seemed to wave a Confederate flag, which vendors hawked, as well as bumper stickers, records, and leaflets. Several women carried placards. One read, "Don't give up your guns, boys." A makeshift lunch counter served Pearl River catfish, hush puppies, shrimp, and hot dogs for $2.50. Vendors also sold soft drinks, potato chips, candy, and popcorn. Many of the judge's sidewalk defenders, thinking race the issue, stood ready to deny that a black woman's life equaled a white man's. One obstreperous street champion croaked into a bullhorn: "It's these younguns you havta watch, drugged and drunk boys like LeShaun Jackson. They don't wanna just vote, they wanna eat and sleep with white women. They already go to school with white kids. Next thing you know, they'll want to marry white women. There ain't no tellin' where they'll stop. Mind you: We're going to have another war between the states unless the atheistic, anti-Christ communists, who are conspirin' with Russia to destroy our country, are rooted out and stood up against a wall."

Inside the courtroom, Judge Bowie said he assumed that the prosecutor and Judge Waters would want to question the prospective jurors. They did not. Did they, based on the biographies of the jurors, wish to challenge any for cause? They did not. Did they wish to exercise any peremptory challenges? They did not. Mr. Mantye, well aware that most of the townspeople knew each other, saw no point in earning the displeasure of the locals by asking for someone's removal. He therefore passed on the twelve (six men and six women, of whom two were black) and four alternates. The courtroom, filled to overflowing, hummed with the sound of anxious spectators and the air-conditioning. Many of those in attendance had never seen the inside of this courtroom or, for that matter, any other. They marveled at the murals depicting scenes of early Louisiana settlements.

With the painting of the elder Montgomery French back on the wall, Rachel reviewed the report for the benefit of her father. "Originally the painting bore the title 'Klansmen.' Your daddy had the painter change the title to 'Kinsman.' My guess is—and I'm sorry to say this—he was one of the night riders who lynched the painter, Godwin Rush, and the young woman who took the picture, Mary Judd. Your articles about the history of Washington Parish often misrepresent; they're fiction. And even your more recent articles—about the civil rights movement—falsify. Is it because you and Judge Waters sided with the Sons of Dixie?"

Her father looked up from the familiar dining room table, where he and Rachel had talked innumerable times. He had been studying the enlarged tributary veins between his wrists and knuckles. "Life often flows through uncharted waters and along the way takes strange byways. In the wink of an eye, things change. My father's generation—and mine—grew up with segregation. Separate but equal. So said the law. But the law did an about-face, expecting people to think differently." He coarsely laughed. "Fat chance! It's like turning around a battleship."

She removed the green accordion file from a large handbag. "These belong to you." Her father eagerly took the damning evidence. "Can you explain bank deposit slips for Geneva and the Cayman Islands and the Bahamas? Frankly, I suspect you have been abetting a criminal."

Without answering her, he said, "You didn't make copies, did you?"

She ignored his question. "I can understand prejudice. I can even understand apologizing or stonewalling, as you are doing now. But I can't understand your need to rewrite history."

Montgomery found it difficult to argue with his daughter. His immeasurable love for her and Miss Ellen and Libby rendered him virtually mute. In fact, his admiration for her as a young woman of independence, his respect for her first-rate education . . . they all militated against his trying to make her understand his motives. He struggled with how to start, and then retreated. Rachel filled the vacuum.

"Tell me. The shooting of that young black state trooper in Varnado: Did you have anything to do with that?"

"No."

"But the man picked up for questioning couldn't afford a lawyer. Who paid for one?"

"The Sons of Dixie."

"A group to which you belonged. And you can sit there and tell me your hands are clean?"

The anger gathering force in his chest rose to his face. He struggled to speak dispassionately.

"I wrote what I did to avoid suspicion. You can call it protective coloration. By sympathizing with the segregationists, I deflected attention away from my family. If people had pried—and you can bet that everyone who had an axe to grind would have jumped at the chance—your life would have been far different. I wanted you to have every advantage. Ellen agreed. We would see you educated and positioned with money and ease. You do realize that the rich have fewer obstacles to clear than the poor?" Rachel nodded, though she said nothing. "Libby would have had an abortion if I had asked. But we both wanted the child. Your borderline skin color enabled us to slip you through the nets and snares of racism so that you could live a good life. To do that I had to create a public image."

"A false one," Rachel added.

"One that would protect you, Libby, Ellen, and, yes, me. As you know, they used to call it 'passing,' when a black person, light enough, passed as a white. I knew you'd be able to pass."

"So you would be safe."

"And you."

"At the expense of my birthright? That's a rather steep price to pay for family respectability."

"I prefer the word *safety*. Blame my judgment, but don't question my good intentions."

"Daddy, please don't use that excuse. That's what every wrongdoer says."

By this time Montgomery had run out of reasons—and patience—to justify his behavior. Until his dying day, he would feel that he had done the right thing. Family eclipsed all else.

"Then I take it," he said, "you removed the painting just to find out what you could about your grandfather, and that Adam's estimate of its value had no basis in truth?"

"Correct."

He breathed deeply and spoke his feelings. "For your well-being I would give my own life, but I know now that for mine you would never give yours."

Rachel tried not to cry, but the tears issued nonetheless. She sniffled, dabbed her nose, and extended a hand. He paused, and then, ignoring her hand, stood and embraced her. Neither spoke.

On the day of the trial, people started lining up for seats at five in the morning. Two or three had spent the night sleeping in front of the courthouse, though according to city ordinances they could have been arrested for vagrancy. Since eight o'clock, every seat had been taken. Adam and Rachel stood at the rear, behind dozens of others. The packed courtroom reeked from body odors: sweat, breath, clothing, flatulence, perfumes, lotions, hair sprays. Women fanned themselves, men mopped their brows, and Judge Bowie wanted to know why the air-conditioning leaked and labored.

Speaking to Judge Waters, the presiding judge said, "You have pleaded not guilty. Correct?"

The judge answered cryptically, "Is there any defense against self-reproach?"

"I'll take that as a 'yes,'" replied Judge Bowie. He then read some general instructions to the jury about how the trial would proceed after the prosecutor and Judge Waters made opening statements. Nodding to the prosecutor he said, "Counselor!"

Walking to the podium, Mr. Mantye shuffled some notes, adjusted his reading glasses, and looked at the judge, "Your Honor!" He then addressed the jurors. "Ladies and gentlemen of the jury, although a person charged with a crime is presumed innocent until proven guilty, once you hear the facts, I don't think you will question that the crime issued from premeditation or that any reasonable doubts exist to mitigate the charge. Mr. Emory Waters is guilty of murder in the first degree, and though caught red-handed, he has pleaded not guilty. Frankly, in light of the overwhelming evidence, I am amazed that this case has come to trial. The facts are indisputable. On the afternoon of Sunday, May 7th, at ten minutes after three, Mr. Waters, working in his garden cottage, heard a knock on his door. Thinking the person at the door someone he disliked, he removed a pistol from his safe, looked through the peephole, saw a brown-skinned cheek, positioned the pistol at the peephole, and pulled the trigger, killing Samantha Larkin. Legally, it makes no difference whether he shot the wrong person. That the person he hoped to kill materialized as someone else has no bearing on his guilt. The fact remains that he fully intended to cause death as he picked up the gun and aimed it, all elements of first-degree murder. Anything he says about being under the influence of drugs cannot alter the reality of this case. He is guilty. No defense can dispel the actual events. In sum, there can be no doubt about the identity of the killer and the identity of his victim. And certainly there can be no doubt that we have a case of premeditated murder."

After leaving the podium, the prosecutor turned to Judge Bowie and said, "I have no more to add to my opening statement." The presiding judge then asked Judge Waters whether he felt ready to speak. The judge said yes, and rose on unsteady feet to make his way to the podium. He carried no notes and seemed disengaged. The bailiff had reported that when he went to the judge's cell to bring him to the courtroom, the accused sat on a stool repeating into the vacant air, "One short sleep past . . . and death shall be no more."

Without a trace of irony, Judge Waters commended the prosecutor "for his brevity and accuracy." Turning to the jury he said, "Counsel has spoken the truth in every regard, and if we wish to live in a just society, then we must heed facts and pay them due respect."

Carl knew that Judge Waters famously praised lawyers and then cut them down to size with his ironic wit. For good reason he now wondered whether the judge would direct his sarcasm at him.

"Mr. Mantye is a first-rate attorney, a Yalie, or perhaps they call themselves Elis or Whiffenpoofs. But then you folks wouldn't be familiar with the songs the privileged Yale boys sing."

"Your Honor," said Mr. Mantye, "this trial concerns Judge Waters, not me. His digression is out of order."

Judge Bowie twisted his mouth, as if moving a wad of chewing tobacco from one side to the other, and responded, "The poor man is being tried for a capital crime that carries the death penalty. The least we can do is to allow him his say at this critical point in his life." He then told Judge Waters he could continue.

"As I remarked, the prosecutor is a well-educated city boy. New Orleans now, but he once worked in Chicago. A real den of thieves that city. It must have taken special skills to deal with that lot."

The jurors smiled and nodded. They clearly loved the judge's rhetoric, a local hero playing to the home crowd with sweetness and folksiness, obstacles that Carl Mantye had considered before he accepted the assignment to prosecute Judge Waters.

"My own legal background can hardly compare. LSU. The law school is named after a man who served as a civilian judge on the Nuremberg Tribunal, Paul M. Hebert."

"Your Honor!" exclaimed the exasperated prosecutor, but Judge Bowie simply held up a hand, signaling Carl to desist.

"We learned Louisiana law," continued Judge Waters, "not big-city or international law. We received an education designed to help the little man, not a Wall Street big shot." He sighed. "So here I stand, a simple man in front of my peers—good, honest people of faith—who have the unhappy job of judging me, as I once judged their neighbors and friends. I know you all, even by your nicknames." He pointed. "There's Butch Berkeley, and there's Boo and Scout and Captain. And over there I see Sweet Mary Jane Withers, whose daddy used to play poker with me." He walked from the podium to the rail of the jury box, but before Carl could object, Judge Bowie shook his head no. "Muffin," he said, and the face of Dorothy Minkus lit up like a Christmas tree. "How's the boy? Over his bronchial asthma attack?" She nodded, "A close call, but we got the ambulance to your house just in time."

Finally the presiding judge felt compelled to act. "Judge Waters, your opening statement, please."

"I got carried away, Your Honor. That's what happens when you come among friends. Sorry." He paced in front of the jury box. When Judge Bowie tried to prod him to return to the podium, the proper place for speaking, he merely smiled and kept on pacing. "As you know, I have already admitted to the crime and signed a confession. What the confession doesn't say, because inadmissible under the law, is that I committed the murder owing to mistaken identity. A door stood between me and Samantha, distorting her voice. My thinking had become confused by drug use. And why did I use drugs? A sad circumstance. My wife's death drove me to seek relief in painkillers. When they proved ineffective, I tried stronger ones, until I settled on cocaine. To obtain the drug I had to rely on dealers. Before long those same dealers started to victimize me, extorting large sums and threatening exposure. There came a point I could no longer stand the fear and anxiety. When I heard the knock on the cottage door, I saw only the person's cheek and thought that person LeShaun Jackson, who had previously tried to blackmail me. In a blind rage, I shot through the peephole." He paused and with the back of his hand wiped tears from his cheek.

The jurors sat transfixed, and the audible sighs of the townspeople in the courtroom spelled sympathy.

"As for Exhibit A, the gun that killed Samantha Larkin, a good friend gave it to me—for protection." He sniffled. "You know the rest." Then he turned to Judge Bowie and remarked, "I see no reason to call witnesses. There's nothing to prove."

Judge Bowie suddenly slumped in his large leather chair. Carl Mantye and Judge Waters had the same thought: Judge Bowie had taken ill. Slowly raising his head, Judge Bowie gestured to the counselors to approach the bench. As the judge spoke, his face sagged and his hands shook.

"Sorry. I get them, ocular migraines." He rubbed his temples. "Suddenly I can't focus. All I see are lines, verticals and horizontals. We can reconvene in the morning. I'll tell the bailiff. Mr. Mantye, I'd like a word with you."

In a few minutes the courtroom stood empty.

Judge Bowie and Mr. Mantye retired to spartan chambers, reminding Carl of how little money the state spent on trials. The judge pointed to a metal chair and fell back into a padded one.

"In my professional judgment," opined Judge Bowie sadly, "you can't win this case. The jury sitting out there will not find Judge Waters guilty. Then we'll all look foolish. Every legal expert in the country will decry this hometown decision. An old boy got off because we failed to change the venue for the trial. And even then, just between you and me, it probably wouldn't have mattered. The moment Emory mentioned Yale and LSU, you lost."

"What do you suggest?

"Think about how we can save this trial and not come away from it looking like fools."

Adam and Rachel left the courthouse together, both convinced that Judge Waters would go free. They had arrived in different cars because Rachel and Pastor Rominy had agreed to meet at the First Baptist Church to discuss Manny Crenshaw. Adam drove to Zoe's house. He wanted to talk to the Naso Indians, but would have to wait for Zoe to translate. In the meantime he watched the couple work the soil as if sifting for gold. He found sitting in her garden a peaceful respite and the presence of the children a pleasant diversion. Zoe returned from work early. Acting as an interpreter, she transmitted Adam's question to the Panamanians, who joined him at the circular garden table. "In Panama, how do the Indian tribes render justice?" They replied that the elders, about ten or twelve of them, listened to the complaint and then retired to consider the fairest way to proceed. In cases of murder the offending member would be exiled from the community, a sentence that often meant death. Alone in the world, the felon had either to join another tribe or live as a hermit. Adam pictured a wandering judge in search of companionship or a means to sustain him—and weighed the fairness of such a punishment.

His mind began to wander. Exile or prison? A person found unfit to live among others ought to wander alone, cast into the wide, windy world, like bread upon the waters. Prisons? They made captives of the warders, and caged the wrongdoer. Better that the person have to make his way in the wilderness or the desert, forced to learn which plants to tap for water and which to eat, which to ease toothache and which to cure snakebite. In the singsong sounds of the Naso language, he found a lilt that his own sharp consonantal language failed to provide.

When Zoe walked him to his car, the sun had retreated to the west, but the pinkish sky highlighted the glow of her soft-brown skin and large dark eyes and swollen lips. He chastely kissed her cheek, and reminded her that she owed him a favor.

"It's true. I did promise to pay you back for keeping the kids." She looked away and closed her eyes, fearing his request would compromise her. "What do you have in mind?"

"Forgiveness. I beg your forgiveness for trespassing."

The welcome surprise of his words led her to hug him. When she disengaged, he saw tears coursing down her face. Driving away, he felt how awful conscience is.

Later that evening he met Samuel at the trailer, where they discussed the possible implications of Judge Waters going free. Samuel admitted that he feared such a prospect.

"Why, just because he did you a favor?"

"No, because I did him one."

"You're speaking in riddles."

"The judge wanted me to find him a new supplier. I sent LeShaun. And the dumb kid tried to interest the judge in a business deal."

"In the Crenshaw case, how did he feel about the manslaughter decision?"

"Delighted, in part because I assured him Manny would never say a word about drugs, as long as he could stand for parole."

"The kid got fifteen years, the first ten a mandatory minimum."

"A lot longer than Manny counted on."

"When Manny escaped, I can imagine what the judge must have felt."

"It scared the holy bee-jesus out of him. But the kid, as good as his word, never spilled the beans."

Adam decided the moment had come for the truth. "I'm the person who abstained."

Samuel looked bewildered. "And yet you stood in front of the courthouse and said the decision 'strained comprehension.'"

"I plead cowardice in the first degree."

"Why vote one way and mouth off another?"

"I feared someone would guess. So I tried to divert attention from myself."

Samuel left the trailer. Adam followed. For a long spell neither man said a word. Then Samuel, looking up at the starry canopy, spoke into the airy thinness. "I voted no, as you might have guessed. In Vietnam, my commanding officer assigned a prisoner to me. He said take this guy to the river, shoot him, and dump his body in the water. I pointed the guy toward the Mekong and gestured for him to swim like hell. Back at camp, I told the officer 'mission accomplished.'" Adam realized that Samuel had told this story to pardon him.

To the former soldier's surprise, Adam hugged and thanked him for sharing the moment. Then he stepped back and said, "Samuel!" His voice tightened. "I owe you an apology." Samuel stared uncomprehendingly. "For my cowardly words and for wanting to make love to your wife."

Samuel laughed. "Doesn't every guy? But what's wrong with yours?"

"At one time I would have said conventional and unimaginative."

"Her crusading for Manny takes some guts."

"I confess she surprised me."

"Maybe she's changing. People do, you know."

Adam wanted to hug Samuel again. Talking to him felt like talking to Larry Weiss. In Samuel's presence, Adam felt shrived and renewed.

"She's a mighty pretty woman," added Samuel. "If I walked in your shoes, I wouldn't be sniffin' around other ladies until I'd experienced all of her perfume." Adam, at a loss for words, shifted from one foot to the other. "Imagine yourself in her skin. Her lot ain't easy, always expected to play a certain role when you know damn well you ain't suited for it. My momma used to say some flowers bloom late, some early. Believe me, she's a good one."

What the "one" referred to, Adam could only guess. But he did have to concede that of late Rachel seemed comfortable in her bones and had begun to flower.

"Zoe once said to me, 'Samuel, can you imagine what it's like living with you?' Until that moment I never gave it a moment's thought. It ain't easy, but just try to step outside yourself and see how you seem to others. I 'spect that when Miss Rachel looks at you what she sees is a handsome guy with broad shoulders, lookin' to all the world like a successful businessman; but actually she knows you don't belong. She sees a guy with a Newark accent who underneath it all worries 'bout his place, worries he's not right for Miss Rachel, wishin' he could remake her into a ball of fire off the streets of New York. So he tries to find in other ladies what he thinks is missin' in his. Trust me, she's the real thing."

Without saying so, Adam saw the wisdom of Samuel's words, but finding the emotional territory uncomfortable, he interrupted Samuel's train of thought and returned to their initial subject, observing that he felt sure the judge would be hospitalized. "I do ask myself, though, what might have happened had Manny lived."

Samuel pointed to the stars. "Do you suppose someone up there knows the truth? And if he does, why ain't he talkin'?" As if needing more oxygen for what he would say next, Samuel inhaled deeply and on the exhale allowed, "A long time ago, I stopped callin' on the Lord. He's either dead or deaf."

"The religious would say that we serve as the Lord's instruments."

"Good," said Samuel, "that's what I needed to hear."

Rachel had hoped that all the elders would be present, but found herself talking only to Pastor Rominy and Mr. Gaylord. They sat in the vestry, and the pastor, still robed, had just conducted an evening service. She tried to read the decision in his expression, but saw in front of her a face fit for poker. Mr. Gaylord looked equally noncommittal. She had told herself that if the decision went against her, she would withdraw not only the offer of a children's center but also her church membership. Pastor Rominy had asked an assistant to bring them hot tea, explaining that a drink of boiling water actually cooled the body more effectively than a cold one. She had the distinct impression that the pastor wished to stall for time. He studied her face. She became anxious. Like the angry parent whose daughter has stayed out late, Rachel began to work herself up to a state of excoriation.

"Anything wrong?" she asked.

The pastor bowed his head and replied, "You remind me of someone." He waited a second before continuing. "My mother . . . the last time I saw her."

Before Rachel could recover from that admission, he said that he had good news. A minute later her composure returned.

The tea came. He held up his cup and toasted: "To our generous benefactress." Mr. Gaylord added, "Here, here!"

"However, the elders have one condition," said Pastor Rominy. Mr. Gaylord looked away as if wishing to distance himself from the condition.

"I'm listening," Rachel said stoically, still prepared, if need be, to unleash her arsenal.

Pastor Rominy took her hands in his and said, "I apologize for keeping you waiting several days. People often have strong opinions. Although the elders have approved your request, they have added a proviso."

"So you said." Her impatience returned, making her wonder whether Pastor Rominy had chosen to exercise the ministerial mode, slow and cautious.

"Namely, that the first check for the children's center reach us within a month's time."

"Do they fear I'll renege on my promise?"

Pastor Rominy shook his head. "You know businessmen."

"Yes, cash on the barrelhead."

"Precisely."

"Is that one of the deadly sins," she asked ironically, "or one of the Christian virtues?"

"I repeat: I am immensely grateful."

She chided herself for directing her anger at the pastor, when the object of her derision—the committee of elders—would escape her wrath. Thanking the pastor, she nodded at Mr. Gaylord. To her surprise, he spoke.

"You are doing a righteous thing," he said, adding enigmatically, "I know what it is to live as a pariah."

"Would you like us to see you to your car?" inquired the pastor.

"No, I think I'll just stop in the sanctuary for a few minutes."

Mr. Gaylord accompanied the pastor out the side door, the two of them looking like gay fellows well met.

Seating herself in the first row of the sanctuary, Rachel stared for several minutes at the stained glass window. Then she stood and spoke in that direction. "Thank you, Will, for your fine words. But apparently payola trumps poetry."

---

As the judge paced his cell, certain favorite verses came to mind, some of lasting literary value and others not. He rearranged words to suit his state of mind.

Had we but world enough and time.
This murder, comrades, were no crime.

He chuckled at the thought of how he changed the next verse.

Hickory, dickory, dock,
The judge removed his sock;
With only one,
He could not run,
Hickory, dickory, dock.

That night, lying on his cot, he dreamed of Miss Julie, and her agonizing death from ovarian cancer. She had long suffered from "women's problems," which had kept her from conceiving. When the cancer spread, it metastasized into her abdomen, causing excruciating stomach pain and aging her overnight. Emory dreamed that when he viewed her in the open casket at the mortuary, her face metamorphosed into Samantha's, and then back again, alternating between the two. Each handed him a note, with the same single word written on it: *When?* He had in fact, at Miss Julie's funeral, leaned over the casket and kissed her cold lips; and at her interment, he had sonorously eulogized her sweetness and once-delicate features. After throwing some dirt on the casket, he had left the cemetery in the company of Montgomery French, who held his arm. But in his dream, he leaped into the grave, embraced the coffin, and cried, "When you get to the other side, remember me. I'll meet you when my days are through. I don't know how long I'll be, but you can trust I'll be there shortly, just wait and see. And 'til that happy day, I'll be loving you, love me."

On the second day of the trial, Judge Bowie looked restored. The color had returned to his face, and he had a bounce in his step. Taking his place at the bench, he expressed surprise that Judge Waters had not yet appeared; as well, the attending bailiff seemed to have disappeared. After a few minutes that felt much longer, the bailiff hurriedly came through the swinging doors behind the bench; whispered to Judge Bowie, who blanched; and handed him a letter. The judge looked seriously ill. The bailiff quickly retired. Obviously some untoward event lurked in the wings. Clearing his throat, the judge announced that Judge Emory Waters had taken his own life. Before the gasps could fade, he read from the letter.

*To Whom It May Concern,*

*As a judge, I kept many a drug user and dealer from going to trial. Except for the most egregious cases, I handled such cases in camera. Why? I felt that I could not try a man for the very crimes I stood guilty of. My drug use and lawbreaking progressed to a point where I could no longer think clearly. Six months ago, in New Orleans, I entered the Cathedral Basilica of Saint Louis just before closing. All the confessional booths stood empty. But I entered one, knelt, and related all my sins to . . . who? Not to a priest. But to God.*

*Now it's time to confess to my fellow man. I killed David Dozier and his son.*

Incredulity swept the courtroom. People moved so far forward on their seats, they nearly toppled over.

*The first cheated me. Having been taught from childhood that a man has to pay his debts, I exacted payment with a bullet. And by confessing, I am paying my debts to the community. I shot Vincent Dozier because I feared that he had learned from his father of our partnership, and that I financed the drug operation. There is also another reason for my shooting David. It concerned some letters that a friend of mine thought might blacken his family's name.*

*But I know from my years of sitting on the bench that the act of murder, no matter how rational it may appear on the surface, issues from a sick mind. Just think of all those Louisiana lynchings in years past, most of them probably the product of men maddened by ignorance and fear.*

*I too had fallen under that spell when I shot David and Vincent Dozier. Crimes are no less crimes for whatever reasons we give. Yes, on the surface I appear as sane as you, but when certain impulses come over me, I cannot control my murderous rage. How else can I explain my behavior: my killing three people; my financing a drug dealer; my laundering ill-gotten money that I needed to hide?*

*The shooting of Samantha Larkin truly occurred accidentally. Because of my poor hearing, I thought someone else called to me through the cottage door. Before God, I declare that I held her dearer than anyone else in my life. Her death was my own. So I am rightly joining her. Where she lies, I will lie.*

*I could continue, but you now know enough to see that I am ill. My confession, I hope, will serve the common good. In addition, I have left some beneficence behind. On the day of Samantha Larkin's funeral, I legally amended my will, donating my house, my property, and my honest savings, which I have kept apart from illicit drug money, for the construction and maintenance of a halfway house, called the Samantha Larkin Retreat.*

In light of the judge's confession, Rachel told her father she would drop by his house the next day "to clear the air." Seated in his cramped living room, they both felt equally uncomfortable. On the tea table between them lay the local newspaper, bearing the headline, "Judge Takes His Own Life." Below the masthead, in smaller bold lettering, it read, "Found Hanged in Cell."

"Why on God's good earth didn't they remove his belt?" exclaimed Montgomery. "They knew his mind had gone off."

"Perhaps he did it to prevent others from pardoning him," explained Rachel. "Everyone expected him to get off. So he did what he knew the others wouldn't do. Even the jurors admitted that none of them thought him guilty. The jailers, too."

"Suicide! It seemed impossible two days ago and still seems so. To my mind, it's as inconceivable as blaming Ivy Methvin for Bonnie and Clyde's death."

"The funeral's been delayed."

"Why?"

"The church elders find it all hard to stomach."

"For Christ's sake, the Waters' family plot goes back two hundred years. Eight generations lie buried there, including Emory's wife, his father, mother, and grandparents. What troubles the First Baptist?"

"Murder, drugs, and suicide."

"Hell, they agreed to bury Manny Crenshaw."

"For a price. And he's still in the morgue."

"The damned hypocrites. They all behave like Judas."

"Libby and I will be speaking to the elders tomorrow. Do you want to join us?"

"Will I help or hinder?"

"Your presence would help. As his oldest friend, you knew him best."

"I'm torn. Like you, Emory lied to me. He told me some cock-and-bull story about the money." Her father paused to suck in his breath. "And you! Gruning told me you made copies of my private papers—at the library."

"I know how undisciplined you are, especially about money. You've never even given me a list of your assets. When death occurs in a family, it's not always easy to locate the person's holdings."

Montgomery mulled over her answer and, though offended by her recent deception regarding the painting, chose to believe her. "Thank you for caring, but you could have asked rather than stolen."

The word *stolen* made her flinch. She shook her head in agreement. "I should have told you the truth. My apologies."

He used the folder in his hands as a stage prop. By rustling through it, he would not have to make eye contact with her. "You're probably wondering about all the large deposits in foreign banks. Well, I got lucky with some overseas stocks."

Rachel had hoped to avoid another unseemly spat with her father. She found it too painful to rehearse his misbehavior. But she could clearly see the anguish in his face. "Daddy, you just upbraided me for lying. If I have to ask which stocks, then you'll have to lie as well. I care for you too much to put you in that position. So *you* tell me about those extraordinary deposits. You already mentioned that Judge Waters told you a cock-and-bull story."

Montgomery, the fierce bantam fighter, looked as if readying himself to enter the ring against a heavyweight, and intellectually that summed up the combatants. "I could tell you," he said, "but I don't wish to add fuel to the fire."

"Daddy, an answer like that only makes me all the more suspicious. You do realize, you could be charged?"

She had dressed in a white summer outfit that emphasized her lustrous skin and hair. Montgomery could see Libby in her face and bearing. Both women, to his mind, exuded nobility.

"I held the money for—" He paused, at a loss for how to continue.

Rachel stared at her father, knuckled her hands, and replied, "Judge Waters."

"A delicate business transaction. I can't go into it."

She smiled. "No need. I understand."

Rachel's statement unnerved her father, who quickly grasped her hands. "Not a word . . . otherwise—"

The fragmentary sentence moved Rachel to give it a noun and a verb. "You'll be the first one suspected of laundering his money."

Montgomery looked utterly defeated. His silent fears had just been verbalized. "A lifelong friend."

Rachel felt nauseous. She feared her father would continue to spend his life in the service of falsehoods. "Tell Judge Bowie the truth," she pleaded. "He'll know what to do."

Her father refused. Rachel left the house and drove off, just as a police car pulled up to the curb, discharging two detectives. Mr. French opened the door. They flashed IDs. He asked them in. They wanted to know whether he could shed any light on the Louisiana drug trade and Judge Waters. A couple of toothpaste tubes packed with cocaine had been discovered in the judge's study. One of the detectives, a young black officer, volunteered that the FBI had taken an interest in the judge's financial affairs and, in particular, illegal money transfers to Swiss and Bahamian banks that originated in Hungamon. Montgomery poured a glass of bourbon and offered his guests the same. They politely refused. "I think," said Montgomery, "we need to talk. Make yourselves comfortable. It may take a while."

The next day, attended by two FBI agents, Montgomery French climbed the front steps of the New Orleans Courthouse and entered Judge Winthrop Steele's private chambers. With the district attorney present, Mr. French immediately agreed to a plea bargain. In return for his avoiding jail time, he would identify and bring back to the United States all the money deposited abroad. He also consented to report once a month, for one year, to a probation officer. Case closed.

Outside the courthouse, Montgomery found Rachel waiting at the foot of the steps.

"We have just enough time to drive back to Hungamon to attend a meeting of the elders regarding Judge Waters."

"If they refuse to let him be buried with his ancestors," he thundered, "I'll never darken their door again!"

"All the more reason for them to say no. I'd advise you to keep your annoyance in check."

"Check! Now you're talking. That's what they want—a donation. All religious institutions draw their strength from fear and threats. Do as I say or no forgiveness, no heaven, no sanctified burial. But . . . if the money is right, we might be able to make an exception for you."

"Whatever it takes," she said.

In the car, father and daughter exchanged hardly a word until they approached Hungamon.

"Speaking of money—"

Montgomery interrupted. "Who?"

"In front of the courthouse, you."

"Well?"

"As you know, I promised the church a children's center. I just thought you ought to know that I intend to use a portion of the money from my trust fund, which you generously created."

"Forget it. That trust guarantees your future well-being. Those thieves don't deserve it."

"No, but the children do."

He hesitated. "Let me mull it over."

A smile shone in her eyes as she lovingly glanced at her father.

They drove directly to the church, parked, and entered the vestry. The elders, all present, greeted them stiffly, as if they resented, yet once again, being asked to bend the rules. Pastor Rominy spoke a few words about the moral responsibility the church shared with the town to maintain the city cemetery. Then the drumbeat of objections began.

"An indifferent churchgoer."

"A murderer."

"A suicide."

"An infrequent donor."

"Infrequent! Hell, never!"

"A drug addict."

"Make that a drug lord."

"A boozer."

"A sinner, living without benefit of marriage to a . . . woman."

Montgomery French stood to make his presence known. Although short of stature, he measured long on courage.

"Judge Emory Waters might qualify as a fallen man, but not an evil one. Consider all the people he kept from jail. Consider his request that his estate go to creating and supporting the Samantha Larkin Retreat." He chuckled. "Consider even his financing a float for our local Mardi Gras celebration. And last but not least, consider that several members of his family helped found this town. Their cemetery plot holds the most important statuary and the greatest number of generations. To ignore all these contributions would make a mockery of the words *Christian charity*."

At this point Rachel feared that her father would launch into a diatribe about church hypocrisy, so she delicately tapped him on the arm and gestured for him to sit.

Mr. Knight, the undertaker, posed the following question: "Given the judge's request to lie next to Samantha Larkin, if we buried him beside his wife, where would Miss Samantha go?"

"To the other side of him!" exclaimed Montgomery. "Why not? He would spend eternity between the two women he loved. I'd want no less for myself."

That stunning admission left the elders speechless.

Before they could recover, Franklin added, "I'll cover the burial expenses for both, including the caskets, which I want in keeping with the Waters' tradition, black mahogany." He conspicuously reached for his checkbook.

Pastor Rominy caught up with Rachel and her father on the sidewalk in front of the church. "They voted unanimously."

"For or against?" asked Mr. French. "When dealing with church people, you can never be sure."

The pastor laughed self-consciously and replied, "For." He smiled awkwardly, thanked Rachel and her father, and returned to the church.

Spying Libby on the walk, Montgomery called, "I'd like a word with you, Miss Larkin."

Rachel reached her first. Fearing that her intemperate father would sever ties to her mother, she whispered to Libby, "Take my arm."

As Montgomery approached, Libby said, "I came to hear the outcome."

The locked arms of the women gave Montgomery pause. "What I have to say concerns both of you." He cleared his throat and declared illogically, though sincerely, "We all know what I think about family. A sacred tree. History begins with it. When family secrets are not guarded, the tree becomes corrupted. In the case of the French family, we will have no more children. Adam's an outsider, a good man, but no gene bearer. So let us agree to keep our secrets dear, and especially those about our family's roots. If you agree, then we can be as before, a sturdy oak."

Her father's racism, which included family, friendship, and sex, made Rachel blush. How could this kindly man have become so steeped in the myths and mysteries of blood that he could not see that his own behavior made him, in his very words, a corrupter? Perhaps that explained his secretiveness. But at his age, it would take a miracle to change him. Bloodlines, Rachel told herself, might create clans and cultures, but nothing could eclipse in strength charitable behavior.

Rachel, the first one to move, embraced her father. Libby, rife with guilt and yet proud of having told Rachel the identity of her real mother, stood stoically waiting for Montgomery to accept or reject her. She also had her pride. A silence that felt like death ended when Montgomery stepped across to Libby and folded her in his arms.

According to the undertaker's custom and calendar, burials took place on Thursday. As the French family requested, Immanuel Crenshaw,

Judge Emory Waters, and Samantha Larkin all came to rest on August 17, 1989. Friends and family attended the burials, including Samuel and Zoe Hildreth. As workmen lowered each casket into the ground, amidst the mosquitoes, one person spoke. Montgomery extolled Judge Waters, Libby praised her mother, and Rachel eulogized Manny, whose parents stood between her and Adam.

Montgomery distinguished himself with one particular line, "Emory's kindness glowed like sparks of fire that warmly befriended me."

Libby cried and swore, "My angelic mother will surely sit at the right hand of God."

But Rachel uttered the words that they talked about later. To the surprise of all, she lyrically eulogized a young man she never personally knew.

"On this sad day, I wish to speak of time and memory, joined each to each. We speak of time as past, as present, and as future, but we cannot live in future time, even as we plan for it. And the present passes in an instant. In fact the words that I have just now spoken have already become relics of the past. But the past is never dead. It is not even past. Every day we live with the consequences of former lives and decisions, which come to us through memory. So important is memory that we call the loss of it tragic. I pray all of us will keep ours, so we can remember this day, when Immanuel Crenshaw came to rest for eternity in a place of his parents' choosing, making loneliness less familiar to his family.

"The survivors of World War II concentration camps, when asked what mattered most to them during their darkest days, said they hoped someone would bear witness. In other words, someone would remember them and what had taken place in those foul and fetid evil camps—and tell the world. Wherever and whenever we can rend the veil of unholy silence, let us not hesitate. At this moment we stand here to bear witness for the sake of Immanuel Crenshaw and his family, and to remember that the talented young athlete for whom so many cheered became an innocent victim of a wayward legal system. I ask that as we bow our heads in prayer, we not be deaf to the varied carols of America singing."

On leaving the cemetery, Rachel felt a tap on her shoulder. Samuel Hildreth wished a word with her. They stepped aside.

"The center you wanna build for the church," he said, "I'd like to help pay for it. Maybe all. But I don't want my name used." Rachel's wonder begged for an explanation, but it never came. "I have the money; don't ask. If possible, I'd like the place called the Crenshaw House or the Immanuel Center, whichever name best suits the church."

A few days later Adam and Rachel, seated at their dining room table, engaged in a discussion that Samuel had unknowingly precipitated. He had confided to Adam that he and Zoe wished to reconcile, and that he would like to work in Hungamon with at-risk youths. The center Rachel planned to build would provide an ideal location. To ease the reconciliation process, he requested that the kids, for the time being, remain with Adam and Rachel. What he did not say, he thought: *The drug money that he had been stashing away for years could not only build the center and sustain it, but also provide a lifetime of comfort for him and his family.* Adam explained the situation to Rachel and asked, "Are you willing to let the kids stay with us until they graduate from the Fry Academy?"

Rachel, suddenly anxious, realized that she faced the very real prospect of the children moving from her home; and given Samuel's mysterious wealth, the Hildreths could always find a larger house, perhaps one outside of town. But she decided, in the interests of fairness, "It would be only right to ask the children about their preference, with Samuel and Zoe present."

A meeting took place at the Shaw house. Without mentioning the hoped-for reconciliation, Zoe remarked: "After all, it's not a lifetime, and we can see them anytime we want. Furthermore, I like the progress they're making in school. But as you say, we'll let Wayne and Lidia decide."

When the children entered the living room, having come from watching television in the den, they pondered the question, looked at one another for a hint of which way to go, then at the Hildreths, and a minute later agreed that staying with the Shaws felt like spending a sleep-over with friends.

"It's kinda like a summer camp," said Wayne, as Lidia shrugged her shoulders, never having attended one.

"Then it's decided," said Rachel with a sigh of contentment.

"Super-duper!" said Adam, wishing he had something more eloquent to say.

The children seemed unfazed and raced to return to their television show.

Shortly after celebrating the New Year, 1990, Adam and Larry Weiss, as planned, flew to Budapest to see if they could, with Mr. Baranyi's information, discover the final resting place of Adam's parents, József and Abagail Rashi. Rachel thought it a good time for the men to go, since the children would be at the Hildreth house for the holiday and Larry's spring semester wouldn't start until the end of the month. Adam would pay for the trip.

Snow and cold greeted them at the Ferihegy International Airport. They took a cab to the elegant Andrassy Hotel and checked in. Larry immediately seated himself on one of the twin beds and made a telephone call. He had done his homework before they left. By means of emails and long-distance calls to the American Embassy, he had helped

Mr. Baranyi identify and locate certain documents. Without unpacking, the two men took a taxi to the Archives. After an initial inquiry, Mr. Baranyi exited an elevator. All smiles, he greeted his "old friends" and said, "Follow me." They entered the elevator and descended to the bottom floor, where rows of records in metal stacks greeted them. On a table that resembled a draftsman's, Mr. Baranyi had laid out some ledgers, which he opened to specific pages. Standing at the table, the three men stared at the documents, written in Hungarian.

After a minute or two, Adam asked, "What are we looking at?"

Larry and Mr. Baranyi exchanged glances.

"Death certificates," said Larry, "for József and Abagail Rashi. They say, 'Killed Sunday, November 4, 1956, fighting Russian troops sent to Budapest to suppress the rebellion against the Hungarian socialist government, 1956. Buried in the Municipal Cemetery.'"

Adam wiped his tearing eyes and asked, "Where is the cemetery?"

"Outside of Budapest," replied Mr. Baranyi.

"I'd like to see it—in the presence of a rabbi."

"That may take some time," said Larry.

Adam replied, "Then we'd better get started."

As they left the Archives, Mr. Baranyi whispered, "Try the Dohany Synagogue."

The next day Larry called and requested the help of a rabbi. No more than thirty minutes later, the secretary called back with a name, Rabbi Jakab Senesh, an elderly man, willing to accompany the two men to the cemetery. The secretary warned Larry that the sage spoke no English, and that it would be a good idea to give him some money for the synagogue.

Adam, when told, replied, "Just so long as he can recite a prayer in Hebrew."

Larry rented a car and the two men drove to the Dohany Synagogue, a building fashioned in the colorful Moorish style and part of the Budapest ghetto during Nazi rule. While Larry entered the sanctuary in search of Rabbi Senesh, Adam waited in the courtyard, where many of the Jewish dead, who had perished from cold and disease in 1945, lay buried in a mass grave. In remembrance of the dead, the courtyard displayed numerous stone tablets, and a metallic weeping willow tree with the names of the dead etched into its leaves. A few minutes later, Larry appeared in the company of a small, wizened man wearing a yarmulke, Rabbi Senesh. Adam held open the front door of the car for the rabbi, and then seated himself in the back. Given that the rabbi knew no English, Adam wanted to position him next to Larry, who had told the rabbi beforehand about Adam's wish to locate, if possible, his parents' graves.

As the car pulled away from the synagogue, the rabbi explained that the Municipal Cemetery, about ten kilometers from Pest Center on the way to the airport, held a special place in the hearts of Hungarians, because here the revolutionary leaders of the 1956 uprising had been buried in a mass grave after execution. The rabbi spoke slowly so that Larry could translate, and frequently ran his tongue over his lips and cleared his throat, as if parched from remembrance. He explained that on November 3, 1956, a Hungarian delegation of "freedom fighters," led by the minister of defense, P. Maléter, had received guarantees of safe passage to attend negotiations on a Soviet withdrawal and an end to the uprising against the Hungarian Socialist government. The meeting, held near Budapest at the Soviet Military Command at Tököl, became a night of infamy. Shortly before midnight the chief of the Soviet Security Police (NKVD), General Ivan Serov, ordered the arrest of the Hungarian delegation. In June 1958, after a secret trial in Romania, the Soviets executed the Hungarian prime minister, Imre Nagy, and two other leaders, and buried their bodies in unmarked graves in the Municipal Cemetery. But in 1989, in an area overrun with weeds, veterans of the uprising discovered the graves of Nagy and other victims. Renewing the site, they honored Nagy and his comrades and reburied them in marked graves, before an estimated one hundred thousand people.

By the end of hostilities, nearly thirty thousand Hungarians and seven hundred Russian soldiers had died, and two hundred thousand people had fled the country.

Adam wondered if his parents had actually been armed and engaged in the fighting, since the cemetery also held the bodies of those innocents caught in the crossfire between the two sides. Many of those graves had markers. In the cemetery office, Rabbi Senesh thumbed through a ledger with the names of the known dead. Among them, he found József and Abagail Rashi. The plot numbers indicated that they had been buried not far from the mass grave. When the three men found the simple plots, both dated 4 November 1956, Adam kneeled and put a hand on each of the markers, J. Rashi and A. Rashi. As he did so, the rabbi softly intoned the prayer for the dead:

*Yisgaddal v'yiskaddash shmey rabboh / B'olmoh dee v'roh chir-usey / V'yamlich malchusey / B'cha-yeychon uvyo-meychon / Uvcha-yey d'chol beys yisro-eyl.*

After Larry placed a small stone on each of the graves, a gesture of remembrance, Adam did the same. As the party left the sites, the rabbi said, "If you would like to have your parents reburied in a Jewish cemetery, I can arrange it."

"No, I think the presence of all the brave men and women buried here does them honor. But I would like to have a plaque that reads: 'József and Abagail Rashi lie joined here in the beautiful silent music of the earth.'"

He had seen a similar inscription in a black cemetery and, having admired it, decided that someday he would use it.

On Friday, July 20, 1990, the First Baptist Church broke ground for the French-Shaw Children's Center. Montgomery French, a major donor, received the compliment of turning over the first sod, followed by Rachel Shaw, whose contribution matched her father's, though neither Montgomery nor Adam could persuade her to reveal the source of the money. In time the community familiarly called the center the Frenshaw House, one letter removed from Crenshaw House. Here Samuel Hildreth counseled troubled youths and Lidia earned pocket money on weekends tutoring children in Spanish. By September, Rachel had cleared her calendar, winnowed her social contacts, and joined the staff to teach preschoolers their ABCs.

The daily routine of introducing restless four-year-olds to the runic mysteries of an alphabet taxed Rachel's patience and skills. As well, she had Lidia and Wayne to look after. But she found the work and the nurturing satisfying, albeit exhausting. Adam suggested that they spend a month or two in Europe during the summer, when the children would be out of school and could stay with Zoe and Samuel, whose fortunes were rapidly changing. The Hildreths had started proceedings to adopt Lidia, and had made a down payment on a large house, with an acre of ground, which could accommodate not only the family, but also the Panamanians.

In July, Adam and Rachel flew to Paris, visiting tourist sites, as well as the Folies Bèrgere and some other ooh-la-la revues. From Paris, they savored the wine-growing country and the south of France, from where they flew to Budapest for a somber stay that included the Municipal Cemetery and the graves of Adam's parents. The plaque that he had requested now rested between the two plots. As commissioned, the words had been engraved in both Hungarian and English.

Their last stop, in August, took them to Martinique, where they remained for nearly the entire month. When they returned to the

United States, Rachel cradled a one-year old child in her arms, Marguerite Valois Shaw, legally adopted from the French authorities. On their return to Hungamon, for some inexplicable reason the presence of Marguerite, zealously protected by Wayne and Lidia, gave the Shaws' life something they had lacked before: an exquisite providential climax.

FINI

# About the Author

Paul M. Levitt is professor emeritus of English at the University of Colorado, Boulder, where he taught modern drama, theater history, and the gangster novel. He has written more than twenty books (six of them novels), radio plays for the BBC, books about medicine, stories for children, and numerous scholarly and popular articles. He lives in Boulder.